Tales for Nodding Sheep

A collection of 32 Short Stories

Kenkonti

First paperback edition 2023

Cover Art: Steve Mackins ©

ISBN: 978-1-80227-854-5 - Paperback
ISBN: 978-1-80227-855-2 - eBook

THUNDERER PRESS

Contact: thunderer-press@outlook.com

Contents

The Doll's House

Waldo Sprinkle raised the roof of the doll's house. Leaning over, he placed the miniature wooden dressing table into one of the bedrooms, positioning it carefully against the thin plywood wall. He then walked slowly back to his workbench, returning with a chair in his hand. With care and precision, he sat the chair down in front of the dressing table, making slight adjustments with his index finger to get it exactly where he wanted it. Taking a step back and putting his hands on his hips, Waldo looked proudly down at his work and nodded to himself in recognition.

"Perfect, she will be so happy with it," he said to himself.

He closed the roof and bent down to the front of the house. Cupping a hand to his mouth, he directed his voice into it.

"It's ready Doris, come see."

Moments later, a door within the doll's house opened, and a tiny elderly lady about five centimetres tall entered the bedroom where he had just placed the new furniture. Noticing it immediately, she clasped her Lilliputian hands together in delight.

"Oh Waldo, it's wonderful!" she exclaimed, shuffling quickly over for a closer look. "It's so elegant, just what I've always wanted."

Waldo smiled.

"Can I try it?" she asked.

He gestured with his hand, instructing her to go ahead, and Doris sat herself down on the chair. She wiggled her back to get it in the correct position, before glancing at her reflection in the dressing table mirror. She smiled to herself for a moment, then turned her head around and looked up.

"It's marvellous, I love it. Thank you so much."

Waldo Sprinkle was delighted.

* * *

Downstairs in the kitchen, Martha Sprinkle was washing the dishes. She had recently prepared and eaten lunch, but a bowl of soup sat untouched on the dining table. A door opened and her brother entered the room.

"It's likely to be stone cold by now," she remarked, "you're always coming down late, I wonder why I bother sometimes."

Waldo sat down at the table and spooned some of the tomato soup into his mouth.

"No it's fine Martha, honestly, it's still warm."

"So why are you late this time?" she asked, but he said nothing.

"Up in your room no doubt, messing about with that doll's house," she continued. "It's all you ever do, hours and hours each day, making silly little things to put in it."

"They're not silly Martha, and they are skilfully crafted." But the comment went over her head.

"What's the point of it? It's not right, a seventy-year-old man playing with a doll's house."

"It's a hobby Martha, surely I'm allowed a hobby in my retirement. Besides, it helps me to relax."

She tutted. "Well it gives you something to do I suppose, it keeps you out from under my feet. I just wish that you did something more normal that's all, like playing golf or bowls, or sitting watching TV all day like Charlie. I get embarrassed when I have friends over and they ask me what you are doing and I have to tell them. And you're always late for your meals, I sometimes think I'd be better off if I were living alone. In fact, I wish I was," she added as an afterthought.

"Well you know what they say Martha, be careful what you wish for."

"What's that supposed to mean?"

"Well, they do say that if you want something bad enough, and wish for it hard enough, it may well come true."

With that, she gave him a disapproving look. "Poppycock," she said, as she left the kitchen.

* * *

It was late evening time in the Sprinkle household. Martha was still awake, sitting in the lounge watching TV. Waldo was upstairs in his room, standing beside the grand doll's house that took pride of place on his bedroom table. Inside, the miniature figures of Doris and Bert sat drinking cups of tea in their cosy lounge that he'd designed for them. A cat lay curled up on the arm of the sofa, but the cat wasn't real, it was plastic, placed there by Waldo just for effect. Bob and Janet, Doris and Bert's companions who shared the doll's house with them, were sitting at a table playing cards, whilst their two children played a ball game on the floor.

Waldo peered in through the window, observing the pleasant family scene. How delightful, he thought to himself, everyone is so happy. When the occupants noticed the big eye at the window they smiled and waved.

"Goodnight all," said the voice from outside, "I'm off to bed now, have a nice sleep everyone, and pleasant dreams."

"Goodnight, see you in the morning," they all replied, as loudly as they could.

* * *

It was a lovely summer's day in the quiet suburb of Cherry Valley. At number seven Primrose Avenue, Martha Sprinkle sat at the kitchen table drinking coffee with her two friends, Betty and Joan. Her brother, as usual, was upstairs in his room, busy at his workbench.

With magnifying glass in one hand and tiny paintbrush in the other, Waldo was putting the final touches to a miniature painting - a still life. With deft hand, he dipped the mono-stranded brush into the paint, peered through the magnifying glass, then dabbed a minute amount onto the tiny canvas. It was the final touch; the painting was finished.

It had not been an easy task for him. From the construction of the frame and securing of the canvas, to the meticulous application of the oil paint, it had taken many hours of his time, but now that the labour of love was complete it had all been worth it - and he felt proud.

"He's up there all the time," Martha was saying to her two friends. "I hardly see him nowadays, only at mealtimes really, and then he's always late. He takes me out to do some shopping once in a while and occasionally cooks the dinner, but most of the time he's up there with his doll's house, making things to put inside it. I don't see the point, really I don't, it's not as if he shows it to anyone, no one's allowed anywhere near it, and I'm not even allowed in the room anymore."

"Well at least he's doing something," replied Betty, "and if he enjoys it . . . well, you know."

"And it keeps his mind active I suppose," added Joan, "it's got to be better than watching TV all day like Charlie."

"I guess so," said Martha, "I just don't get what he sees in it that's all. I mean, I could understand a train set, it does something doesn't it, ... it moves."

"Well as long as it keeps him happy I wouldn't worry

about it," said Betty.

"Mmm," Martha responded, sort of agreeing. "But he isn't much company for me, I sometimes wish he wasn't around at all to be honest, it'd be one less to cook and clean for."

"Well be careful what you wish for," Joan remarked.

"That's exactly what he says," concluded Martha, rolling her eyes.

*   *   *

It was late morning; a parcel had just been delivered to number seven Primrose Avenue and Waldo Sprinkle was opening the brown cardboard box with eager excitement. Unwrapping the paper and removing the item revealed a red and yellow box. Bold writing across the lid read:

Build-Your-Own:
Miniature Grandfather Clock.

Slightly smaller text below stated:

Special deluxe edition - a perfect working model!

Very small text at the bottom of the box read:

Made in China.

The recipient was utterly delighted. He quickly turned the box over to scroll down the contents list printed on the reverse: Instruction leaflet, 2 x sheets of balsa wood, 1 x glue, 8 x screws, 1 x mini screwdriver, adhesive clock-face, glow-in-the-dark decals, fully functional clock mechanism with key.

"Splendid," he said to himself, he couldn't wait to get started.

*   *   *

Over the following weeks, Waldo worked studiously, meticulously assembling the grandfather clock to the best of his abilities, and when it was finished he was thrilled with the results.

So one morning, he slowly and quietly opened a lower-front section of the doll's house, then positioned the timepiece carefully in the main hallway before closing it back up again. Walking back to his workbench to clear away his tools, he smiled, just one thing left to make and then I'm ready.

A short time later, he made his way downstairs to join his sister at the kitchen table.

"I think I'll go into town today," Martha called out, "to buy a new dress. I've seen a nice one in Tinley's, it's similar to Joan's only better. The quality at Tinley's is always good. I'm not sure what colour to go for though, maybe yellow or blue, either will go with my new white shoes don't you think?"

But her brother wasn't listening, he was staring into space in deep thought.

"Are you paying attention Waldo? Did you hear anything I said?"

"Yes of course Martha, I'm listening."

"Well it didn't seem like it, I wonder why I bother wasting my energy. I may as well be on my own, I'd probably be better off, I sometimes wish it were just me and the goldfish."

*   *   *

Waldo Sprinkle was bending down, talking into his doll's house once again. A little figure was looking up at him and smiling; it was Doris.

"Oh it's fantastic, it keeps such regular time. Bert loves it, he's always wanted a grandfather clock."

"It's a true replica," said the maker, "a special deluxe edition."

"Really?" replied Doris, seemingly impressed by the comment.

"And made from grade A balsa wood."

"Wow, that's incredible."

"And the hands are luminous, you can see them in the dark."

"Yes we noticed. It's fantastic, and it looks so good standing in the hallway next to the new picture. You know we all love that painting so much; you are so talented."

"I'm glad to hear it," he said. "It wasn't easy, but I thoroughly enjoyed doing it. I used to paint a lot you know, when I was younger. My sister however, said that I wasn't any good at it and shouldn't waste my time, but doing that little painting made me realise how much I've missed it."

"Well you did an excellent job that's for sure."

"I've got the house to myself today Doris, Martha's gone shopping. She should be out for quite a while so won't bother me, as you know, whenever she goes shopping she does likes to make the most of it."

"Well that's wonderful, I'm so pleased that you are going to have a good day."

"I certainly will," he said. "And how are you today?"

"I'm feeling good, as right as rain."

"And Bert and Tom, and Janet and the children?"

"Oh they're splendid," said Doris. "Bert is downstairs listening to the radio that you rigged up for him, Bob and Janet are exercising in their bedroom, and the kids are playing hide-and-seek."

"Wonderful," he replied.

"You know Waldo, we really are grateful for everything that you do for us, you are so kind."

"Oh it's my pleasure. Doing things for you all, it gives me a purpose in life, and when I see you all smiling in your happy home, it makes me happy too."

"Well, we all appreciate it."

"Thank you Doris, and if there is ever anything you need don't hesitate to ask."

"We certainly will," she said.

Then, with a deep and thoughtful expression on his face, Waldo bent down closer to the tiny figure looking up at him.

"You know Doris, some people say that if you want something badly enough, like really really want it, and you wish for it hard enough, it will come true. Do you believe that to be so?"

"Of course it's true," she replied, "you should try it sometime."

"Well I might just do that," he concluded, "I might just do that."

With that, he said goodbye to his little friend and walked over to his workbench. Opening the toolbox, he took out some precision tools and laid them on the surface. He then slid open one of the drawers and took out his latest project - a little wooden rocking chair.

* * *

One afternoon, in early spring, Martha Sprinkle was in the kitchen. Sitting on the table was an untouched plate of cold baked beans on toast.

"Late as always," she grumbled to herself.

But on that particular day, her brother was later than usual, it was lunchtime and he hadn't even had his breakfast.

She walked along the hallway to the bottom of the stairs and shouted up.

"Waldo! Waldo! Your beans are stone cold, come down this instant!"

She carried on with her business, but several minutes passed and there was still no sign of the man about the house, so she decided to climb the stairs. On reaching the top, she walked along the creaky landing with the faded, patterned carpet, until she came to his bedroom - and she knocked loudly on the door.

"Waldo! What are you playing at? Your breakfast has been sitting on the table for hours."

But there was no response, no noise at all came from the bedroom, which she thought odd.

Her brother had strictly forbidden her from entering his room, but as she'd already tried knocking and calling out, she felt that she had no choice. So, ignoring the *Keep Out* sign, Martha opened the door and slowly entered the bedroom, and when she did she found it empty - Waldo was gone!

* * *

The following morning, Martha Sprinkle sat at the kitchen table drinking tea. Her friends, Betty and Joan, were consoling her.

"Fancy that, just upping and going after all these years," said Betty.

"And without saying a word," added Joan.

Martha sat with handkerchief in hand, feeling sorry for herself. She was however, enjoying the attention she was receiving, plus, hearing the detrimental things being said about her brother was making her feel better.

"Well good riddance to him, that's what I say," said

Betty, "he never did anything anyway, just spent all of his time up in that room of his making toys. If you ask me, you're better off without him, it'll be one less person to cook and clean-up after for a start."

"Yes, Betty does have a point," added Joan, "he wasn't much company for you, and you always said that you wished he wasn't around."

"That's true," Martha concluded.

* * *

So, life at number seven Primrose Avenue, in quiet Cherry Valley, carried on for Martha Sprinkle. She got used to living without her brother, and if she were honest with herself, it was a bit better for her. Betty and Joan would visit most days, Thursdays was bingo night, and she now only had to cook and clean for one - besides, she still had the goldfish and the TV to keep her company.

Martha thought of her brother sometimes of course, and even fondly of on occasions. Out of respect, she never went into his room, it was left exactly as it was.

"It's what he would have wanted," she would say.

So nothing much changed in Waldo's bedroom; his bed, his lamp, his chair, and his workbench, were exactly as the day that he disappeared.

But there *was* one little change. Inside the doll's house that stood proudly on the bedroom table, sat Doris and Bert, having a cup of tea in the dining room. Bob and Janet were sharing the sofa with their two children, and on a miniature rocking chair next to the fireplace, with his slippers on and smoking a pipe, sat Waldo Sprinkle - as happy as could be.

High-Strangeness Day

Sara awoke from her night's sleep. As she gradually adjusted her thoughts to the morning, she realised what day it was - it was the fourth of June, High-Strangeness Day. As she lay, still and quiet in her bed, she wondered to herself, along with everyone else around the world who was waking up that morning - what was going to happen this time?

She thought back to when it had all started, the very first time that strange things had happened simultaneously all over the world. It must have been six years ago, she calculated, when she was just nine years old. As she recalled, her and her sister had been playing outside when they immediately stopped what they were doing. They'd stood together, motionless and wide-eyed, as coloured balls rained down from the sky.

She could visualise the scene clearly in her mind, even after all this time. They were the size of tennis balls, perhaps slightly smaller, and all different colours, floating down in their thousands to land softly on the ground. She remembered that she had bent down and picked one of them up. It was soft and light, and spongy too, which explained why they had floated down so gently.

The pair had run home as fast as they could, thinking that their mother would surely have an explanation for what was going on, and to make sense of it all. But when they reached the house, their mother was standing outside gazing around, perplexed, with no more of an idea as to what was happening than they did. So, the three of them had stood together in the front garden just looking up at the sky, as the coloured spheres cascaded down all around them.

Looking back on it now, the whole episode was like a dream sequence, only it wasn't a dream of course, it had really happened. She recollected that after watching the phenomenon for a while, they had gone indoors and her mother had turned on the TV set to check the news. It showed the same extraordinary scene, the bizarre spectacle was happening all over the world, everywhere, in towns and cities to the remotest places - and no one could explain why.

It was a while before the balls eventually stopped falling, by which time the entire ground had become a mass of different-coloured dots, like a composition created by the dabbing of an assortment of felt-tipped pens on paper. It wasn't until much later in the day that they started to disappear from the ground, not melting away slowly like snowballs, but simply popping out of existence one by one. By the next morning they were all gone, but the whole world was talking about the extraordinary event of the previous day. No one had any explanation however, and there was no evidence left to examine.

* * *

As the weeks and months went by, people stopped talking about the event so much, it became just another one of those unsolved mysteries in the world. But then, the fourth of June came around again the following year - that was the year of the domes.

They began to appear all over the place, materialising out of nowhere, sometimes right in front of someone's eyes. They were the size of a small house, but round and featureless apart from a single door. They popped up everywhere, in various colours but always shiny and metallic.

As with the previous year, people had gathered around

their TV sets for an explanation as to what was going on. Once again, it showed that the occurrence was happening all over the world, it was a global phenomenon, and just as before, the news offered no explanation as to how or why; although it did reveal something about the nature of the domes - they were portals. If someone entered one, it would immediately transport them to a different dome someplace else. The location could be anywhere in the world, a city, a beach, the centre of the jungle or the top of a snow-capped mountain, and you wouldn't know where you'd end up until you stepped out at the other end. To return, you simply retraced your steps.

Sara visualised the dome that had materialised close to her home, a friend had discovered it in a field at the end of a quiet lane and had alerted everyone. All the kids had run over excitedly to see it, but when the parents arrived they told the children to keep away and sent them home, but she'd never forgotten how it looked. It was a silvery-purple colour, and made of the shiniest metal she had ever seen. As it sat there, glistening in the sunlight, it was like something from a different world.

The TV reported that day, that some people had been using the portals, but as far as she knew, no one ever used the one by her home, although she did hear that a man from a neighbouring town had tried one out. Apparently, when he stepped out at the other end, he found himself standing on an open plain in Africa, gazing out at giraffes and elephants with the roar of lions in the distance. What an experience that must have been, she thought to herself.

That was certainly a remarkable day. The following morning, not one dome remained, everything was back to normal. The extraordinary event had, just like the one from the previous year, baffled everyone. There was no doubt that something odd was occurring across the planet, but was there any significance to the fact that both events had happened on the same date? That was the question people were asking. Many were convinced that there was, others said that it was merely coincidence. There was only one way of knowing for sure of course, and that was to wait for the next June the fourth.

* * *

One year later, the whole world waited with anticipation. Nothing out of the ordinary had happened since the appearance of the domes, but as the fourth of June approached there was much expectancy and not a little excitement. Would something extraordinary happen again this year, they wondered. When the day eventually arrived, those that had hoped so were not disappointed - it was high-strangeness of the utmost kind.

As people awoke in their beds that morning, they sensed that their bodies felt different. They didn't seem right, a bit peculiar, and they felt lighter somehow. Some thought that they may be coming down with something, a touch of the flu perhaps, or maybe it was something they'd eaten the night before, but when they remembered what day it was, they suspected that it might have something to do with it.

Their suspicions were confirmed as soon as they stepped out from their beds, because when they did their feet never touched the floor, literally, they were floating a foot off the ground. This extraordinary occurrence was happening to everyone, to every single human being on the planet, and it lasted throughout the whole day, no one walked with their feet on the ground, everyone floated. Sara recalled how strange it had felt, and how if she put a thought in her mind of where she wanted to go, she would simply drift over to it. She and her sister had so much fun that day with their friends, it was a day they will never forget.

Of course, after the third incident it was clearly no coincidence that the events had all happened on the same day of the year. So the date of June the fourth was officially declared High-Strangeness Day, and became a global public holiday. People all over the world would celebrate it. Happy High-Strangeness Day cards were sent and unusual gifts were given, and the more unusual they were the better. The night before became known as High-Strangeness Eve, when friends and families stayed together overnight so that they could wake up excitedly the next morning to find out what would happen. No one could ever guess what the day was going to bring, although some tried, and most people began to look forward to June the fourth with great excitement.

* * *

Sara remembered the two most recent High-Strangeness Days very clearly; it was as if they'd happened only yesterday. Two years ago to the day, everyone awoke to find out that they were invisible. Nothing else had changed, the surroundings were the same, matter still had substance, including their bodies, only they were unseeable.

She thought back to how peculiar it was, walking around doing normal things but not being visible, and everyone talking to each other as usual but not actually seeing the person with whom they were conversing, just hearing a voice in mid-air. She smiled to herself when she recalled her pet dog, who could never quite work out what was going on. It was a crazy day for everyone, and so much fun. The invisibility had lasted until early evening, then everyone began to fade slowly back into view.

Then of course there was last year, which was a totally

different experience altogether, with the flying ships. The whole day, fantastic machines criss-crossing the sky, each one different to the next but no less bizarre. None of the craft landed, they just went to and fro above people's heads throughout the day and no one had any idea who was flying them, if indeed someone was flying them. The craft came in all shapes and sizes, some were sleek and futuristic, like spaceships from a far-off planet, others were mad, like something conjured up from a crazy person's mind. Some had wings but many didn't. There were silent ships and ones that made strange noises, some had tailpipes emitting puffs of smoke whilst others appeared to have no visible means of propulsion.

Sara smiled to herself when she remembered one particular craft that she and her sister had watched fly over their back garden. They had named it the Flying Teapot, because that's exactly what it was, a huge floating teapot complete with handle, lid, and spout, and that was just one of many extraordinary things that they saw up in the sky that day. A lot of people said that it was their most favourite High-Strangeness Day so far.

* * *

The reasons for, and causes of, High-Strangeness Day are still not known. Some are adamant that it's the work of a higher source somewhere, trying to awaken human beings to the fact that there is much more going on around them than they realise, whole worlds beyond the limitation of their five senses. Others say that it's an attempt by the creator to bring the people of the world together. Some claim that a wizard is responsible, that he's just having a bit of fun with everyone and will eventually get bored and stop doing it. But even if the latter were the case and the strange occurrences stopped, and June the fourth reverted back to being just like any other day of the year, the date would continue to be known as High-Strangeness Day, in memory of the events that had happened, and perhaps to serve as a reminder that unexplainable things can happen at any time.

* * *

Perhaps this is the year when it all stops, Sara thought to herself, now fully awake in her bed. She hoped not, along with Christmas it was her most favourite day and she wanted it to go on forever. That morning though, everything seemed to be just the same as always. She checked her body, it was exactly as it should be, she looked around her bedroom, everything appeared normal.

Although it was still very early in the morning, she decided that she would get up, maybe wrap up the High-Strangeness Day presents that she'd bought for her family; a ring for her mother that changes colour depending on the mood of the wearer, and for her sister, a small pot-plant that smells of chocolate. She doubted she could get back to sleep now anyway, even if she tried, because she was itching to see if anything was different.

Stepping down from her bed, Sara walked out of the bedroom, down the stairs and into the lounge; nothing untoward happened along the way. She considered turning on the TV to check the news but realised that it was probably too early, plus she didn't want to wake anyone.

Looking out through the window at the garden outside, there wasn't anything that stood out as being out of the ordinary. She looked up at the sky, it was just as it should be, there wasn't anything falling down from it or flying across it. Still in pyjamas and slippers, she slid open the patio door and stepped outside. It was a gorgeous day, the sun had risen and was proceeding to warm everything up with its golden rays, so she sat herself down on a wooden bench to catch the gentle sunshine and to savour the peace and stillness of the early morning.

As she sat, still and quiet, she thought that she heard a croaky voice beside her, it sounded a little bit like it had said good morning. She ignored it, putting it down to her state of mind due to the fact of what day it was. But then, she heard it again, even clearer this time, and it definitely did sound like someone had said good morning to her. Looking over toward the direction of where the voice came from, she noticed a frog sitting on a rock at the side of the garden pond. She felt silly in even doing so, but hesitantly, she addressed it.

"Did you happen to say good morning to me?"

"I most certainly did," replied the frog, "It is a beautiful morning don't you think?"

Sara was startled. "It certainly is, and a rather strange one at that."

"Naturally," said the little green amphibian, "surely you expected nothing less."

Just then, a pair of striped bumble bees passed by her ear. She could clearly hear that they were having a discussion about which flowers in the garden were the best for pollen. Sara leaned back on the garden bench and smiled.

"It's going to be a very interesting day," she said to herself.

Snowbound

1908 seemed like any other year for the residents of a small rural village in southern England called Borley. However, when the winter months came around, something happened there that was anything but ordinary - and unlikely to ever happen again.

* * *

Late October had brought the first of the frost, lightly dusting the fields in the early mornings before dissolving into the earth. With the onset of November came thicker layers, which was nothing out of the ordinary or unexpected for the time of year, but when the latter part of the month arrived there was a noticeable change. The sky became much whiter, individual clouds could no longer be made out, up above became one single blanket of stark whiteness. The villagers were experienced enough to recognise the signs, the sky's appearance and the bite in the air told them that heavy snow was imminent.

They'd dealt with such situations before; it wasn't a problem. Everyone in the village was always prepared, stocked-up with food and well-equipped with firewood and candles - they could survive in their homes for several months if needed. But days passed and nothing happened, not a single snowflake fell, yet all the while the sky became ever whiter, more dense, evidently heavily laden with snow. An eerie atmosphere now pervaded the air, as though something ominous was about to happen.

Then one morning, as a young child gazed quietly out from the window of their home, a tiny speck landed on the outside of the glass pane. Moving closer to examine it, the child noticed how pretty it was. Its body was star shaped, with six protruding arms. The arms were identical, and they themselves had different shapes coming out from them, and the whole thing glistened in the light - the first snowflake had fallen.

Within a matter of minutes, snow was falling upon the whole village thick and fast - it was a beautiful sight. In less than an hour it had settled on the ground, and snow continued to fall for the whole day. When evening time came around, everyone looked out from the windows of their homes where, from the glow of the street lamps, they could see that even larger snowflakes were now cascading down from above.

* * *

The snowfall continued throughout the night, so when the villagers awoke the next morning the view outside was one of pristine white; it was quite wonderful. The snow was clean and fresh, a pure whiteness, so much so that the ground appeared to glow.

The children were delighted, it was the first decent snowfall they'd had in a long time, so they were quickly outdoors with sledges, throwing snowballs and building snowmen. The snow fell throughout that day too, and once again the whole of the night, so by the second morning the depth of the snow had doubled. It was now a struggle to open front doors, shovels were needed to clear pathways, and smaller children had to remain indoors.

On the third day, most of the villagers had decided that it was probably better to stay inside. The level of the snow had reached halfway up the door, so going outside was proving difficult, if not impossible. The children viewed the astonishing spectacle through their windows, watching as one thing after another disappeared; bicycles, benches, and bushes, all consumed by a sea of white.

When the villagers awoke on the fourth morning, the snow was so deep that it covered all of the doors and almost the whole of the windows too; just a small gap remained at the very top. The children stood on sofas and stools to look out where the gaps were, and when they did, they could see that the snow was still falling. By that time, anything that had been on the ground was no longer visible, it was mostly a flat white landscape with the occasional mound where a tree stood. But it didn't stop there, because the following morning it wasn't even possible to look out through the tops of the windows at all, for they were totally covered. From inside each and every home, windows now appeared as large white squares and rectangles hanging on the walls.

It took just a few days more for the houses to be completely covered from top to bottom. The village of Borley was under snow, all that could be seen of it were the tops of chimneys poking out. It was a remarkable sight to see for the one person who was able to witness the spectacle from outside, one Percival Bishop, an eccentric hobbyist who was out in his hot-air balloon with his dog Archie. The pair had set off from a nearby village to view the landscape as they had never seen it before, and as they passed over Borley they looked down and were astonished. Where they usually saw numerous cottages, all that they could see was a scattering of brick squares poking out from a sheet of white, the tops of chimneys emitting smoke. Percival couldn't believe that it was the same place that he had seen so many times before, he smiled at the sight of it and Archie barked with delight. As for the villagers, well they were safe and sound inside their homes beneath the thick white covering, snuggled around log fires with toasted crumpets and cups of hot chocolate, passing the time away by telling stories and playing games.

* * *

Now in 1908 in small villages, there was no electricity, so fires and candles were used to light up the homes so that those who lived inside them could see; it was a primitive way but very cosy. And there were no such things as mobile phones either in those days, or even landline telephones for that matter, but despite being snowbound and separated, the villagers still found a way to communicate with each other. How they were able to do this was quite remarkable - they used mice.

The thing about mice is, they are much smarter than people realise, and the ones that lived in the village of Borley at that time were very smart, because they built a network of tunnels beneath the snow from which they could travel from one place to another. The tunnels that the rodents created, connected to the letterboxes of every house in the village, which the occupants realised could be put to good use - and they devised and developed an ingenious way to send messages to each other. They did this by writing a note on a piece of paper, folding it into a little square, and then handing it to a mouse. The mouse would take it from them, run through the tunnel with the note in its mouth, and deliver the piece of paper to its destination.

Now how on earth did the people of the village manage to get the mice to do this, you are probably wondering, and how could they get the little creatures to deliver the notes to the intended location. Well, it was quite simple really, it was all to do with training and reward. The mice knew that they would get a particular treat from a certain house; at number five for example they would get a peanut, whilst at number seven they would receive a piece of broken biscuit. So, it was possible to send a mouse to a particular house simply by drawing the correct symbol on the note. If the mouse saw a sketch of a peanut for instance, then it would know to go to house number five, whereas a picture of a biscuit meant that it should go to number seven, and the mice knew that if they did what was required of them, they would always be rewarded. At house number two they would get a piece of fruitcake, at number eight a raisin, whilst number ten would reward them with a cube of fresh apple, and so on and so forth. So, the mice knew exactly where to go to get their treats, and always delivered their assignment to the correct location.

It was an ingenious system that worked perfectly, one that was reliable, efficient, and rapid - much better than the local postman at the time to be honest. The villagers could send notes to whomever they wanted and whenever they wanted, and the mice were kept well fed during the harshest of times - it was a beautiful example of man and creature working together in perfect harmony.

* * *

The village of Borley remained entirely under snow for several weeks. It was a bizarre time for all those who went through the experience, although actually, most people quite enjoyed it if they were honest, especially the children who found it exciting. Snuggled up beside a cosy log fire beneath the surface, the villagers lived off their food supplies and obtained water by melting snow in a bucket over a fire, all the while staying in touch with each other with the help of their furry friends.

Then, one morning, everyone awoke to find that

something had changed; gaps had appeared once again at the tops of the windows. The gaps were just wide enough to peek through, and when they did, they saw that it was no longer snowing - at last the white stuff had all been used up. It took a further week for the snow and ice to thaw enough so that the people of the village could step out from their homes once more, and when they did it was nice to see the outside world again. The villagers shook hands with each other in celebration, and eagerly shared their hibernation stories, which were many. A few weeks later, it was Christmas.

* * *

The summer that followed was a splendid one. The sun shone down and the grass grew green, butterflies fluttered in the air and birds sang from the trees. As the villagers soaked up the hot sun, they remembered their extraordinary winter, which now seemed such a long time ago. During one balmy sunny afternoon, a hot-air balloon passed over the village. It was Percival Bishop, and as he looked down on everyone from his wicker basket he smiled and waved - and Archie barked happily.

THE LEGEND OF ALBERT HUBBLE

Imagine that your body is leaving the ground, floating slowly upwards towards the sky. If you keep on going you will eventually reach the clouds, pass through the clouds and you would be in what is known as the stratosphere. Continue, and you will travel through the mesosphere, the thermosphere, then eventually find yourself in the outermost layer of the Earth's atmosphere, the exosphere. At this point, you will be about halfway to the moon - but let's not stop here.

Continue on, past the moon, and it might be said that you were floating around in the solar system. This is a fantastic place, with its star at the centre which we call the Sun, and several orbiting planets, of which our Earth is one. There are other things here too besides planets, like comets for instance, which are masses of dirty snowballs, and asteroids, millions of them drifting around in space. Asteroids are metallic rocks, some as small as the pebbles that you would find on a beach, others are as wide as four-hundred football pitches.

Now from this point on, if you chose to go one way you would head towards the sun, but as it's a huge ball of fiery gas then let's go in the other direction. You will reach Mars first of all, then Jupiter, and then Saturn, where you may choose to stop for a while to admire the fascinating rings that surround it. If you look closely, you will see that the rings are made up of tiny particles of ice and rock.

Beyond Saturn, you will pass by the blue planets of Uranus and Neptune, until eventually you would reach what was once known as the outermost planet of our solar system

- Pluto. Is Pluto a planet or is it not a planet? Well, we aren't exactly sure at this moment because it's still being debated. Owing to the fact that Pluto is so small, astronomers can't quite decide, so for the time being I think we should simply call it a dwarf planet.

So as you float around the dwarf planet of Pluto, you would be in what's known as the Milky Way. This is the name of our galaxy, so called because it's made up of so many stars that when you gaze up at it from Earth, you don't see the spaces in between them, you just see a vast area the colour of milk. But the view from up here is much better than the one down on Earth, and it feels kind of strange here too, floating around in space. The Milky Way is only one of the trillions of galaxies that make up our universe, so it's fair to say that our universe is pretty big, and there are trillions of other universes beyond that.

Now you might decide to spend some time here, which would be a cool and amazing thing to do, drifting in orbit around Pluto, enjoying the peace and quiet and admiring the magnificent view. But, if you did decide to go on just a little further, then you might be in for a surprise, because, as you floated slowly and silently out from the solar system, you may well come upon . . . . Albert Hubble.

Now who is Albert Hubble you may be asking yourself, or perhaps more importantly, what is he doing sitting on an asteroid, fifty-billion miles out in space? Well, here's how it all happened . . . . . .

* * *

Albert Winston Horatio Hubble, to give him his full name, once lived in Stoke Newington, England. Why we now find him in deepest outer space is to do with the fact that he was once Science Teacher at the local primary school. He wasn't however, just any old science teacher, for he was also an inventor, which meant of course that he was partial to an experiment or two - and experiments can sometimes go wrong.

As Science Teacher at Stoke Newington Primary School for Boys and Girls, Mr. Hubble, or Hubble the Bubble as the children called him, was thought highly of. He spoke softly, never shouted, was always polite, and was so preoccupied with doing experiments that he rarely gave out a detention. Because of this, he was generally liked by his pupils, although it's fair to say they did think him a little odd. This was due partly to his appearance, of outdated suits, spotted ties, and little round glasses, but also to the fact that throughout the day he drank nothing but Burke & Burge's Best Cream Soda. He virtually lived on the stuff and would always have at least four or five bottles scattered about his person, the necks of the bottles sticking out from his many pockets.

* * *

Albert Hubble was dedicated to science, if he wasn't teaching it in school then he'd be experimenting or inventing something in the house that he shared with his mother. There were just the two of them at number 32 Winifred Road: Albert was an only child. He and his mother were much alike and he'd inherited many of her ways: the need for routine, attention to detail, aversion to noise, as well as being somewhat obsessed with cleanliness. Yes, the schoolteacher hated grubbiness of any kind and would often lecture his pupils about the importance of cleanliness, reminding them that it was next to godliness.

His biggest gripe of all was dirty ears, they were unacceptable to him, so at the end of each lesson he would always remind his class not to forget to wash behind them. It was usually to no avail however, weekly ear inspections were not a pretty sight, which used to get the teacher down somewhat. But it did happen to spawn his very own 'Eureka' moment, when the idea of the automatic instant body-wash machine was born.

As soon as the concept had been conceived, the inventor got to work, devoting all of his spare time to the project. So, whilst Mrs. Hubble sat downstairs knitting pullovers and darning socks, her son was up in his room planning and constructing. He was determined to do it, and lo and behold, just six months after its conception, his baby was born - a machine with the potential to clean a child all over in a matter of seconds. And it was easy to use, the subject simply needed to take their place in the apparatus, push a few buttons, then sit back and let the positive and negative ions do the rest. They would emerge spotless, their body, their clothes, even behind their ears, everything would be as clean as a whistle.

"What a magnificent gift I have bestowed upon the world," the inventor proclaimed to himself triumphantly. "Dirty kids will be a thing of the past, and the name of Albert Hubble will go down in history."

All that was left to do was to test his invention. So one night, under cover of darkness and with the help of his mum, he transported the automatic instant body-wash machine to his school laboratory, from where tests could begin.

Initial results were promising. Tea stains from canteen cups disappeared instantly, grubby fingerprints from textbooks were totally removed, and the pot plant from the headmaster's desk had never looked so radiant. When the local zoo had let the teacher borrow Charlie the chimpanzee for a supposed anatomy class, they were over the moon when he was returned, saying that it was much appreciated but there really was no need to have given him a bath and full body scrub before handing him back.

All was going fantastically well, and the inventor was ready to proceed to the final stage, but for that he would require a human guinea pig. Luckily, he knew exactly where he could find one, lots in fact - he had a whole classroomful.

* * *

It was Thursday morning for the pupils of Stoke Newington Primary School for Boys and Girls, which meant double science. There was a noticeable apprehension amongst the children that morning however, as they sat waiting for Hubble the Bubble to arrive, a definite tension filled the air. And it was with good reason, for it had not gone unnoticed that the behaviour of their teacher over the past few weeks had been even stranger than usual, and suspicions were magnified when, at the end of their last lesson, he had not reminded them all to wash behind their ears as they left the class. This had never happened before; he was definitely up to something.

Now if alarm bells were not already ringing, then the sight that greeted the pupils that Thursday morning must have surely set them off. Because, sitting in the middle of the classroom, was the most hideous contraption they had ever seen. Looking like a cross between a photo-booth and a robotic octopus, it filled them with deep unease. Painted on the side of the monstrosity was an inscription that read: The Hubble 3000.

* * *

When the teacher eventually arrived, he said nothing about

the 'thing' sitting smack bang in the middle of the room. He chose instead to give an address, an emotive speech if you like, not so much about famous inventors, but more about their heroic accomplices. Those brave souls who have gone down in history as assistants to the great inventors, and without whom, important discoveries would never have been made.

"Alexander Graham Bell had his Thomas Watson, Marconi his William Holwell, and Pavlov his dog, their names forever written in the annals of history because they saw their opportunity and seized the day."

When he'd finished his speech, the fear level amongst the pupils had reached an all-time high, and it was then that the teacher chose to enlighten them about the mysterious object in the middle of the room. He explained confidently and eloquently, what it was, the enormous benefits of it, and how it was going to revolutionise the world. The teacher and inventor then went on to tell them what a momentous day this was, and how fortunate they were to be able to witness history in the making. Finally, with arms out wide as if offering their heart's desires, he asked which one of them would like to go down in history as the first person ever to use the Hubble 3000.

"Carpe Diem children!" he proclaimed, "Carpe Diem!"

The expected raising of numerous grubby hands never happened. In fact, there were none, just a deathly silence filled the room. Furthermore, the children seemed to have froze to their seats with a look of fear on their faces. Even Beefy Baxter the school bully, who was usually up for anything, looked terrified. The teacher was hugely disappointed by the negative response, and even tried offering a bottle of his Burke & Burge's Best to anyone who volunteered, which had always worked in the past, but even this was to no avail:

no one was going to take up the offer.

Albert Hubble, however, was a determined man, and he wasn't going to abandon his dream simply because of a lack of courage and ambition from his pupils. So, he announced there and then, to the whole class, that he himself would demonstrate the automatic instant body-wash machine. As soon as the pupils heard this, as if in rehearsed unison, a collective sigh echoed around the room. The atmosphere instantly changed, tension was replaced by relief, fear by almost excitement, and the whole class became suddenly interested.

* * *

The children watched on, both perplexed and intrigued, as this obviously mad, someone plump man, in a striped suit with spotted tie, and bottles of cream soda sticking out from every pocket, squashed himself into the hideous contraption. With much effort and grunting noises, the teacher managed to sit himself down inside the Hubble 3000 and close the door behind him. Hushed silence followed, then excited anticipation as the onlookers waited with bated breath. A snigger was heard coming from the back of the classroom, it was Beefy Baxter, like a spider in its web eyeing an unsuspecting fly, he sensed impending misfortune and was enjoying it immensely.

There was a whirring sound as the machine came to life. Lights came on and buzzers buzzed. The floor shook, and sparks flew. After about half a minute, from amidst the whirring and banging came a noise from deep inside, one that seemed to emanate not from the machine but from Mr. Hubble himself. It was a sound not dissimilar to the one made by a plughole as the last bit of water drains away in the bathtub. And then . . . a sudden explosive flash as a huge plume of smoke rose to the ceiling. And finally . . . . . quiet.

The pupils looked on, half expecting their teacher to emerge out from the Hubble 3000 cleaner and brighter than ever before. But nothing happened. So they waited, and waited, for several minutes in fact, as the smoke settled to the floor of the classroom and the contraption made clicking and clacking noises as it cooled down. But no movement came from within the machine. The pupils looked at each other - something had gone wrong.

It was Beefy Baxter, being the bravest of them all, who decided to take charge. He got up from his chair, walked slowly over to the Hubble 3000, and cautiously pulled on the handle to open the door. The sound of a click broke the silence, and then . . . gasps. The opening of the door revealed an empty seat, the science teacher was gone - Hubble the Bubble had popped off.

* * *

Stoke Newington Primary School for Boys and Girls was headline news. There was excitement in the scientific community, naturally, but scandal in the newspapers. Aside from inventing the world's first instant body wash device, it seems that their science teacher had inadvertently invented the world's first teleportation machine. Unfortunately, no one could fathom out how it worked, where the poor man had gone, or indeed, how to get him back.

Theories were put forward of course. Maybe he simply dissolved into the ether, or shifted into another dimension. One top scientist suggested that the high level of sugar in the teacher's blood system from the Burke & Burge's Best Cream Soda may have reacted with the photons and neutrons, causing his molecules to be dispersed into two-zillion pieces. This in fact wasn't too far from the truth, the only thing they failed to add was that Mr. Hubble's molecules then travelled at two-hundred times the speed of light through time and space, until they met an object consisting of suitable components to reconstitute them. In this case, it happened to be an asteroid made up of 20% iron, 20% silver, and 60% carbon, which also happened to be floating about in the outer edges of the solar system, just beyond the dwarf planet of Pluto.

* * *

Over time, the excitement of this extraordinary event faded somewhat, but it was never forgotten. Especially in Stoke Newington, where a bronze statue proudly stands in the town square, of a strange-looking man wearing odd clothes, and holding in his hand what appears to be a bottle of pop. An inscription at the base of the statue reads:

A. W. H. Hubble: Inventor and Explorer - the first man in the world to go . . . . somewhere.

THE LIGHTHOUSE

It was my first visit to the southwest of England; a family holiday. I was young at the time, around twelve years old, and the location that my parents had chosen was perfect, the archetypal Cornish setting of old stone cottage surrounded by cliffs and coves. Our home for the week was an original smugglers' dwelling perched high on the cliff edge, with the coastal path right outside our door. The path runs the length of the Cornish coastline so we could walk for miles in either direction, taking in the magnificent cliffs and the crashing waves of the sea.

Cornwall certainly is a mysterious place, steeped in folklore and entrenched in fables of pirate ghost ships, smugglers caves, and things that come out at night. And something mysterious certainly happened to my brother and sister and I during our stay, a reminder of which still hangs on my wall to this day - not that we would ever forget.

* * *

Our rented property stood all on its own. There were neighbours around but none close by, and despite being small and somewhat isolated, the accommodation had all that we needed: electricity, running water, and a good supply of logs for the fire. A narrow stone pathway led down to some local shops in the bay where we could buy essential supplies. There was a grocery, a small gift shop, newsagent, bakery, and an antique shop too. If you followed the pathway past the shops it led to the seafront, with its tearoom and tavern. Running adjacent to the beach was a picturesque row of traditional fishermen's cottages facing out to sea, each one painted a different colour.

My brother and sister and I spent much of our time exploring. At that age it was like being in a different world, and we spent hours on the beach, paddling in the sea and messing about on the sand, or searching for something interesting that may have washed up on the shore. Pirate ships once frequented these waters and even to this day, artefacts from that romantic time can still drift in with the tide.

We did the coastal walk many times during our stay, in both directions, enjoying the spectacular views. Ravens dipped and dived over the cliffs, seals bobbed up and down in the water, and we sometimes sighted a peregrine falcon surveying the area for food. Following the path west, for about forty minutes, took us to an old abandoned tin mine which was great for exploring. It felt strange to imagine how it must have been hundreds of years ago when the mine was a hive of activity.

We did some night walks too during our stay, which were a whole different experience to walking in the daytime. With our torches in hand, it's fair to say that they were slightly eerie, but exciting too, and it was on one of these nocturnal excursions that we had our strange experience.

* * *

For this particular night walk we'd decided to take a different route to the one that we usually took. Instead of joining the coastal path directly from our house, we took a narrow pathway that led inland through an area of high grass and bushes, before it curved around through some small trees and then up to join the coastal path there. We had already done the route before during the day so were familiar with the path, and we all agreed that it would make an interesting walk when it was dark.

I remember it clearly, even to this day. In one area there were hundreds of glowworms dotted around, their green luminescence lighting up the tall grass, it was quite magical to see, and bats had swooped around our heads as we came out from the coppice of trees. It was a great walk, and interesting, yet nothing too out of the ordinary to begin with. But as we made our way up the path towards the cliff, things started to get rather odd.

It all began when we noticed that an area of the clifftop in the distance was lit up by a faint light. We couldn't tell from where the light was coming from exactly because part of the cliff was obscuring our view, but we immediately thought it a bit strange. As we continued on, we discussed what it might be. Night fishermen perhaps out in their boats, but the source of the light was coming from the land and shining outwards, not the other way around, and besides, it would have to be a big boat to cast its light across such a large area, and all the fishing boats that we had seen were small wooden vessels. Maybe it was campers spending the night beside a fire on the clifftop - we would soon find out.

The nearer we got the more intrigued we became, and as we came close to the cliff edge our view was no longer obscured, and that's when we saw it - an old lighthouse standing tall and mysterious on the rocks.

* * *

We couldn't understand how we had never noticed the Lighthouse before, as we'd walked past the same area during the day, on more than one occasion. Standing there on the clifftop, with the expansive dark sea below us, it felt eerily silent. In the hazy glow of the light, the three of us walked slowly towards the tower. It looked very old, and when we eventually stood beside it, it was like we had somehow stepped back in time.

The building was solid, thick walled, and its foundation had been constructed from the same large rocks as the cliff upon which it stood, making it appear as if it were rising up from the ground itself. As the structure went up, the rocks got smaller, eventually becoming normal-sized bricks at the top, but ones that had been carved from the same stone. There were a couple of lookout windows on the sides, and at the very top was the classic glass dome feature of all lighthouses.

There was no electricity inside the building we concluded, because the internal light that shone on the inside of the windows continuously flickered, so the source must have come from either lanterns or candles. We all agreed that the beam of light coming out from the top was a bit odd. Although it spanned a reasonable area it was quite dim, too dim in fact, not the bright shining light that we assumed a lighthouse should emit. None of us had seen a lighthouse close up before, it certainly was interesting, and exciting too - but definitely a bit spooky during the night.

We stood outside the big wooden door for a while, and we could see that it had a thick, black, iron door handle. I can't remember whether it was my brother or sister, but one of them tried pushing down on it, probably just out of curiosity, not really expecting it to budge. But to our surprise, the handle moved and the door unlocked, so we entered, but cautiously. I recall the door being very heavy and hard to push, we all had to contribute to get it to open.

As soon as we stepped inside, we became strangely absorbed by our surroundings, as though under some kind of spell. The three of us stood at the bottom of the musty old tower, looking around at the inside of the walls and the stairway that spiralled upwards. I remember thinking about how old it must have been, and that someone hundreds of years ago had once stood in the same spot, seeing the exact same thing as we were now seeing. We discovered that we were correct about the inside light source, which turned out to be candles, they'd been placed on narrow stone ledges on the inside of the walls. The flames flickered with the gentle wafts of air, creating eerie shadows that danced around on the damp brickwork.

All three of us made our way up the stone steps that hugged the wall, our torchlight adding even more shadow shapes to the ones that the candles produced. We passed by the lowest of the windows and were just able to see out from it, then continued up to the level of the second window, but having tried looking out through that one we could see nothing, the glass pane looked totally black. Up and up the spiral steps we went, eventually reaching the top, where we came upon the lantern room - so we entered.

The lantern room was small and compact, but there was enough room for all of us to walk around the machinery in the centre, the workings of the lamp. I didn't want to look directly at the source of the light, but the surrounding light wasn't too bright so I could see the rest of the apparatus without hurting my eyes. I remember seeing a large metal tube upon which the light sat, and at the base was a circular tray. Knowing what I do now, I would say that what I saw was an oil lamp, and the tray at the bottom would have been used for catching the drips; I do recall it having a peculiar smell.

My brother and sister and I looked around for a while inside the lantern room, just the three of us. We had thought that there might have been a lighthouse keeper, but there was no one but ourselves. I can remember the lamp gave off a nice heat, it shone gently out in all directions and through the glass we could make out the rocks and the sea below which were lit up by the glow. Looking out across the land, we were surprised. From being so high up, and what with it being night time, we'd expected to see the lights of the towns and the houses that were scattered along the coast, but there was hardly anything, just a couple of tiny lights in the distance and what looked like a wood fire from a nearby cove.

After a while, we decided to make our way down, carefully traversing the stone steps in the candle and torch light. It was much easier going down and we soon reached the bottom, and after pulling open the big wooden door we stepped outside. The difference in the air was immediately noticeable, cooler and much fresher than the stale air inside.

It was as we were walking away that something peculiar happened. We had all turned around to have one last look before leaving, and that's when we noticed that there was someone looking out at us from the bottom window. It was unmistakably a man, we could all make him out, he had a beard and a cap, and seemed to be wearing an old black overcoat. It must have been the lighthouse keeper we all thought, but we couldn't understand how we had not seen him when we were inside. He couldn't possibly have been in there when we were, we were absolutely sure of it. He was certainly not in the lantern room as we would have seen him, and there were no other rooms coming off from the staircase either. The building had only one entrance in and out, and we hadn't passed anyone on our way down. We couldn't work it out, it was a mystery.

After what seemed like about a minute, the figure looking out at us disappeared from view, and that's when we decided to head off home. We followed the pathway back to our cottage, and on the way we spoke of nothing else, trying to reason an explanation for the man at the window.

* * *

The following morning, we told our parents all about the incident and what had happened on the clifftop. They knew nothing of any lighthouse in the area, as far as they were aware the nearest one was at Lizard Point which was many miles away, not even visible from where we were let alone close enough to walk to. However, they did say that they would ask he housecleaner who was due in later that morning, she had lived in the locality for many years and knew the area well. Following breakfast, there was only one thing that my brother and sister and I had in mind to do, we were going back to the same spot, to take a look at the lighthouse in the daylight. If we were lucky, we might even get to meet the mysterious lighthouse keeper.

We retraced our steps, doing the exact same walk as the night before. Through the grassy fields where we'd seen the glowworms, out from the small trees where the bats had swooped around our heads, and then up the slope to the clifftop. As we got close we were all quite excited, eager to see the lighthouse again, this time in the clear light of day. However, when we reached the spot where the lighthouse was, it wasn't there. Where it stood, there was nothing, just some scattered rocks and flat ground.

We wondered if perhaps we were in the wrong location, that we had somehow followed a different path, but it didn't seem possible. There was only one single pathway through the fields and bushes, and besides, everything around us looked exactly the same as when we were there the night before, the only thing missing was the tall stone tower rising upwards. We spent some time searching the area, but we never found anything. On the way back, we checked if there were any other pathways that led off from the main one that we may have inadvertently taken, but just as we had thought there weren't. We had definitely gone to the same place.

* * *

Back at our property, we told our parents that we were unable to find the lighthouse again. It was then that they informed us that the housecleaner had told them that there were no lighthouses in the area, but they did offer an explanation as to what may have happened. They explained that we had probably stumbled upon an old abandoned cottage, one that must have had a workshop or mill attached to it, which would account for the tall staircase and the strange machinery. As for the man looking out from the window, it was just a trick of the light and shadow combined with our overactive imaginations. And the reason why we didn't see the house when we returned was simple, we hadn't gone back to the same spot.

We never said anything, but we were sure that what our parents had told us could not have been possible. It was a lighthouse that we had seen, from both outside and within, there was no mistaking it. We had climbed the steps, many of them, and seen the lamp at the top, and we had looked down at the rocks below, and we had clearly seen the lighthouse keeper looking out from the window. We realised that we had experienced something very strange that night, something out of the ordinary.

* * *

That wasn't the end of the story though, because something else happened before we left, something that explained the mystery in one way yet added to it in another.

It was on the final morning of our stay, the three of us had taken the walk down the steps to the village shops to buy some gifts and souvenirs to take back with us before going home. After visiting the gift shop, we went into the antique shop on the corner to have a browse around. We were only in there a short time when my brother yelled out, telling my sister and I to come quickly. When we did, he pointed to an old framed photograph hanging on the wall. It was the lighthouse, the same one that we had seen, just as we had seen it and seemingly in the exact same location on the clifftop.

We asked the shopkeeper if she knew anything about the picture, and fortunately she did. The lady informed us that the photo was very old, and that it had been taken not far from where we were. She explained that the lighthouse was no longer there, it had been severely damaged a long time ago during a bad storm, which had blown off the lantern room and brought it crashing down into the sea. Following the unfortunate occurrence, the lighthouse was subsequently inoperable and eventually fell into ruin. Over time, as the many years passed, more and more of the structure collapsed and fell into the sea, until nothing remained of it.

We thanked the shopkeeper for telling us about the photograph and the history of the lighthouse, and we said our goodbyes. Before departing though, we put some money together and purchased the picture. The old black and white photograph of the lighthouse on the clifftop still hangs on my wall to this day, a reminder of this strange event that happened to us.

Nine White Clouds Above an English Village

If you venture deep into the English countryside, you may stumble upon a delightful little place by the name of Foggy-on-the-Moor. One fortunate enough to do so might choose to stay a while, to stop for lunch perhaps or to admire the views, and those who do, well they may be inclined to think that Foggy-on-the-Moor was just a typical English village much like the rest - but they would be wrong. Because, if they looked closely, they would realise that things aren't entirely as they should be, and that there is something rather curious about the folk who live there.

They will notice, that whilst chatting to each other, the locals will often stop for a brief moment to look up at the sky. Some will smile, some will appear to be deep in thought, whilst others will simply shake their heads before returning to their conversations. An observant onlooker would notice this for sure, but the very observant ones, those rare folk who tend to spot the little nuances and peculiarities that most people miss, will detect something more, something very peculiar. For they would realise that the villagers were not simply looking up at the sky, they were actually looking up at a small clump of white clouds sitting high above their heads, nine of them in fact.

Now this is rather odd in itself, but what's even odder is the fact that this small cluster of clouds are in the same place above the village every single day. They never move, no matter what the weather, no matter how strong the wind, every day, every week, every month, the same nine small fluffy white clouds sitting motionless above the village. And there is a reason for this, and why Foggy-on-the-Moor is not such a typical English village after all. To know why, we will need to go back a few years, to a time when a certain person lived there, someone by the name of Ernest Cumberpatch . . . . . .

* * *

It was a lovely morning; the sun had risen in all its splendour and was shining down brightly upon Foggy-on-the-Moor. Most folk were awake and going about their usual business, like one Ernest Cumberpatch, who was up bright and early and taking a stroll through the local high street to buy some bread. He was a friendly sort of chap, always liked to stop and chat with anyone he bumped into - although the villagers weren't always so keen to talk to him.

On this particular morning, he encountered Mrs. Harrison waiting outside the Post Office, so he took the opportunity to exchange pleasantries.

"Ah, Good Morning Mrs. Harrison," he enthused, "and how are you today?"

"Oh, err, not too good I'm afraid, in fact, I should get home as soon as possible. Goodbye, have a nice day." And off she went.

"Oh, good day," Ernest called out, as she disappeared down the street.

As he continued on, he came upon Mr. Clarke who was just about to open up the bank.

"Hello Thomas, fine morning don't you think?"

"Hello Ernest, yes, it is a pleasant morning indeed. Oh, but I must get on, sorry, got things to do."

Mr. Cumberpatch strolled on to the bakery, and just as his nostrils caught the warming aroma of freshly baked bread, he saw dear Mrs. Bumble walking her dog.

"Oh, good day Betty," he said, bending down to stroke the little Yorkshire terrier at her feet, "and how is the furry fellow today?"

"Oh he's very well thank you" she replied, but then immediately seemed to change her mind. "Oh no, actually he isn't, he isn't well at all, poor little Tyson has an upset tummy so I must get him home this instant. Goodbye."

"Oh I do hope he isn't too bad, he certainly looks okay," Ernest called out, as Mrs. Bumble dashed off down the road with her dog in tow. No one seems to have any time to talk nowadays, he thought to himself, a sign of the times I suppose.

When he entered the bakery, Mr. Miller was putting out newly baked cottage loaves onto the shelves and they smelled delicious.

"Good morning," enthused Mr. Cumberpatch.

"Oh good morning," said the baker, somewhat nervously. "And what would you like today Ernest?"

"Well, this morning I would like one of your finest loaves. I plan to make myself a nice heartwarming sweet potato soup and I thought a slice of your . . ." But before he had a chance to finish the sentence, Mr. Miller had placed into his arms a large fresh wholemeal bloomer.

"There you go, this is exactly what you need, my finest and most popular. Thank you and good day to you sir."

"Oh, oh thank you," said the grateful recipient, "but I haven't paid yet, let me see, what do I have in my . . ."

"Oh don't worry about that, I'll put it on the slate, you can pay me another time."

"But you always say that."

"That's just fine, you hurry along now, it's lovely weather outside and you don't want to be stuck indoors on a day like this."

"Well thank you very much. Yes you are right of course, it is a lovely day."

With the loaf of bread under his arm, the cheery customer proceeded to leave the shop, but as he reached the door he stopped momentarily and called back to the baker.

"Although we should enjoy the nice weather while it lasts, I've seen the forecast, at five o'clock it's going to be raining cats and dogs."

Mr. Miller walked over to the lone wooden chair sitting behind the counter, slumped down into it, then put his head in his hands.

"Oh dear, oh dear, oh dear," he said solemnly to himself.

* * *

Throughout the rest of the morning and afternoon, everything was as normal as could be hoped for in Foggy-on-the-Moor, people went about their regular business and the day was calm and uneventful. However, as five o'clock approached it became almost too quiet, something didn't feel right, as if it were a lull before a storm. The villagers were apprehensive, they had felt this feeling before, but only one of them had an inkling as to what might be coming.

Peering out from his bakery shop window, was Mr. Miller. He was looking up at the sky, his eyes fixed on a substantial rain cloud that had recently drifted over and positioned itself directly above the village. A feeling of dread began to manifest deep within his stomach, the great cumulonimbus hung overhead like some harbinger of doom.

The fearful baker continued to gaze upwards, watching and waiting . . . . and then it happened. Five o'clock arrived on the dot, and something emerged out from the cloud and began falling down to earth. Mr. Miller watched as it descended, he could tell that it had form, a shape. Looking closely, he could see that whatever it was had a body, and a head, and if he focused his eyes he could just make out a tail. Then more and more began to tumble out from the cloud, until there were many, all descending on Foggy-on-the-Moor.

As the shapes came closer, it became obvious what they were: Beagles, Dalmatians, salukis, Pekinese, poodles, peekaboos, sausage-dogs, and terriers of all kinds - dogs were falling from the sky in their hundreds. But it wasn't just animals of the canine variety, there were felines too: ginger toms, Persians, Siamese, American shorthairs and Japanese bobtails, and others he didn't know the names of, dropping thick and fast to land safely on the ground. As the animals rained down, the villagers ran for cover, panic-stricken, locking themselves inside their homes for safety.

The cats and dogs ran amuck. Bins were trashed and shops were looted, and there was barking and caterwauling throughout the evening and all through the night, the noise was unbearable. No one got any sleep, apart from the occupant of number 10 Lupin Drive that is, a certain Ernest Cumberpatch who, tucked up in his bed, snored peacefully, totally unaware of the mayhem that he had caused. Mr. Cumberpatch had struck again, and just as he had said, at five o'clock it had rained cats and dogs.

* * *

No one in the village knew how he had come to have such an ability, or curse as most called it - the Cumberpatch Curse, but their lives had never been the same since the day he'd arrived. They were pleased to have him at first, Mr. and Mrs. Cumberpatch seemed pleasant enough, respectable, ordinary people, but it didn't take them long to realise that there was something not right about *him*.

The thing was, he liked to talk, which is fine in itself, but when Ernest Cumberpatch talked he liked to use phrases, and when he quoted a phrase it would often come true, literally. So if he told one of the ladies that she had a bee in her bonnet, a bee could suddenly appear and start buzzing beneath her hat, and if he remarked that someone was the black sheep of the family, the person might immediately go down on all fours and begin munching on the grass, occasionally lifting their head to say "baa" in a confused tone.

It was an unfortunate situation, and because of it, everyone was afraid to talk to the local resident for fear of what he might say. What made matters worse was that Mr. Cumberpatch himself was oblivious to it, totally unaware of the drastic consequences of his spoken words, even when the other residents tried to tell him, even when something happened right in front of his eyes, and even when something happened to him himself. Such as the occasion when he addressed the assembly in the local village hall, and had asked the audience to excuse him because he had a frog in his throat.

* * *

The morning after the village had been terrorised by wild cats and dogs, a clean-up operation was put in place, with most people taking the day off work to assist with the tidying up and repairs. The army were called in to round up the animals and transport them to Battersea Dogs & Cats Home.

Thankfully, by evening time things had returned to normal once again, which was a huge relief to everyone. But the locals knew that normality was only a temporary thing in their little world, and that it was only a matter of time before another passing remark from a certain person would cause mayhem and chaos once more. Some were not prepared to simply stand by and wait for this to happen, and Mr. Garvey the fishmonger was one of them. He was hit harder than most by the incident of the cats and dogs, his fish stocks had been totally cleaned out, all that remained were hundreds of fishbones scattered over the shop floor. He for one had had enough, and he'd decided to have a word with the man who was responsible.

* * *

It was a week or so before Mr. Garvey had plucked up enough courage to proceed with his plan, so one Tuesday lunchtime there was a knock at the front door of number 10 Lupin Drive. The occupant of the house got promptly up from his easy chair and made his way along the hall to answer it. When he opened the door, he was delighted to see Mr. Garvey standing outside.

"Oh Gilbert, how wonderful to see you, please do come in. It's so nice of you to come to see me."

"Well, I won't be able to stay long I'm afraid, I've just popped in for a quick word."

"Oh you're always welcome you know that, I don't seem to get many visitors nowadays. I'll tell you what I'll do, you sit yourself down and make yourself comfortable and I'll put the kettle on and make us both a nice cup of tea."

As Ernest Cumberpatch pottered about in the kitchen, Gilbert Garvey sat nervously on the flower-patterned sofa in the lounge. He could hear the host in the adjacent room, opening and closing cupboard doors and mumbling away to himself. The feeling of unease that the fishmonger felt this morning had now developed into a sense of impending doom. What had seemed like a good idea one week ago now appeared utter folly, in fact, he was regretting having gone there at all.

Just as he was considering getting up and leaving, the friendly host entered the room carrying a silver tray, upon which stood a teapot, two cups with saucers, and what looked like fruitcake. As he placed the tray down on a small wooden table, he noticed that his friend and neighbour had turned rather pale.

"Are you okay Gilbert?" he asked, in a compassionate tone. "You look a bit . . . ill."

His guest shook his head nervously. "Oh it's nothing for sure, just a slight indigestion that's all," he replied, then quickly added as an afterthought, "Perhaps I should be going home."

"No, no, of course not, have a nice cup of tea, I'm sure it will make you feel much better. You know Gilbert, it's so kind of you to come to see me, I was starting to get the impression that people were trying to avoid me, but then I tell myself that I'm being silly, that it's just my imagination. You see, I do like a nice chat, and since Mrs. Cumberpatch disappeared six months ago, well, I haven't really had anyone to talk to."

"Oh yes, poor Mrs. Cumberpatch," replied the visitor, "and how strange, disappearing just like that."

"Yes indeed, it was like she vanished into thin air."

"And you've no idea where she went?"

"Haven't a clue, there was no note, nothing."

"Well it's a mystery I suppose," said the fishmonger, his anxiety level rising by the minute.

"It certainly is, I will never forget the night that it happened, I remember it like it were yesterday. As I recall, she seemed a bit tired that evening, so I advised her to go to bed and get some rest. I made her a nice cup of cocoa and tucked her in, kissed her goodnight as always, and instructed her not to worry. I told her to close her eyes, relax, and she would soon be in the land of Nod. When I returned to the bedroom not long afterwards, she was gone."

"Oh dear," said Mr. Garvey, now a bag of nerves. "Oh dear, oh dear."

"Anyway, enough about me," said the host, sitting comfortably in his easy chair and sipping this tea, was there anything in particular you wanted to talk to me about or did you just feel like coming to see me for a pleasant chat?"

"Well, mm, actually there was something. It was, err, well, you see, erm." The fishmonger was struggling to find the right words, any confidence and bravery he had mustered prior to coming was gone, he was a nervous wreck and found it difficult to speak.

"Well, it's, what I mean to say is, it's like this . . . . . . you see, Mr., mmm, Mr. Pundercatch, ..." Gilbert Garvey stopped speaking and began trembling like a jelly.

Ernest Cumberpatch looked perplexingly at his friend. "Oh do speak up," he said, "what is it? What on earth is the matter with you Gilbert? It seems the cat has got your tongue."

There was a moments silence, then Mr. Garvey held his mouth in horror, if he wasn't totally speechless before, he certainly was now. At the same time, next door at house number eight, Mrs. O'Grady had gone into the kitchen to feed her pet cat.

"Caesar, oh Caesar darling, where are you? Time for din-dins."

Her beloved moggy entered the room and strolled nonchalantly towards her. When it arrived at her feet, the gentle kitty looked up at its owner with loving eyes, and Mrs. O'Grady recoiled in horror at the sight of the long pink rubbery thing wriggling and writhing in the animal's mouth. When she bent down to take a closer look, she realised what it was and let out an almighty scream, so loud that it was heard all over the village.

* * *

Twenty-four hours later, things had thankfully calmed down. The tongue had mercifully reappeared in the mouth of its rightful owner, who lay in the small-local hospital bed recovering from severe shock. In the bed next to him lay his next-door neighbour, recovering from severe trauma.

The news of the event travelled around the village like wildfire, the locals were talking and they were not happy, the night of the cats and dogs and now this. Clearly something had to be done, so an emergency meeting was called, and everyone bar the occupant of number 10 Lupin Drive was invited.

* * *

On the evening of the meeting, the village hall was full. Everyone attended, emotions were running high and they all wanted their say.

"Enough is enough," proclaimed Mrs. Mills, the schoolteacher, "we have to do something."

"I agree, how will it all end?" asked Mr. Clarke, the bank manager.

Mrs. Oliver put in her two pennies worth. "I don't mind the little harmless things to be honest, like when he told Miss Shaw that she had a chip on her shoulder, or when he said that Mrs. Thomas had made a pig's ear of the cake."

"Or when he told the Mayor to put a sock in it," a man shouted from the back of the hall, which raised a few sniggers and lightened the mood somewhat.

"But it's becoming very worrying now," Mrs. Oliver continued, "some of the things that have happened recently have been frightening, I mean, what is he going to say next? Poor Mr. Garvey with his tongue, and poor Mrs. Taylor last month when he told her that you are what you eat."

"Yes indeed, poor Mrs. Taylor," uttered a lady in a floral dress sitting beside her and shaking her head, "not to mention Mrs. Cumberpatch, where on earth has she gone?"

It was hours before everyone had had their say, and when they were finished they were in total agreement; urgent action was needed. So they concluded the meeting by devising a plan. It was a very clever plan, one that was meticulously thought out and crafted to perfection, and one that with luck, would put an end to their problems once and for all. A few days after the meeting in the village hall, a note was dropped through the letterbox of number 10 Lupin Drive. It read:

The Residents Committee are pleased to announce that for this year, Foggy-on-the-Moor will be hosting a special awards night. The purpose being, to give recognition to an outstanding citizen of the community. The event will take place next Thursday in the village hall at 7:00pm. The award will be presented to the one who has made an outstanding contribution to village life over the past year. It will be an award of honour and pride for whoever wins. Please attend.

How splendid, thought the recipient, I will most certainly be there. I wonder who the winner will be.

* * *

When Thursday evening arrived, the village hall was full once again. There were the initial exchanging of pleasantries and formalities, followed by some announcements regarding some local affairs, and then a brief Q&A. After the tea & biscuits interval, the time had come that everyone was waiting for - the announcement of the winner of the Outstanding Citizen Award.

When the winner was declared, and Ernest Cumberpatch discovered that he had been bestowed with this honour, he was plainly delighted. He was also very surprised, although he did notice that no one else seemed to be, it was almost as if everyone in the hall had expected it.

There was a round of applause as the victor mounted the stage, and after receiving the presentation, Mr. Cumberpatch was obliged to do a short speech. There was silence as the proud man stood atop the stage clutching the trophy to his chest. He took a deep breath, composing himself, whilst contemplating how to begin. The onlookers sat with their fingers crossed, with contrasting feelings of hope and trepidation.

"My dear friends," the winner commenced, "thank you so, so much. I am both privileged and honoured to be receiving this award. I have to admit, it has come as a bit of a shock, I didn't know that you felt this way about me. You have all been so good to me since I arrived here and I am grateful for that. I know how busy you all are, and that you don't always have time to stop and chat, but this prize makes me realise that you do have a fondness towards myself. Foggy-on-the-Moor has welcomed me and I am happy to be here. You are looking at a very proud man, one who will always cherish this day, so I say thank you once again, to each and every one of you."

The prizewinner proceeded to leave the stage, but before he could do so, the compere stopped him.

"Oh but Ernest, please do tell us more, tell us all how winning this award makes you feel."

"Well, as I have said, I feel honoured."

"Yes, but what else?"

"I feel proud." said Mr. Cumberpatch.

"And?"

"Well, I feel happy." he said, now looking a bit puzzled.

"Yes, but how does it make you feel inside?"

"Well, I feel special I suppose."

"Yes, but how would you sum it up? Please do tell us."

"Well, I guess if I were to sum up how I feel right now, I would say that I am on cloud nine."

A silence fell around the hall, all eyes were fixed on the figure standing on the stage. The audience watched, waiting expectantly, and then . . . 'pop', the man on the stage vanished into thin air.

A huge sigh of relief was heard all around - had their masterplan really worked? Everyone dashed out through the double doors to see, to stand outside and look up. They saw a small cluster of clouds directly above their heads, the only clouds in an otherwise clear evening sky. The villagers quickly counted them, there were nine - it was all the confirmation they needed. They knew for sure that sitting on the ninth cloud, was one Ernest Cumberpatch, and that from now on they no longer had to live in fear, their lives would at last return to normal.

* * *

So this is the reason why there are always nine little white clouds sitting over Foggy-on-the-Moor, and why the locals sometimes, for seemingly no apparent reason, stop what they are doing to look up at the sky.

Today, everything is tickety-boo in the village. The people who live there are sure that Ernest is happy on his beautiful fluffy white cloud, with the fantastic views of the land below, and they are happy too, because they can go about their daily lives without having to worry what someone might happen to say to them.

But as fine as it all seems, beneath the calmness and contentment there is a slight unease, a little concern brewing inside some of the locals. Because, Mr. Cumberpatch has been on his cloud nine for some time now, and when people are all alone for a while they tend to start talking to themselves. Some think that Mr. Cumberpatch is already doing this, and that it is only a matter of time before he says something to himself along the lines of . . .

"Oh I do miss my friends, we got on so well together. In many ways we are like birds of a feather, and like birds of a feather, we will flock together."

AMAZON EXPEDITION: 1866

I have in my possession a very old and interesting little book. Its worn and tatty cover bears testament to the fact that in the year of 1866, it accompanied the great explorer, Stanley Shuttleworth, on his legendary expedition through the Amazonian jungle. The artefact, which is in fact the logbook from the expedition, I recently discovered whilst sorting through the contents of a rather battered travel case.

The scribblings on the pages are a real treasure, because not only was it the first ever expedition to this remote region of the world, but also because what happened there has remained a mystery to this day. For it was a trip from which no one ever returned, neither Stanley Shuttleworth nor his three companions were ever seen or heard of again. So perhaps, the clues that I have unearthed can shed some light on what exactly took place there, all those years ago.

* * *

The aforementioned travel case, which I stumbled upon whilst clearing out my attic, contained other items too. Some curious stuff, but nothing that merits mentioning here, apart from a handful of very primitive black and white photographs which serve to bring the owner of the travel case to life. Images of a bygone age, Stanley Shuttleworth, the archetypal eccentric Englishman, sporting characteristic moustache and beard, posing next to a variety of natives from around the globe. One of the pictures, however, is of great importance in trying to solve the enigma of the 1866 jungle endeavour, because it was taken at a place called

Ayo-Wa-Ka, which was the intended final destination for the crew, and it's the only snapshot that we have from the expedition.

The photograph adds proof to the fact that Stanley Shuttleworth did in fact reach Ayo-Wa-Ka, which apparently when translated means, *the land of the crazy mind.* The reason why we have just one solitary picture of the man can only be conjecture of course. It could be that the other photos were simply lost in transit, perhaps when the travel case made its way through the jungle on its return. Or it may have been that the leader of the expedition was saving the limited use of his slides for when the team reached their final destination. If this were the case, then the reason for just one photograph can be easily explained, because Shuttleworth would've had to have instructed one of the natives on how to use the camera to take it, because none of his colleagues would have been there to do it, as you will soon discover.

With the aforementioned logbook, this solitary photograph acts as the only evidence we have that might reveal something about what actually happened. Scribbled handwriting on the reverse of the picture may also reveal a clue. It simply reads:

'Me and a Snort being. Ayo-Wa-Ka, deepest Amazon - Sept 25th, 1866.'

So the diary and the snapshot are real gems, because no one has any idea what took place all those years ago, and why the group never came home. Various theories have been put forward, naturally, but no one is sure, and it's fair to say that even after reading the notes in the book and seeing the evidence provided by the photograph, nothing is totally clear - some may even argue that they actually serve to add further to the mystery. What is evident, is that during the course of the trip the four men became separated, that Shuttleworth lost touch with each of his companions one-by-one, and when he entered the final words into his journal he was alone - and in a very strange place.

* * *

According to the records, the explorers had set off from London on January 17th, 1866, for destination Ayo-Wa-Ka, a remote location deep in the Amazonian jungle. It wasn't stated why this particular spot was chosen, there may or may not have been a reason, we will never know, but what is clear is that the team left with high hopes and eager excitement.

The small group were well acquainted with each other, good friends in fact, and apart from Little Sid, for whom this would be his maiden voyage, they were very experienced, having been on many exploits together. This was to be their most adventurous undertaking yet, but with the right preparation they were confident they could do it. The party comprised: Stanley Shuttleworth - team leader, Percy Collins - doctor, Bertie Mee - retired banker and philanthropist, and the youngest of the group, Little Sid.

* * *

The logbook reveals that the four men had reached the Amazon basin by mid-February. After a few days rest and acclimatisation in the Manaus region they were keen to press on, so they decamped and headed down river in dugout canoes. The notes, although brief, do conjure up a picture of how it was for the explorers as they ventured into unexplored territory, traversing through the thick undergrowth with their packs, finding food and setting up camp along the way. It seems they toiled throughout the day and spent the evenings under the stars, eating and drinking around campfires and reminiscing about past adventures - all very romantic.

The men had to endure a few setbacks along the way, as one might assume. As well as having to adjust to the climate, which was always hot and humid, there were occasional torrential downpours to deal with, plus, the animals and insects in the forest needed to be treated with utmost respect. But food was plentiful and finding clean drinking water was never a problem, although it appears that the juice of a certain fruit became their preferred method of hydration and a prominent feature during the trek; the fruit was called a dungsap and was apparently delicious. Dungsap juice was so tasty in fact, that after a relatively short time in the jungle, all four men were drinking it regularly throughout the day - it was around that time that things began to fall apart.

* * *

Little Sid was the first to go. The team had made basecamp along the river, at a picturesque spot known as the Po-Po Delta.

Sid had gone out very early one morning to collect yuk yuk root for breakfast. When he returned much later, he told the others that he'd met a sweet little native girl by the name of Suki. Sid went out to collect yuk yuk root for lunch too, and also dinner, in fact, over the next three days the party ate so much yuk yuk that, to quote Shuttleworth's very own words, "*we were sick of the damned stuff.*"

When it was time for the group to move on, Sid hit them with the bombshell: he told them that he would not be going with them. He had fallen in love, he would be marrying sweet little Suki and spending the rest of his days with the Po-Po tribe. Now it was his choice of course, and

Stanley, Percy, and Bertie, although saddened at having to say goodbye to their friend, were very happy for him, albeit rather surprised. Shuttleworth records that Sid asked one last favour of his mates before they departed, requesting that they attend his wedding. In his diary he wrote:

'The ceremony was unusual, as might be expected, but the strangest thing of all was when the bride appeared. It seems that Suki wasn't quite so sweet after all, or indeed little for that matter. In fact, she bore a remarkable resemblance to the local river hippopotami.'

And then there were three.

* * *

Just two months after saying their goodbyes to Little Sid, Bertie Mee, the retired banker and philanthropist, deserted them. On June 10th, 1866, Shuttleworth wrote:

'Bertie gone AWOL. Five mornings ago awoke with high fever, his whole body covered in green spots - ghastly sight. Also hallucinating, claiming that pink donkeys were coming into his tent. Dr Percy said never seen anything like it in his life. We travelled half a day up river to a local medicine man, who informed us that our companion had a severe case of Green Monkey Disease. Suggested we keep Bertie there overnight for treatment and Percy and I agreed, but during the dark hours, Bertie escaped and was seen by some natives running off into the jungle making monkey noises. Did not return. Been searching now for several days but to no avail. Will press on.'

An interesting entry related to the event appeared in the diary almost two weeks later:

'Astonishing incident today. Percy and I got a glimpse of Bertie. He was spotted swinging through the trees naked with a group of howler monkeys. We called out to him but he didn't respond. Both agreed that he looked happy though, and it's comforting to know that he has found

some new friends.'

And then there were two.

* * *

Stanley Shuttleworth and Dr. Percy Collins continued on, determined to complete their mission. But sadly, when they were just days away from reaching their destination, Percy was taken by a spaceship. The pair were sitting around a campfire drinking dungsap juice and eating stinkwort, when apparently the UFO appeared out of nowhere. It hovered right above their heads, and both men were in shock as the huge illuminated craft descended upon them.

'The damn thing was huge, it must have been at least fifty foot in length. It was no more than a hundred feet above us when it sent down a beam. I was unable to move, paralysed from my top to my bottom. I couldn't turn my head in either direction, but I was able to move my eyes and I could see Percy floating upwards inside the traction beam. I could do nothing to help, all I could do was follow his ascent with my eyes. I watched as he went up and up, when he reached the underside of the craft a door slid open and he floated inside. Just seconds later, the beam retracted and the spaceship shot off at an incredible speed. Only then was I able to move again.'

The explorer does make a note in his journal, that prior to leaving England, there had been reports of spaceship sightings, but that, '*the middle of the Amazon jungle was the last place I expected to see one!*' According to the records, Shuttleworth reported the abduction the following morning to the local tribe, the Tikki-Takki, with whom he had become acquainted. They conveyed to him that it was not uncommon for spaceships to visit the area, and to even come down and whisk someone away, in fact, it was looked upon as a privilege for this to happen. This didn't really make him feel any better, but he did take comfort from the fact that in honour of his dear friend, the Tikki-Takki had named a spider after him. So the deadly White-Spotted Percy probably hunts the deep undergrowth of the Amazon rainforest to this day.

And then there were one.

* * *

Stanley Shuttleworth did eventually make it to Ayo-Wa-Ka, on August 13th, 1866, seven months after he and his colleagues had left London. It was after he'd befriended the local Ga-Ga tribe that he discovered the meaning of the name - *the land of the crazy mind*. Now if the adventure up until then hadn't been bizarre enough, then what happened in Ayo-Wa-Ka certainly was, because it seems that the place was inhabited by strange creatures whom Shuttleworth called Snort beings. He referred to them frequently in his final logs:

'*They have big round bellies and long noses. Thanks be to God that they are friendly.*'

And in another entry:

'*The Snort are sociable creatures, who spend much of their time chatting to each other and playing games like belly bouncing and nose pulling. I've managed to pick up some of their language, I can communicate with them now and even join in some of their games.*'

It appears that Stanley Shuttleworth thought very fondly of the Snort and enjoyed his time with them immensely. It seems that life was good for these curious creatures, the land gave them everything they needed, being abundant in delicious food like stinkwort, quangosteen and yuk yuk root. So, they spent much of their time relaxing, playing games and roaming the forest, and they occasionally sailed down the river in boats made from hollowed out giant chuker fruits.

Apparently, during the night, the Snort slept on clouds which they had gathered in from the sky. Stanley reports that he once witnessed how this was done, and it was quite remarkable. With a bow, and a hooked arrow that was attached to a long coil of rope, a Snort being would gaze upwards and scan the sky. It would select a small cloud that it felt was the ideal size, then fire the arrow at it. If it hit the target, the cloud would be collected in and used as the softest of beds.

The Snort did have an enemy of sorts, they were called the Hag and they lived on the opposite side of the river. The Snort and the Hag would occasionally attack each other, but it would never amount to anything more than a brief excursion across the water to shout out names and throw rotten fruit at before running off. The logbook also mentions that the Snort would sometimes have ceremonies, and interestingly, Shuttleworth claims that he often partook in these:

'*The ceremonies are quite remarkable. They gather themselves together around fires, feasting and drinking dungsap. Dried grumpweed is sprinkled onto the open fires and when the smoke given off enters their nostrils it makes them dance around wildly for hours, until they fall into a deep coma which lasts for several days.*'

* * *

The idyllic existence in Ayo-Wa-Ka did not last, because something happened that changed things for those who lived there. It was all to do with an animal called a Kava Bear, a furry thing with big teeth that unfortunately also had a liking for dungsap fruit.

Kava Bears roamed the jungle in one large herd, and would totally clear an area of the delicacy before moving on - and one day they passed through Ayo-Wa-Ka. Shuttleworth records that there were hundreds of them, in a matter of days they had stripped all the dungsap trees of their fruit. The delicious delicacy that the Snort and Stanley loved so much were no more, so the Snort subsequently upped and left to seek out richer pastures where dungsap was plentiful. Stanley awoke one morning to find them gone.

* * *

The final entry in the logbook was written on February 2nd, 1867. The explorer mentions that it was time for him to leave the land of the crazy mind, to go in search of the Snort and the coveted dungsap fruit. He must have known that he wasn't going to return to civilisation, because before he set off he placed his few belongings into his travel case, which included his logbook and the 'Me and Snort being' photograph, both of which were later to come into my possession. It seems that he handed the case to the natives, with the instructions that they pass it along the river from one tribe to the next until it reached Manaus, from where it should be shipped back to England - which is exactly what happened.

And then there were none.

* * *

So the legendary explorer, and my Great Great Grand Uncle, Stanley Shuttleworth, was not seen or heard of again, nor were his three companions: Percy Collins, Bertie Mee, and Little Sid. I like to think that it was because they chose not to, that they never returned to England, that they found their place in the world where they wanted to live out the rest of their days, and also that they were happy in their new lives.

I have browsed through the archives of every Amazon expedition undertaken since the one that my distant relative and his friends took, and can find no mention or sighting of a Snort creature, or anything remotely resembling it. Which brings me to the picture of my Great Great Grand Uncle with the Snort being. The photograph does indeed show Stanley, standing upright and proud in full camouflage regalia, somewhat glazed-eyed and smiling. But alas, that is all there is, nothing next to him but an empty space.

Anna

Anna stood in the corner of the room, very still. She always stood, never sat, and always silent, never a sound. She was just seven years old.

Her little room at the top of the house was originally an attic, it had been converted to a bedroom before she was born. Now, having been neglected for many years, it had regained the air of being an attic once again.

Thick wooden beams spanned the underside of the roof, and a layer of dust settled over everything below them. Just one small window, built into the side of the roof, let in light, so the living space was generally dark and dingy; but this was exactly how Anna liked it. She wanted seclusion, to be hidden from the outside world.

She liked the old wooden floorboards. Walking around barefoot, the feel of the wood on her feet felt good. In fact, everything about the room was perfect for her, it was her sanctuary, her own private little world where no one bothered her.

For a couple of hours during the day, the sun would be in a position to shine its beams directly into the room. At such times, a bright rectangular shape would appear half on the floor and half on the wall, and the room would become much lighter. So, Anna would retreat to a darkened corner; she much preferred the softer luminescence that diffused in from the outside street lamp at night.

*   *   *

Anna had resided in the room since the day she was born,

and from that day on had spent most of her life there. She now lived all by herself, although it hadn't always been that way. She once shared the room with her mother, who left one day and never returned. Shortly after that, an elderly lady shared the living quarters with her for a while, but she went too.

Although she now had the upstairs attic room to herself, she was not alone in the building. A young man occupied the rest of the house below her, she always knew when he was at home because the wooden floorboards would vibrate when he played his music. But Anna didn't mind him, he rarely bothered her and she never bothered him. Sometimes, the man from downstairs would come into her room. He never knocked, there was no need to, and the door was always unlocked. It was his house, Anna understood this, he'd inherited it from his mother - the elderly lady with whom she had once shared the room.

In the beginning, when the man from downstairs had first started coming into the room, it would startle Anna and she would run for cover. But over time, she learnt that he wasn't going to hurt her, so whenever he visited she would just stand still and watch him. The man had gotten used to seeing her too, so they would look at each other briefly, in silence, never saying a word. Sometimes, when their eyes met, a little smile would appear on the man's face; it seemed to please him to know that she was there.

* * *

Anna rarely left the dusty old room at the top of the house, there was no need to. If she did, it was simply to take a walk outside to stretch her legs and get some fresh air, or perhaps to find some food. She would mostly take her walks at night, she didn't like to be seen and it felt safer, and she never went far and was never gone for long. She preferred the solitude and security of her room, which is why she spent most of her time there, doing very little. Occasionally she would weave, she was a good weaver, it was something that she'd inherited from her mother, who'd inherited it from her mother before that.

The little room provided Anna with everything she needed: safety, warmth, and shelter. The old sink in the corner with the dripping tap supplied her with water, and being so small she ate very little. On occasions, an insect would come into her room through the gap in the window and she would catch it and eat it.

* * *

One day, in early autumn, the man from downstairs came into Anna's room. He'd brought up some cardboard boxes filled with paperwork to place in storage, which he occasionally did. As always, he scanned the room briefly to check that she was there, but this time she was nowhere to be seen - Anna was gone.

From that day on, he never saw her again, but the man from downstairs never forgot her. He remembered her whenever he came into the room, and he always had a quick glance around to see if she had returned, and when he saw that she hadn't he wondered to himself where she might be. He had somehow grown attached to her, in a strange sort of way, after all, it was he who had given her the name, Anna. And in a strange sort of way he missed her - Anna, the little spider in the room at the top.

The Dream-Bed

A car pulled to a halt on the pebbled driveway. Two children in the back seat peered out through the window, looking at the big old house for the very first time; it was to be their accommodation for the next three nights. Emma and Lewis glanced at each other and smiled; they liked what they saw.

"Radical!," said Emma.

The children's father switched off the engine then turned around to face them.

"Okay, we're here," he said. "It's getting late, so you'll need to unpack, wash, and then straight to bed. It's been a long day and there'll be plenty of time for exploring tomorrow." He gave them both a look, to let them know that he knew that this is exactly what they were itching to do.

"Don't make too much noise, and try not to break anything," their mother added, "remember, it's not our house."

Carrying their luggage, Lewis and Emma followed their parents through the big front doors; the inside of the house was just as impressive as the outside. The reception area was huge, and although the dwelling gave the impression of being somewhat strange, it did have a cosy, welcoming feel to it, accentuated by a log fire that burned gloriously in the hearth. An impressive-looking chandelier hung down from the centre of the ceiling and heavy curtains bordered the windows, patterned rugs covered the floor and paintings of old-fashioned ladies and gentlemen adorned the walls. The furniture appeared old, like antiques, and standing proudly in one corner was a grandfather clock, still working perfectly after all these years as it showed the correct time.

The owner of the property was waiting to greet them at the desk: Mrs. Armitage, a polite, elderly lady who both worked and lived on the premises. After the welcoming formalities, she began to give them a brief history of the house, explaining when it was built and how it had been passed down to her through the generations. As she was speaking, some wooden cabinets alongside one of the walls caught the family's attention, not so much because of the cabinets themselves, but more because of their contents. Positioned behind clear glass panes were various ornaments and artefacts that were somewhat unusual. There was a wooden carving for instance, of a peculiar looking creature with six arms, and a canopic jar, and a bronze statue of a figure with an elongated skull. Sitting atop one of the cabinets was a pair of African masks, staring disturbingly out at them.

The owner noticed their curiosity. "It was my late husband," she declared, "he was an ardent traveller and explorer, and liked to collect things from all over the world, the stranger the better. He would either bring them back with him or, if they were too large, have them shipped over from wherever he happened to be at the time. I never knew what was going to turn up next, you'll find them all over the house I'm afraid."

They chatted for just a little longer, it was getting late and Mrs. Armitage could see that her guests were tired after their long journey.

"Breakfast at eight-thirty," she said, as she locked up the drawer of the reception desk with a chunky brass key.

She then addressed the children specifically.

"Just the one bed in your room I'm afraid, but it *is* rather large so there's plenty of room for both of you."

"Goodnight," the children said in unison.

"Goodnight," replied the owner, "and pleasant dreams," she added, giving them a rather mysterious smile as she did.

* * *

Emma and Lewis' bedroom was in keeping with the rest of the house, with dark wooden furniture, a plush woven carpet, and elaborate wallpaper covering the walls. The bed looked very interesting, as soon as the children saw it, it brought to mind what the owner had told them, that all over the house were strange objects that her late husband had discovered on his travels. Looking at their bed, it certainly seemed to be one of those. It was large, just as she had mentioned, a four-poster made from solid oak. It looked very old, but this was no ordinary antique piece, there were elaborate carvings sculptured all over the bed-frame: animals, birds, trees, and strange objects that they didn't recognise. There were mysterious creatures and odd-looking people too, it really was quite bizarre, the two children had never seen anything quite like it.

Adding further curiousness, was the fact that protruding out from the headboard was a pair of carved wooden hands. They had been meticulously sculpted and perfected to a smooth finish, and they were holding out a carved wooden bowl which seemed to be beckoning someone to put something into it, like a begging bowl asking a passerby for a coin. It was all very interesting and Emma concluded that it might in fact be a magic bed, because she'd also noticed that the curtains that went around the bed-frame had moons and stars printed all over them.

"I can see what she meant now, about never knowing what was going to turn up next," said Lewis.

"It really is odd," replied Emma, as she took off her

yellow woollen hat and threw it into the carved wooden bowl of the bed. "It's a great place to keep a hat though."

It wasn't long before the two children were feeling sleepy, the long journey having worn them both out, so they promptly washed and brushed their teeth, changed into their pyjamas and tucked themselves in for the night. They were delighted to discover that although the bed was definitely unusual, it was also extremely comfortable. The mattress was the perfect firmness, the pillows were sumptuously soft, and the bed linen smelled of fresh lavender. They were certainly going to sleep well.

"This house is radical," Emma said quietly to her brother as they lay still.

"I can't wait to go exploring tomorrow," he replied, and that's all they had time to say to each other, because seconds later they were both in deep slumber.

* * *

Emma found herself alone, and became aware that she was sitting in a small, yellow, wooden boat, which was gently swaying on water. When she glanced down, she saw that the water was yellow also, and taking a closer look, it appeared to be very thick, like custard, but the cleanest, purest custard ever. She looked up at the sky, it was yellow too, and as a flock of lemon-coloured flamingoes flew over her head, Emma realised that she was in a yellow world.

The boat was floating slowly toward a small island, and looking out she could see that there were trees on the island, which were yellow of course. It wasn't long before the boat had drifted up to the shore, and Emma was able to step out onto the sand. As she did, she was unable to resist the temptation of dipping her finger into the thick yellow sea and tasting it. Her hunch was right, it *was* custard, and it tasted delicious. 'Radical,' she thought to herself.

She stood alone on the shore, looking around to take in her surroundings. The sky was clear, apart from a few pale clouds that floated lazily along with the breeze. A golden sun shone down, warming Emma's body, but not harshly so, it was a gentle heat that felt good. She could feel the sun's rays healing and rejuvenating her, so she stood for a while soaking it up. She then decided to walk towards the trees, the ones that she had spotted from the boat, and as she got closer she could see them in much more detail. They had large, fan-like leaves, and hanging down from the branches were clumps of bananas.

As she looked beyond, a pair of yellow dolphins leapt playfully out from the sea, and it was then that it suddenly dawned on her - she must be dreaming! That would explain everything, she thought to herself, although it did seem real, she was lucid and thinking clearly, which isn't usually the case with dreams - but real life isn't all in yellow, so it had to be a dream.

* * *

As Emma stood alone, thinking about what was happening, a voice close by broke her from her reverie. The words were clear and audible, but spoken in a whispered tone.

"Emma, Emma."

It was a voice she recognised, and when she looked around she saw her brother coming towards her.

"Lewis!" she cried with surprise.

"Emma, is that really you? he said.

"Yes it's me. Are we in a dream?" she asked.

"I think we must be. It feels so strange, to be in a dream and to know that you are."

"Yes, I agree," she replied.

"Have you seen the sea? It looks like custard," said Lewis.

"It is custard," Emma informed him, "I've tasted it."

"I've seen a yellow turtle," he said, "and it talks, it said hello to me."

"Really? How bizarre, but I guess it doesn't surprise me, not here anyway, I suppose if we are in a dream then anything can happen."

"I suppose it does," her brother concluded.

Suddenly, something came flying through the air, bounced off of Lewis' head and then fell to the ground - it was a banana.

"I've just been hit on the head by a flying banana!" he exclaimed.

His sister saw the funny side and started to laugh, but as she did, another banana came hurtling over and bounced off of her head too. The children were puzzled as to what was going on. Who, or what, was throwing fruit at them?

It soon became apparent, a raucous laughter echoed out from over by the trees and when they looked, they spotted a group of monkeys sitting on some branches. They were all different shades of yellow fur, and they were looking over and laughing. When the hairy animals realised they'd been spotted, they instantly clambered down from the trees, and with seemingly big grins on their faces began running towards Emma and Lewis - and they were carrying bunches of bananas.

"Quick," cried Emma, "let's run!"

The children sped away as fast as they could, they were both fast runners but the monkeys were pretty quick too, and as bananas flew all around their heads they could hear the noisy primates cackling behind them. Emma and Lewis began to laugh as well, they found the situation rather amusing, it was like some crazy game that they were playing. They continued to run, but the riotous mob followed closely behind, chattering and whooping loudly as they did so. Along the golden sand they went, the two children running ahead with the hairy apes in hot pursuit, and bananas flying everywhere.

They dashed quickly up a sand dune, trying to escape, and when they came down the other side they saw several enormous seashells resting on the sand, they were the biggest seashells they'd ever seen, bigger than both of them.

"Quickly," cried Emma, "let's hide inside one of these, they won't find us in there."

Inside the shell was like entering into another world. The furore from outside was completely shut out, the only thing to be heard was a gentle whooshing sound, like when you hold a seashell to your ear. The children felt safe, they had escaped from the mob. Just then, a soft tinkling sound started up from within the shell. The beautiful music began to surround them, and they weren't sure how, but they became aware that they were listening to the sound of yellow. They somehow knew that every colour has its own harmony, and because in the real world the lives of humans are so busy and their world so noisy, they can't hear them. But here, in this strange dreamworld that they found themselves in, Emma and Lewis were able to.

"We should rest here for a while," said Lewis, "until they're gone. It's so peaceful."

"Definitely," replied his sister, "I like it in here, it feels safe, and the music is so soothing."

As they nestled inside the shell, making themselves comfortable, the gentle sound started to have an effect on them. They began to feel very relaxed, and then drowsy, and it wasn't long before they closed their eyes and succumbed to the soft music.

*   *   *

The next thing the children knew, they were back in the bedroom of the old house, lying awake in the four-poster bed - it was morning. Emma immediately began to tell her brother all about the radical dream that she'd had, the yellow world that she'd found herself in, and the fact that he was in her dream too.

The remarkable thing was, Lewis had had the same experience. They recounted to each other what had happened and their stories matched exactly: the custard sea, the golden beach, even the banana throwing monkeys and how they had managed to escape from them by hiding in a huge sleeping-seashell. It was clear that they had both been in the same dream at the same time.

"It must be something to do with the bed," remarked Lewis, "it has to be, just look at how strange it is, the carvings in the wood and the pictures on the curtains, I think the bed caused us to have the dream."

"So it is a magic bed after all," said Emma.

"Yes, a magic dream-bed," Lewis concluded.

As they sat discussing the dream, Emma noticed her hat, still sitting in the carved wooden bowl where she had left it the night before.

"Look Lewis!" she gasped, "my yellow hat, perhaps that is what caused our dream to be in yellow. Maybe that's what the bowl is for, whatever colour you put in the bowl is what colour dream you have."

"You could be right," he said, then began to think deeply.

"I wonder," he added thoughtfully, "I wonder what would happen if tonight, we put something in the bowl of a different colour?"

"Radical," Emma concluded, "let's do it, and that way we will know for sure."

* * *

At the breakfast table, the two children did not mention their dream, although it hardly left their minds. They listened politely as Mrs. Armitage told the family more details about the house, as well as informing them of some local attractions that they might want to visit while they were there. She expressed that during their stay, they should treat the place as their own and feel free to go wherever they wanted. The children were pleased to hear this as they couldn't wait to go exploring, and as soon as breakfast was over, that is exactly what they did.

The whole day was spent searching the house, and not only the house, the gardens too. They had a great time and discovered many things. They found even more unusual items scattered about the property, and new rooms and hallways too, even a secret staircase and a hidden cupboard. The house and its grounds were much bigger than they had realised, and there were several gardens, too many to explore. Some had statues and ponds, and one of the gardens even had a maze made out of Yew bushes; they got lost in the labyrinth for half an hour before eventually finding their way out.

It had been such a busy day, so that evening, after a hearty dinner, they were feeling tired and thinking of sleep. And thinking of sleep made them both think of their bed, and they remembered the dream they'd had the night before, and the plans they had made for tonight. Would they both have the same dream again? Had it really been Emma's hat that had caused everything to be in yellow? Was it anything to do with the bed at all? Tonight, they would find out for sure.

* * *

The two children stood in their pyjamas, looking at the carved bowl that protruded out from the headboard of the four-poster bed.

"I'm really not sure what to put in it," Emma said, "but it shouldn't be my yellow hat again, we should try another colour to see if it works, besides, I don't want to be chased by any more monkeys."

Lewis looked around the room. He noticed a pile of freshly laundered sheets on a dressing table, the sheets were of the purest white. He took the one from the top of the pile and held it up.

"How about white?" he asked his sister. "No one has ever had a dream before that was totally in white."

Emma agreed. "Brilliant, let's do it," she said excitedly. "If we have a dream that is all in white then we know for sure that this really is a magic dream-bed." With that, Lewis placed the folded sheet into the bowl.

As they lay together, despite being tired, the children's minds were initially too active for them to go straight off to sleep. The events of the busy day kept going over in their minds, as well as images of the dream they'd had the previous night, and wondering if they would have a similar one this night. But after a while, their tiredness started to get the better of them and they both began to feel drowsy. It was Lewis who fell asleep first, drifting gently off as his head sunk into the soft pillow.

"Are you asleep?" whispered Emma. But there was no response. Moments later, she too, fell into a deep slumber.

* * *

Lewis found himself standing in a twilight, surrounded by a mist. Peering through the haze, he was able to make out a light off in the distance, so he headed towards it. As he made his way through, the air was cool on his skin, and it felt fresh when he breathed it in.

He quickly realised that his walking created a crunching sound beneath his feet, and when he looked down, he discovered that he was stepping on snow. It was pure white, crisp and clean, and there were no other footprints around, just the fresh ones that he himself was making.

He continued onwards, heading towards the source of the light. As he did so, the thickness of the mist began to lessen, becoming patchy in places, and soon there were clear areas where Lewis was able to see around him. It wasn't long before he'd stepped out from the mist altogether, and when he did, he observed the most delightful scene beyond.

Looking out, he could see that the snow-covered road on which he stood led up a hill, and at the top of the hill was an enchanting little town. There were houses, like old-fashioned cottages, he wasn't able to see the roofs because they were covered in snow, but from their shapes he guessed that they were probably thatched roofs.

As Lewis stood, marvelling at the wonderful snowscape, he heard a faint voice in the distance. It was coming from behind him, from within the mist cloud from which he had emerged. The voice was soft, but it was getting louder all the time, and it was calling his name.

"Lewis, Lewis, can you hear me?"

He listened intently.

"Lewis, it's me Emma, are you here?"

"Emma," he cried out, "I'm over here, I'm over here."

"Where are you? I can't see you, it's too foggy."

"Head towards my voice," he said loudly, "and you will come out from the mist. Look for my footprints in the snow, follow them and you will reach me."

"Okay, I'm heading toward the sound of your voice, keep talking."

"You're getting close now, I can hear you well."

"Yes me too, and the fog is getting thinner, I can see much better now and I can see your footprints."

"Keep going, keep heading in the same direction, the mist will clear and you will come out from it."

"Lewis, I can see you, I'm over here."

Lewis spotted his sister as she ran enthusiastically over to him.

"It worked, it worked!" she exclaimed. "It really is a magic dream-bed, we are both in the same dream again - and everything's white!"

"Yes, look at all this beautiful snow, it's incredible, and it's all because of the white sheet that we placed in the bowl."

They were both very excited, and Lewis gestured towards the snow-covered picturesque town up on the hill.

"And look at this amazing view," he said.

"Radical!," was all that his sister could say.

* * *

Time in the children's dream must have been distorted because, as they stood on the pristine white snow, the surrounding light suddenly dimmed as if night were falling. It was still possible to see, as a full moon had suddenly appeared and was bathing everything in a magical glow. The village beyond was a delightful scene, hundreds of tiny lights twinkled from the windows of the houses. Where is this place? they both wondered. All was quiet and still, it seemed that everyone in the village was sleeping, unaware that they were even there. A warm glow emanated from within some of the cottages, lanterns perhaps, or the last endeavours of logs that continued to radiate light and heat long after they had been abandoned.

They walked over to a street lamp that was close by, and Lewis realised that it must have been the distant light that he had followed to make his way through the haze. Now, standing beneath it, the lamp lit up the space around them, wrapping the pair in a delicate cocoon of light.

Snow began to fall thick and fast from above, and the sight of it made the children's eyes widen with delight. They tilted their heads back, to look up to the sky, and in the radiance of the lamplight they could see the masses of snowflakes cascading down on them, swerving and weaving as they fell. Emma stuck out her tongue, a snowflake settled on it before instantly dissolving, then Lewis did the same. They could feel the flakes landing gently on their skin, whilst others fell to the ground around them to merge with the snow.

As they stood together in the twilight, a strange feeling engulfed them both. They became aware of how incredibly silent it was, and there was a mystical stillness in the air. They were completely absorbed in the moment, totally at peace, and they could feel the energy of everything that surrounded them. Remarkably, they were able to hear the gentle sound of the snowflakes as they landed softly on the snow. The children said nothing, they just surrendered to what was happening, absorbed in the wonder of the moment.

A powerful loving presence could be felt, one that penetrated deep within, to their very souls - and it was bliss. Emma and Lewis were at peace, and seemed connected, not only to one another but to everyone and everything.

To all the creatures on the planet, and the plants and the trees, and the earth itself, and then beyond the earth, to the moon and the stars and the cosmos, and the creator. They felt connected to it all, from the smallest insect to the vast universe beyond, it was a wonderful, spiritual experience that they didn't want to end. They closed their eyes in the rapturous state, and as they did so, their bodies began to drift upwards, they were floating.

The next thing the children knew, they were opening their eyes and staring up at the ceiling, it was morning and they'd awoken in their bed. They immediately began discussing what had happened, and once again their dreams matched, they had found themselves in the same place at the same time, this time in a white world.

* * *

There was just one day left at the big house, and the children's parents had planned a day out in town. Throughout the day, although their minds kept thinking of it, Emma & Lewis said nothing about their dreams, or the bed. They somehow knew that if they told anyone, the bed would cease to work and the dreams would stop happening, that keeping its secret was like a condition for using it, which would also explain why the owner had not mentioned it to them outright.

The day was an enjoyable one, the family looked around a historic castle and museum, and had lunch in a tearoom. Afterwards, they'd strolled around some local shops, one of which was an old-fashioned sweetshop with sweets of all kinds. The children bought a mixed selection, enough for the whole day and for their long car journey home that was to follow the day after.

When they arrived back at the house, Mrs. Armitage had already prepared dinner, which would be their last, for in the morning they would be leaving. It had been an amazing trip for both of them, one that they would never forget, but it wasn't over just yet, because they still had one more night - which meant one more night-time adventure.

*   *   *

When evening came, the children informed their parents that they were tired and were going to their room. If truth be told, they couldn't wait to try out the magic dream-bed once again.

"Our last night," said Emma, in a slightly disappointed tone.

"Yes, it's such a shame that we have to leave," replied her brother, who then became upbeat and added, "But at least we have tonight."

"What colour shall we choose?" Emma said, enthusiastically, "have you any ideas?"

"Well, orange would be good," said Lewis.

"Or purple, imagine a purple world," said his sister.

"Blue would be nice, there might be a beautiful blue sky and a deep blue sea with magnificent blue whales leaping from it."

"What about a green world, we could walk on the lushest greenest grass ever and pick limes from trees."

"And talk to a friendly grasshopper," Lewis remarked, and they both laughed.

"How about a red world, wouldn't that be exciting, with a fantastic red sky."

"And volcanoes spurting lava that looks hot but doesn't burn."

"Yes, you could dip your finger in and it would taste like raspberry jam."

The children laughed again at the thought of it, then

concentrated back to thinking about what colour they should choose.

"Oh it's so hard, I wish we were staying for two weeks so we could try out all the different colours," Emma remarked.

As soon as she'd said this, she saw her brother's face light up.

"Of course," he said, "I've got it."

He rushed over to his coat, the one he'd carelessly slung over a chair when they had returned from their day out. Putting his hand deep into one of the pockets, he pulled out the bag of sweets they'd bought from the sweetshop, then opened it up. They both peered inside.

"Wow, look at all these fantastic colours," said Emma, "but what one shall we choose?"

Lewis looked at his sister with wide eyes, "Why choose just one?"

Emma realised what he was thinking. "Yes of course," she said, "we could put lots in, of all different colours."

"Better still, why not put them all in?" And with that, he tipped the whole bag of sweets into the carved bowl of the bed.

"Do you really think it will work?" Emma asked.

"Well, we'll soon find out."

"Radical!," she said, and they smiled and jumped into bed.

The eager pair immediately switched off the bedside lamp, they couldn't wait to go to sleep to see what would happen.

"Goodnight," they said to each other, "Pleasant dreams."

The two children lay on their backs, looking up at the fabric that covered the top of the bed. They took in some deep breaths to relax themselves, then closed their eyes.

Snuggled up in the ultra-comfortable bed, despite having excited minds, it wasn't long before they both fell fast asleep.

* * *

Emma and Lewis opened their eyes, both at the same time. They were laying in the same position as when they had fallen asleep, but they were no longer looking at the bed, they were looking up at millions of stars. The sheer depth and vastness of what they were seeing was breathtaking. They sat up and looked around them. The sides of the bed were no longer there, and the bedroom furniture was gone too, even the walls had disappeared. The only thing surrounding them was the open sky, up above and to the sides, and it looked magnificent, a mass of silver twinkling stars amongst different shades of purple. Clearly something strange was happening - the children knew that this must be the start of their dream.

The magic dream-bed upon which they lay began to move, very slightly from side to side, and it then started to undulate, up and down. The mattress felt different, firmer somehow. Suddenly, to their surprise, as if out from nowhere a huge, long, pink-feathered neck reared up in front of them. At the end of the neck was a head with two big white eyes and a yellow beak. Then two massive wings began flapping up and down on either side, creating wafts of air as they did, and the children felt themselves rising up from the ground. The children looked around to find out what was going on. They saw the long-outstretched neck of a flamingo in front of them, its pink and black wings were by their sides, and behind them a tall plume of tail feathers. They realised that they were not on their bed at all, they were on a giant bird and were now flying through the air. They looked at each other in amazement.

"How radical is this!," cried Emma.

"It's fantastic," replied Lewis. "I think it's going to be our best dream yet."

* * *

As they soared through the air, with the purple sky all around them, the soft breeze blew warmly and gently on their faces, it felt invigorating. Looking down, they could make out land below, rolling hills of various shades of green and yellow, and there were little houses of all different colours. A bright blue parrot crossed their path, and as it did so it nodded to them as if to say hello. The pink flamingo nodded back and the children laughed, flying on a giant bird was the most fantastic thing ever.

After a while, Emma suddenly pointed forward. "Look ahead!," she cried, "it's a rainbow!"

When her brother looked, he saw the biggest, most colourful rainbow he had ever seen, and they were heading straight towards it. As they got closer, the rainbow became even larger, and the colours even richer. The red was like the deepest strawberry red you could ever see, the blue, the most intense deep blue sea you could imagine, and the yellow shimmered with different shades of brilliance - the children were awestruck. When they reached it, the flamingo landed gently on top, and Emma and Lewis could not believe what was happening as they slid down the pink-feathered bird's long neck to stand on top of the rainbow. The flamingo gave them a nod to say goodbye, then flew off in the direction from where it came.

"Goodbye," shouted Emma.

"And thank you," yelled Lewis, as the friendly bird left them.

*   *   *

Walking on top of a rainbow was incredible, beneath their feet felt solid, yet soft at the same time. Each step that they took was cushioned, and as they stepped, tiny sparkles sprinkled up around their feet and ankles.

"No one is going to believe us when we tell them," remarked Lewis.

"I totally agree," replied his sister.

The two children made their way along the top of the rainbow, making sparkles as they went, and as they did so it began to slope downwards. After a while, the incline became so steep that it was difficult to walk.

"It's getting tricky," said Emma to her brother.

"Yes I know," he replied, "it's like trying to walk down a slide."

As soon as he said this, they both had the same idea, they looked at each and realised that they were thinking the same thing.

"Let's do it," Lewis said, "we know it's a dream so nothing can harm us."

So Emma held her brother's hand. "Let's go," she cried, and the two children sat down and began sliding down the rainbow.

They were soon zooming along a multicoloured slide, with all the colours flashing beneath them: red, yellow, orange, green, blue, indigo and violet, it was so much fun that they never wanted it to stop. But they knew that it would have to at some point, because eventually they would reach the bottom.

*   *   *

The children's first thought as they landed, was that the grass on which they stood was not as soft as they'd expected, in fact, it was very hard. When they looked down at their feet they discovered the reason why, they were not standing on grass at all, they were standing on a pile of large gold coins; it seems they had landed in a pot of gold. So there really is a pot of gold at the end of a rainbow, they both thought, at least in dreamland anyway. The coins shimmered and glistened, and jangled when the children disturbed them with their feet.

"It's a shame we can't take one of these back with us," Lewis mentioned, "just one would make us rich forever."

The two children clambered over the gold coins. They reached the edge of the pot, where they were able to scramble over the side and down onto the ground. This time, they were standing on grass, and it was the softest grass they had ever felt. The two of them stood for a while, to catch their breath and to compose themselves after the helter-skelter ride that they had just taken. Looking around, they noticed a white stone pathway winding its way ahead, so they proceeded to walk it. As they went on their way, three pink rabbits hopped across their path, and overhead, they noticed that the colour of the sky had changed, a large crimson sun now showed, causing streaks of scarlet, orange and white.

The pathway took them through an orchard of all different types of fruit trees: lemon, lime, cherry, peach, and some with fruits that they had never seen before - there was even a tree with strawberries hanging on it. The children noticed that there was one particular tree up ahead, one that was covered in all different coloured dots. They presumed the dots must be fruit, but when they got close they realised that it was not fruit at all, they were birds sitting on branches - birds of paradise with spectacular colours.

* * *

When Emma and Lewis emerged out from the trees, they found themselves in a magnificent garden. Beautiful butterflies flitted around them, landing and taking off from vibrant-coloured flowers, and striking, fluffy, yellow-and-black bees buzzed happily from one plant to another. The scent from each of the different flowers was delightful, and combined they filled the air with one exquisite aroma.

Emma bent down to smell a creamy-white flower.

"Wow, that's amazing," she remarked, "it smells of vanilla."

Lewis smelt one of the green flowers. "And this one smells of apples."

The two of them spent several minutes sampling the different flowers, each one had an amazing and unique scent. The red ones smelled of cherries, the blue ones of blueberries, the orange ones of oranges, and the pink ones smelled of bubblegum. They noticed a very interesting looking tree, with large brown bell-shaped flowers hanging down from it. Simultaneously, they both stood on tiptoes and inhaled.

"Mmm, chocolate," they said with delight.

At the far end of the garden were some giant foxgloves, with huge petals of mottled pink and white - they seemed to be beckoning the pair to come to them. Together, Emma and Lewis were drawn slowly over to the flowers, and when they arrived they put out their hands to touch them - it was the softest, silkiest thing they had ever felt. The act of disturbing the petals made the flowers release a scent into the air, an enchanting sweet aroma that made them feel suddenly drowsy. Looking into the centre of the flowers at their marbled, coloured patterns was hypnotic, the children were now in a trance and felt very sleepy. They both slipped gently into a giant foxglove of their own, and into a deep slumber.

* * *

When they awoke the next morning, Emma and Lewis talked about their fantastic dream and everything they'd experienced; it was the most remarkable adventure ever. When they'd finished going over and over all that had happened to them, it was time to start packing their cases to leave.

When breakfast was over, the family was ready to depart. Their parents had already packed up the car and were saying goodbye to Mrs. Armitage, thanking her for their lovely stay; she told them that it was pleasure to have met them. As the parents walked away, the children took the opportunity to thank the owner for themselves. Lewis informed Mrs. Armitage that he'd had a fantastic time, and Emma told her that the house was 'radical.'

"I'm so glad to hear it," she replied.

Before they went off, the owner bent down and whispered quietly to the children, "And I hope it was colourful enough for you," before giving them a little wink.

* * *

As the car pulled away on the pebbled driveway, Emma and Lewis took one last look at the old house.

"What a remarkable place," their mother said, "we shall have to visit again sometime, what do you think children?"

"Definitely," they replied, and looked at each other and smiled.

The Wise Old Man and his Beard

In olden days, a small village nestled beneath the Kunlun mountain range of southern China. The people who lived there lived a simple life: they worked the land, tended to their animals, and fetched water from a nearby river.

The constructions which they called their homes were simple affairs, made from natural materials such as bamboo, wood, and plant fibres, but they served the needs of the people perfectly: they provided clean living spaces for eating and sleeping, protection from wild animals, and offered shade during long hot summers. Wintertimes were not a concern, the climate was such that temperatures never dropped very low and the mountains gave them protection from strong winds, so the basic dwellings easily sufficed to get them through.

* * *

Everyone knew of the old man who lived at the far end of the village. His age was not known, but no one could remember a time when he hadn't been there, and some claimed that the man had been in the village since its very beginning - which would have made him four-hundred years old.

People would sometimes visit the man to ask for help or advice, and they would always be given guidance. They consulted him on such matters as health and wealth, business, marital issues, and even on how the weather was going to turn out; which he often predicted with remarkable accuracy. There was seemingly nothing that he didn't know about, so he was revered and respected by all, and thus became known as the Wise Old Man.

Now befitting wise old men of that time, he had a long

white beard. This was fine in itself, however, there happened to be an issue with this particular beard, because it grew remarkably fast, and for some reason the old man had stopped cutting it. It thus became a problem. The beard grew all the way down to the ground, and then some. It began to get in the way, and people started to trip over it, in fact, it grew so long that some of the villagers thought to ask the man if he might not want to cut it off, or at least trim it up a bit. These were mere suggestions at first, but as the beard grew longer and longer they became polite requests, then not so polite requests, eventually sounding more like demands. But the old man would not budge. "Certainly not," he would say, "my beard is the most important thing in the village."

So the old man's facial hair continued to grow, and it began to crawl along the floor of the living room, in the little wooden dwelling that he called home. It extended into the next room, and then up the stairs, but it didn't stop there, it eventually filled up the whole house. When the hairy mass proceeded to creep out from the windows and into the street below, the neighbours started to talk. As time went by, the big white beard began to travel down the street, winding its way around fences and posts as it went, and that's when the residents became concerned. They pleaded with the Wise Old Man to have it removed, but he would have none of it. "Certainly not," he would say, "my beard is the most important thing in the village."

* * *

There came a time when the situation was getting too much for the villagers to bear, something had to change. So, they devised a plan. The idea was, for the village baker to make the old man his most favourite dish, which happened to be quince and sea slug pie. They would then present him with the offering, explaining that it was in gratitude for all the help and advice that he had given them over the years. The Wise Old Man would be delighted, he would nosh the whole pie down in one go, then tell them how delicious it was and how it was the best quince and sea slug pie he'd ever tasted. He would be so grateful in fact, that when they asked politely if the barber might be allowed to cut off his beard, because it was beginning to be a bit of a nuisance, he would say, "Of course you can, be my guest."

So the children of the village were sent out to pick the finest quinces they could find, and the fishermen sailed out in their little wooden boats to collect the fattest, juiciest sea slugs. The bounties were then handed to the master baker, so that he could make the most delicious quince and sea slug pie ever made; which is exactly what he did.

The villagers marched down the street with the pie, and knocked on the door of the little wooden house. When the Wise Old Man answered, they informed him that they had brought a gift, in gratitude for all the help and advice he'd given them over the years. The recipient was delighted, his eyes widened at the sight of the steaming hot crust of the pie, and his nostrils twitched when they smelt the hearty aroma. There and then, in front of them all, he noshed the whole lot down in one go.

"Delicious!" he proclaimed, "that was the best quince and sea slug pie I have ever tasted."

The onlookers were thrilled to hear this. Tentatively, one of them stepped forward and politely asked the man if the barber might perhaps cut off his beard, as it was beginning to cause a few problems for some of them. The Wise Old Man looked down at his empty dish, and then up at the group who stood waiting patiently for an answer.

"Certainly not," he said, "my beard is the most important thing in the village."

* * *

The poor people were despondent, at a loss as to what to do, and all the while the long white beard continued to make its way further along the street. It snaked its way through gardens and weaved in and out of houses, suffocating trees and blocking drains as it went. Some of the villagers' personal belongings became entangled and were impossible to retrieve: hats and glasses, books and bicycles, umbrellas, saucepans, toys and musical instruments, all kinds of things became absorbed within the mass of white hair. There was even a lavatory trapped somewhere in the middle of the beard, and rumours went around that someone was actually still sitting on it.

Eventually, the people could take no more, something had to be done, the plan of the quince and sea slug pie had not worked but they could not give up. If the old man would not have his beard cut off when they asked him, then they would have to tell him. So a petition was compiled, signed by everyone in the village, and once again they marched down the street to knock at the front door of the little wooden house. When he answered this time, the group politely but firmly informed the occupant that they had come to present him with a petition. One of them stepped forward to read it aloud:

"*We, namely the villagers, do so demand that the big white beard, belonging to the said man known locally as the Wise Old Man, must forthwith and without delay, be removed immediately.*"

The Wise Old Man took the piece of paper and read it over again, slowly to himself, before handing it back. He then addressed the group.

"Certainly not, my beard is the most important thing in the village."

The poor residents were beaten, resigned to the fact that they would have to get used to living with what had now become known as 'the big white monster'. So they stopped visiting the man to ask for help or advice, after all, he couldn't be that wise if he didn't even know when it was time for a beard to be cut. And they ceased calling him the Wise Old Man too, referring to him simply as the Old Man, or other things which weren't so polite. It seemed the only ones who appreciated him were the birds who built their nests in his beard in springtime, and the stray cats and dogs that slept inside it during the winter months.

* * *

Now if things weren't troublesome enough for the people of the village, then they were about to get a whole lot worse, because one winter, they had weather like they had never known before. Instead of the relatively mild temperatures that they were used to, winter hit them with arctic-like conditions. It snowed regularly for weeks on end, temperatures plummeted to unknown depths, water turned to ice and the whole village froze.

The cold spell went on and on, it seemed like it was never going to end, and it had taken everyone by surprise. The basic homes in which the villagers lived were ill-equipped to withstand the severity of such conditions, they could not survive the cold much longer, and they didn't know what to do.

As a last resort, the people decided to turn once more to the old man who lived at the far end of the village. They hoped and prayed that somehow, within him, he could find one last bit of wisdom to save them. So a small assemblage gathered themselves together, wrapped themselves up in their warmest clothes and blankets, and marched their way down the street. They fought their way through the blizzard, and through the white hairy mass, to locate the little wooden house. When they found the front door, they knocked; the old man had been expecting them.

"Please, do enter," a voice calmly spoke from within the house. So the freezing mob made their way inside, to find the man sitting in his wooden chair, and when they were all facing him, one of them spoke.

"We are desperate," he cried. "Our wooden huts cannot keep out the cold, we will surely perish. Is there any advice that you can give us in our time of great need?"

"Of course," replied the man, "go fetch the barber and cut off my beard."

So the big white beard was detached forthwith, and from then on, it became a free-for-all for anyone with a knife or scissors to take from it as much as they needed. There was plenty to go around, the beard was so big and thick that it provided enough insulation for every house in the village. The people made blankets from it too, and used it as fuel for their fires, there was even ample to keep the animals snug and warm.

* * *

Mercifully, the extreme winter eventually passed, temperatures rose, the ice thawed, and the village returned to normality once again. The old man and his beard, although a much shorter one now, had saved the day. So he was once again referred to as the Wise Old Man, and the people came to visit him just as before, to ask for his help and advice.

When summertime came around, the villagers decided

to make the Wise Old Man a quince and sea slug pie, to thank him for saving them. When they presented it to him, he noshed it down in one go.

"Delicious," he said, "that really was the best quince and sea slug pie I have ever tasted."

He then surprised them all, by asking if the barber might trim his beard for him whilst he was there.

"I've been thinking," he said, "perhaps it is a bit too long for this hot weather, and besides, it would probably make life much easier for everyone if my beard were trimmed regularly and kept to a respectable length."

The people of the village looked at each other, then looked at the old man and said,

"Certainly not, your beard is the most important thing in the village!"

GREY WOLF AND THE FIREFLY

The following story was told to me many years ago, when I passed through a rugged and somewhat beautiful part of North America. Extraordinary as it is, many of the people there claimed that it was true, that it told of real events that had actually happened, that had simply been passed down from generation to generation. Others said that the story is just what it is, a story, the work of someone's imagination. As for whether it really happened or not, I will leave that for you, the reader to decide.

* * *

As the sun sets behind the great western mountain range of the North Americas, the heat of the day gives way to the coolness of evening. The Sequoyah tribe gather around their campfires, which crackle and pop as the sweet smoky aroma of burning pine and hickory fills the air. Fire is the Sequoyah's friend, it cooks their food and heats their water, it gives them warmth and comfort, and it brings everyone together at the end of the day.

When gathering firewood, the tribespeople will never chop down a tree as this would end its life. Instead, they will break off twigs or lop branches because, like the cutting of hair or nails, they will soon grow back, and they will always ask the tree for permission before doing so - or they might simply collect dead wood that has fallen naturally to the ground. The Sequoyah live in harmony with nature, and they have many ways of communicating with it.

Gathered around their evening fires, the people of the tribe will eat and drink, talk of the day's events and sing to celebrate life, and each one of them will give a blessing for what the great spirit has given them. Sometimes, they will tell stories, some old, some new. Anyone can tell a story if they so wished, although it is often left to the official storyteller of the tribe who is the most skilled at this pastime, and who tells the best tales.

* * *

Many moons ago, there was one such storyteller by the name of Grey Wolf. He was remarkably gifted at it, when Grey Wolf told a story everyone would listen. His accounts of extraordinary characters and fascinating journeys took the listener away to other worlds, and both children and adults would sit captivated as he narrated his tales of adventure. He had inherited his talent for storytelling from his father, Red Sun, who had been the tribe's storyteller before him, for many years. But Red Sun eventually grew old and left the earthly plane for another realm, but before doing so, he handed down the legacy of storyteller to his son.

There was something magical about sitting around the glow of an open fire on a warm summer's evening, with the star-filled sky above, and listening to Grey Wolf speak. The legend of Grey Wolf, however, is not so much about him being one of the greatest storytellers the tribe had ever had, but more because of something that would often happen when he told a story - and it was quite remarkable.

It began as soon as he started his new role, when he told his very first tale, and it continued to happen many times after that. It occurred so regularly in fact, that as the years went by, those who witnessed the phenomenon got so used to it that they thought it quite normal, but it was actually something rather extraordinary. Because, as the Sequoyah sat around their campfires and Grey Wolf began his narration, a firefly would appear. It would show up as soon as he started to speak, and it would hover around for the duration of the story. As soon as the tale was finished, it would leave, and would not be seen again until the next time, when it would suddenly appear from out of nowhere to fly around them once more. The tiny, luminous beetle seemed to be listening to what Grey Wolf was saying, and would occasionally glow brighter when he spoke, as if communicating its enjoyment and appreciation of the storyteller's words.

Having the glowing firefly hovering around as they sat listening to stories was quite something, and many of the tribe believed that their mysterious visitor was in fact Red Sun, their previous storyteller and Grey Wolf's father. That he was temporarily taking the form of the insect, so that he could drop-in to join them around the fireside once more, to spend some time amongst friends and to listen to his son's anecdotes.

*   *   *

Many years passed. Grey Wolf continued to entertain his fellow tribespeople, and the mysterious firefly regularly came to visit when he did. But there came a time when Grey Wolf's spell on earth also came to an end, and he too, just like his father, went to join the great spirit in the sky.

Before he moved on however, Grey Wolf handed down the legacy of storyteller to *his* son, whose name was Little Bear. When this came to pass, there were many who believed that they would never see the mysterious firefly again, that there was no need for Red Sun to visit them any longer now that he had been reunited with Grey Wolf. They would know for sure of course, once Little Bear began telling his stories.

*   *   *

It was a delightful summer's evening; the air was still and warm and the sweet-smelling smoke from campfires wafted over the hills. There was a glorious cloudless sky, seemingly millions of stars twinkled and sparkled overhead, and the Sequoyah tribe gathered to hear Little Bear's very first story.

Everyone was silent as he prepared to speak, and he began a tale about a wild coyote and a majestic eagle. The eagle had saved the coyote from danger when it was just a few weeks old, and the pair had become best friends. Little Bear was recounting the adventures of this unlikely couple, when, as everyone sat quietly absorbed in what he was saying, something happened that made them rejoice - the mysterious firefly appeared. It seemed that Red Sun *had* come to listen to his grandson's story after all. But there was something else, something that was even more wonderful, because the firefly was not alone - there were now two fireflies joining them around the campfire.

Tale of Walt Pepper

Walt Pepper was a no-nonsense kind of chap, a junior clerk for a small bank in his hometown. The pay wasn't so good, but he enjoyed his job, especially when he was sent to do errands out of town. This would not happen often, but when it did it was usually to do with title deeds and such matters, or to tie up loose ends for wealthy clients, and Walt would always jump at the opportunity to see a new place and meet new people. On one such occasion, he was sent to a place way out in the sticks, a little village which had the unfortunate name of Witches Crag.

Now, young Walt was a materialist, he didn't believe in anything that he couldn't feel with his own hands or see with his own eyes, and he ridiculed anyone who did. "Ghouls, ghosts and goblins, all of it hogwash," he would say. But that was before he visited Witches Crag, because not only was it odd by name, it was also odd by nature, as our poor protagonist would discover, and something happened there that changed his way of thinking forever.

* * *

The bank clerk had arrived at the village early one morning and he'd immediately found it a bit strange, although he did like the place; his first impression was that it was like stepping back in time. He'd been sent to do a report on a property, and to survey some land for a long-standing customer. It wasn't hard to find his intended locations, what with the village being so small, and he was eager to get down to business.

The only place for visitors to stay in Witches Crag was at the local tavern, called the Green Man. Walt didn't mind that, the room at the inn looked warm and cosy and the food seemed good, besides, it would give him an opportunity to get to know the locals. The Green Man was the social hub of the village, if the yokels weren't working or at home then they were likely to be in there.

As Walt was discussing the room and the terms & conditions with the landlord, he couldn't help but overhear a conversation that some of the patrons around him were having. They were discussing the strange things that had happened in the village over the years, and they spoke of the supernatural, of spirits and superstitions. Walt couldn't refrain from telling them his feelings on such matters, that he didn't believe in all that mumbo jumbo, and they were fools if they did.

The countryfolk were not surprised to hear him say this of course, being a townie, he'd had no experience of anything unusual or otherworldly. They did offer him some friendly words of advice though, they told him to be careful during his stay, for the surrounding hills and moors contained goblins and sprites and suchlike, not to mention the McCracken.

"Because such characters are pranksters by nature," they warned, "and there's no one they'd rather play a trick on than a non-believer."

"Poppycock," Walt said, "and what is a McCracken anyway?"

"Ahh, 'ave ya never heard of the McCracken?," one of the locals answered, "it's the craftiest critter of 'em all, a real cheeky-chappy that's for sure."

"Well he'd never fool me," Walt replied, "even if he did exist, which he doesn't. It's all superstitious nonsense, he's no more real than the man in the moon."

*   *   *

The new visitor soon settled in Witches Crag, and it's fair to say that he felt comfortable there. He spent his daytimes out and about, taking care of business, and when his work was done he'd be downstairs in the snug bar with the locals. They were a friendly bunch, albeit a bit peculiar, and it wasn't long before Walt knew them all by name. He would chat regularly with them and have a bit of a laugh, although his evenings were largely spent sitting alone at a table in the corner, having a sandwich whilst doing his paperwork.

On one such evening, as he sat in his usual place, someone came into the Green Man that the bank clerk had not seen before. He was a curious-looking chap, craggy with wrinkled skin. His hair was messy, like straw, and his clothes were somewhat tatty and worn. Walt concluded that he must be one of the original residents of the village, an old farmer perhaps.

The man came over and sat himself down at Walt's table, and when he spoke it was with a gruff-sounding voice. They chatted for a short while, and despite being odd, Walt enjoyed the man's company. He was friendly and somewhat amusing, and he had a permanent grin on his face which Walt found intriguing, but there was definitely something curious about his demeanour.

Walt also noticed that the chap never had anything to eat or drink the whole time that he was there, which seemed rather strange, and another thing that became apparent as the pair sat talking, was that the man never made any attempt to speak to anyone else in the tavern apart from himself, and no one in the pub bothered to acknowledge the strange man's presence either. Perhaps the old man is a bit eccentric and only likes to talk to outsiders, Walt thought to himself, maybe the locals know that so they leave him alone.

*   *   *

A few evenings later, the strange fellow came into the Green Man again, and as before, joined the bank clerk at the table. He looked exactly the same as the previous time, with the noticeable craggy and wrinkled skin, messy straw-like hair, and he wore the same clothes. When Walt offered to buy the man a drink he declined, and once again, he showed no interest in anyone else around him other than Walt, which was again reciprocated. Walt wondered if perhaps the man had done something in the past to upset the villagers, and that they didn't mind him being in the pub so long as he didn't bother them; the landlord certainly didn't seem to mind him sitting there without ever buying anything.

It was during this second meeting that Walt noticed something else that was a bit peculiar. As the pair chatted away to each other, some of the other patrons of the inn would occasionally glance over seemed to be laughing to themselves. Perhaps they find the man amusing, he thought to himself.

As they conversed this time, the curious chap revealed to Walt that he had a proposition for him, something that could be beneficial to both of them. The man explained that he required his help, that there was a job that needed doing which he couldn't do himself. It would only take a couple of hours, but as it was a considerable task it needed a young man to do it, and for which the requital would be amply adequate. Walt wasn't sure, and he asked the man why he didn't ask one of the locals to do it.

"I doubt any of them would be willing to 'elp me," the man said, "besides, what I'll give you in return is something rather special, and I wouldn't want any of them to 'ave it anyway."

With that said, he discretely took out a small pouch from his ragged coat pocket and opened it up so that Walt could peek inside. The young bank clerk could not believe his eyes, for inside the pouch was the shiniest gold coin that he had ever seen. For a brief moment he was speechless, but was then able to explain to the man that he couldn't possibly take it for it was far too much to pay someone for doing one little job. The fellow leaned forward and spoke quietly and discreetly, he said that he was going to let Walt into a secret, something that none of the others in the village knew. He revealed that he was a very rich man, and that he didn't just have one gold coin, he had hundreds of them, so giving one away meant nothing to him.

The job at hand sounded straightforward enough, to move a large stone from one place to another, but for some reason that wasn't divulged, it had to be done that very night. It would be a laborious task, the stone would likely be heavy, and it was at the top of the hill and needed to be carried all the way down to the bottom, which is why the old man couldn't do it himself. But Walt was young, fit and healthy, it was certainly something he could do, but he was curious as to why the stone had to be relocated in the first place. When asked, the man explained that he was the keeper of the moor, and that Walt would never understand the ways and traditions of the countryside, but the location of stones on the moors is very important.

"They all 'ave a function," he said, "each and ev'y one of 'em, and it's my job to ensure that they are all in their correct place."

He was right, Walt didn't understand, but it didn't really matter. His junior clerk post paid a pittance, the gold coin was worth more than he could earn in ten years, and the man had plenty of them so why not? Besides, he would be doing the chap a favour. Walt could not resist the offer, and shook on it. The old man was so pleased that the grin on his face became even broader.

Walt finished off his drink, and the unlikely couple left the tavern. As he said goodbye to the other patrons on the way out, he got the distinct impression that some of them were sniggering. They probably think I'm mad going out into the night with this crazy bod, he thought to himself, but little do they know what I'm going to get out of it.

* * *

The pair walked together, all the way to the top of the hill, where the man revealed the stone that needed to be moved. It was even bigger than Walt had expected, and he could see why the old fellow couldn't move it for himself. The man further explained what needed to be done, that he should carry the stone down to the bottom of the hill, until he came to a stream. Once there, he would see a big willow tree on the side of the bank, he must place the stone on the ground under the tree. The man then took the pouch from his pocket and handed it to Walt, wished him good luck, and disappeared into the night.

With effort, Walt lifted the stone and placed it on his shoulder. What a strange place this is, he thought to himself as he set off down the hill, these countryfolk certainly have some weird ways, and fancy paying someone a gold coin just to move a stone. Perhaps the old man couldn't ask any of the locals to do it because they would have been afraid to, what with all their superstitions and suchlike, maybe that's why he'd asked me, because I was the only who wasn't too scared.

But as he carried the stone down the hill in the dark, Walt realised how spooky it was to be alone on the moors at night. He had to keep reassuring himself that he wasn't going to encounter any goblins or leprechauns or banshees on the way, or any MacCrackens for that matter, because such things do not exist.

* * *

It was an arduous task, the walk down the hill was a long one and the stone seemed to get heavier and heavier the further he went, but Walt knew that if he reached the stream it would all be worth it: and eventually he did. He made it down to the bottom of the hill, and he saw the stream and the big willow tree just as he had been told, and he placed the stone beneath the tree, relieved to offload it. It seemed crazy, as Walt looked around he saw other large stones on the ground that looked just like the one that he'd carried all the way down the hill. All that work to move a stone that was just like all the rest, he didn't understand it, but the job was done and he had his gold coin. He could now make his way back to his room at the tavern for a good night's rest - he had certainly earned it.

Before he turned in for the night, despite being exhausted, Walt wanted to have another look at the gold coin. So he took it from its little pouch and held it in his hand. It was even more impressive than he'd remembered, the thick gold coin sparkled in the light, it was beautiful. Walt rested his head on the pillow, and with a big smile on his face fell into a deep and restful sleep.

* * *

But that wasn't the end of this adventure for young Walt

Pepper, because a few evenings later, he sat once again at his regular place in the tavern, with his little pouch containing the gold coin secure in his pocket; he wasn't going to let it out of his sight. The bank assignment was now pretty much complete, all that was left to do was to write up a final report; he would leave Witches Crag the next day.

As he sat at his table in the corner, dotting the i's and crossing the t's of his paperwork, he was surprised when the same character came into the Green Man once again, and as before, joined him at the table. It was the first time he'd seen the old man since he'd left him at the top of the hill a few nights before.

The peculiar chap thanked Walt for his hard work, and said that he had done a very good job, but he then divulged the reason for coming to see him yet again. The man explained that he had unfortunately made an error, and had instructed Walt to move the wrong stone. It was in fact, an adjacent stone that should have been taken down the hill, a much smaller one that he himself could carry. Walt was naturally disappointed to hear this, but was immediately reassured when he was told that he could still keep the gold coin - they had 'made a deal,' and Walt had done what was asked of him. It did mean however, that the stone that he'd placed beneath the tree would need to be returned to its rightful spot, and Walt was then told that if he was to put the stone back in its original location, he would get another gold coin.

The thought of carrying the stone again was not a pleasant one, but the thought of a second gold coin certainly was. Walt considered the proposal. It was his last night in Witches Crag, he would be leaving the next day and would probably never see the place ever again. The young bank clerk knew that he would never get another chance to earn another gold coin, and for just a few hours work. So he accepted the offer - two gold coins were worth more than he could earn in twenty years.

* * *

The unlikely pair stood together atop the hill once again, looking out at the vast expanse of the moor. This time, the scene was bathed in the light of a full moon which produced an eerie glow over the lay of the land, and there was an unearthly feeling in the air too, one of mystery and uncertainty.

The man instructed Walt to take his pouch from his pocket and to open it, and when he did, he dropped into it another gold coin just like the first one. So there were now two shiny gold coins in the small bag, quite a little collection, Walt thought to himself. The curious fellow seemed perfectly happy to pay for the job in advance. The bank clerk knew that he had the man's trust, he knows that I am a man of my word and will get the task done, he realised.

They said their goodbyes for the very last time, Walt knew that he would never see the remarkable person again. Standing on the lonely moor, he watched the craggy old fellow go off into the night, turning to look around one last time as he did, with his characteristic grin seeming even bigger than ever.

"What an extraordinary chap," Walt said to himself, "I will never forget that grin for as long as I live."

* * *

Walt was as good as his word, and immediately set off down the hill. He made it to the bottom in no time at all, without any load to carry the hill wasn't half as big, and when he reached the stream he saw the big willow tree and recognised the stone on the ground beneath it, just as he had left it a few nights before. So once again, he hoisted the lump onto his shoulder, then proceeded to make his way - up the hill this time.

He hadn't thought of it before, but he soon realised that carrying the stone downhill was one thing, but carrying it uphill was another thing altogether. The old man must have known that, he told himself, perhaps that's why he'd had such a crafty big grin on his face as he left.

The weight of the stone seemed twice as heavy going up, the young bank clerk wasn't even sure if he could make it to the top. And there was something else - in the full moon, the moor seemed even spookier than ever. The moonlight cast dark shadows all around, long black fingers ran along the ground as if reaching out to grab him, and poor Walt began to make things out from the shapes of the bushes and the trees. And there were strange noises too, he had no idea what they were. He had to tell himself over and over again that it was just his imagination, his mind playing tricks on him, perhaps brought on by fatigue. He had to keep reassuring himself that he wasn't going to encounter any goblins or sprites and suchlike, because none of them are real, but in the current situation it wasn't an easy thing to do, even for a staunch disbeliever like himself. However, he'd made a deal and he had to go on, and besides, he wanted to keep that second gold coin.

Walt persevered through the night. He sweated and toiled, and had to take regular stops on the lonely moor to rest a while and to regain his breath. His legs became weak, so much so that he could barely stand. But he made it in the end, he carried the heavy stone all the way up the hill and he placed it on the ground, in exactly the same position as it was originally.

He was exhausted, two nights of carrying the stone had taken its toll. His back was aching, his hands were rough and blistered, and his body had never felt so tired - but he'd done it. Taking a deep breath in, and looking up to the stars, he thanked the heavens, his work was now complete and he was a very wealthy man.

When Walt Pepper eventually got to his room that night, he collapsed on the bed. He mustered one last drop of energy to take out the two gold coins from his pouch, to look at them lovingly before going to sleep. As they glistened in the palm of his hand, he felt an immense sense of achievement, proud to have carried the big stone all the way back up the hill in the dark. And what's more, he had proved himself right, because he'd spent several hours alone on the moor at night, with a full moon to boot, and he'd encountered nothing. No spirits or goblins, no leprechauns or banshees, and no so-called McCracken, just as he always knew, they were figments of the mind, they didn't exist. Having not even washed or removed his clothes, he fell into a deep slumber - with a big contented smile on his face.

* * *

He awoke late the next morning. Despite having a long rest, his body still ached, but he was happy. All he needed to do now was to take a hot bath and pack his few belongings, he would have lunch in the tavern before saying goodbye to the locals. When he left he would probably never see Witches Crag again, and when he returned to his hometown he would be a very wealthy man.

* * *

Walt went downstairs to the saloon, where he was met by the usual faces, he knew them all so well now and felt slightly sorry to be leaving them. The patrons of the Green Man were pleased to see the lodger once again, and greeted him with big smiles. After a hearty meal he felt much better, most of his energy having now returned.

As he was preparing to leave, the young bank clerk chatted with the locals for the final time. They asked him if, after having stayed in the village for some time now, he still thought that their superstitions and beliefs were hogwash.

"Of course," he said, "more than ever in fact, but if you countryfolk want to believe in such things then it's fine by me, you just won't get me believing in them that's all."

"Is that so?" they replied.

He started to leave, but then stopped for a moment.

"Could I ask just one thing before I go?" he said. "Who was the strange-looking fellow that came to sit with me at my table, and why didn't any of you acknowledge him?"

What strange-looking fellow was that?" they replied.

"The old man of course, who sat with me in the corner, for three nights in all."

"But you were alone at the table all the time," said one of the regulars.

"That's right," said another, "no one sat wiv you at all."

"But I was talking to him, you must have seen us."

"Well, we saw you, you were sitting there talking to ya'self quite a bit, it did look amusing, did ya not notice any of us 'aving a little laugh?"

"Well yes, but I thought you were laughing at him."

"So tell us," one of the villagers asked, "this man that was supposedly sitting with you, did 'e buy a drink at all?"

"No, nothing."

"So 'e sat there for three evenings without even buying

a drink?"

"Yes that's right, I did think it a little odd."

"Well let us tell ya something son. The landlord 'ere is as frugal as they come, and there is no way on earth that anyone is going to sit in 'is tavern for one evening without spending so much as a penny, let alone for three. Sorry lad, there was no one else wiv ya."

Poor Walt was puzzled, and confused, and didn't know what to say.

"Did 'e 'appen to tell you 'is name at all?" One of the locals asked.

"Well actually no, he didn't as a matter of fact, and I never thought to ask," replied Walt in a bemused tone. "But I *was* talking to him, someone must have seen it."

"No one was wiv ya, you were talking into thin air."

"So what did this chap look like?" someone wanted to know.

"He was peculiar looking I must admit. He was old, and his skin was wrinkly."

"Aha, and was 'is 'air like straw by any chance?"

"Yes it was."

"And were 'is clothes ragged and tatty?"

"Yes they were."

"And did 'e seem to have a permanent grin on 'is face?"

"Yes that's him!" Walt exclaimed, triumphantly, "you know him."

"Yes we know 'im alright, but we never saw 'im, it sounds to us like you've had an encounter with our friend the McCracken."

Walt Pepper was stunned when he heard this, totally speechless. He turned to walk away. Had he really been made a fool of by some mythical goblin that he doesn't even believe in? But then, as he was about to leave the tavern, he suddenly remembered his gold coins - of course, he had evidence there in his pocket! He turned around to face the patrons of the inn once again.

"But I have proof, I did some work for him, he gave me a job to do and paid me handsomely in gold coins, I'm a rich man so I wasn't fooled."

"Really?" said the locals.

"Yes, and I can show you, I have two gold coins here in my pocket, they will prove that he is a real person and that it really happened."

Everyone in the tavern watched and waited, as Walt Pepper hastily pulled out the little pouch from his pocket. He opened it up in front of them all, and tipped the two gold coins into his open hand. Only they weren't gold coins that fell out, they were two small brown stones, just like the millions of other little brown stones scattered all over the moors.

"So the McCracken is hogwash is it not?" one of the locals called out, and the tavern erupted with the sound of laughter.

The Big Old Tree

The splendid oak tree was loved by everyone, from the animals and creatures that lived on its branches or fed on its fruit, to the children who played happily beneath it. On hot sunny days, people would sit in its shade, and occasionally a passerby would stop beside its trunk, stretch out their arms as long as they could and give the tree a hug.

There were others that would even talk to the tree. It couldn't talk back of course, but it did have its own way of communicating that some people, if they were that way inclined, could understand. And if anyone ever sought the tree's help or guidance, it would listen, and some were sure that the tree responded, sending out thoughts of wisdom and insight. Because of this, some people said that it was very wise.

* * *

The big old tree stood all alone in the field, strong and proud. Its sturdy trunk and thick knotted branches had witnessed the passing of many years, and the coming-and-going of countless seasons. Springtimes, when the surrounding fields came alive with colour and birds sang exuberantly from its branches. Summertimes, when wonderful aromas filled the air and bees and butterflies came to visit. The oak tree loved the autumn, as the wind blustered through its leaves it felt invigorated and alive. And lastly, winter, which was a time for rest and to reserve energy. So, like the hedgehogs that hibernated safe and secure under the leaves within the crevice of its trunk, the big old tree spent much of the time asleep, awaking only on occasions to take a peek. Often, when it did this, all around would be covered in a blanket of white, and thick snow would be cascading down from above - it was quite magical.

At such moments, the tree would sometimes become aware of a strange feeling in the air, a kind of mystical stillness. There would be a surrounding sense of peace and serenity, accompanied by a powerful and loving presence. The energy that was perceived seemed to be alive, and the tree felt somehow connected to it. It called this the 'special feeling,' when it knew that someone was looking over it and that everything was perfect in the world, and exactly as it was supposed to be.

* * *

One autumn, the tree was feeling somewhat melancholy. Standing alone in the middle of the field, it felt lonely. It had felt this way before, although this time the sensation was stronger - but it then had an idea. The tree remembered the special feeling, and the connection they had, and how this wonderful loving presence seemed to be able to listen to its thoughts. So it decided, that when the special feeling next appeared, it would ask if perhaps this powerful loving energy could help in some way.

It so happened, that during the month that followed, the special feeling came around again, and the tree did exactly as it planned - it explained how it felt and asked for help.

* * *

A few nights later there was a big storm, one that swept across the land. Houses shook and trees swayed, thunder roared and lightning flashed across the sky, and rain poured down continuously throughout the night - it was a storm like never before.

When morning came, all was calm once more, the hushed stillness a marked contrast to the tumult of the night. Fences and roofs were easily repaired, things soon returned to normal, and no one was any worse for wear because of what had happened. In fact, in a way, it was a positive thing for many people, because most of them had actually enjoyed the storm, especially the children - there is something about the power of nature that is awe inspiring and exciting to see. Also, the people did like to talk, and the 'Great Storm,' as it was to be called, was something they would be able to talk about for many years to come. The tree was happy about all of this, but decided that it was probably better not ask for anything again from now on. It blamed itself. I must have made the special feeling angry, it thought, because I asked for something for myself, how selfish I have been.

* * *

The remainder of the year passed uneventfully, and those who had been through the Great Storm spoke about it with a sense of pride, that they had been there to witness the event.

During the wintertime, something happened that made the tree feel much better. It had awoken from its slumber to discover that it was snowing, all around was pristine white and it was quite beautiful. The air felt fresh and clean, and the glow from the sky created a magical twilight. There was a surrounding stillness, a pure silence, and the tree felt the peacefulness and wonder of the world that it was living in.

As usual with such moments, the special feeling was there too, but this time the powerful comforting presence was even stronger than ever. As it stood alone in the field, the big oak tree was engulfed by love, in a state of bliss, and in awe of simply existing. The special feeling then spoke to the tree, reassuring it and letting it know that all was fine, that everything was exactly as it was supposed to be. The tree felt good.

* * *

When spring arrived in the new year, everyone was delighted, happily noticing the changes taking place around them as nature came to life. The woodland animals emerged from their hibernation, and new leaves sprouted from the once bare branches. Delicate snowdrops gave way to the bold colours of crocus, and daffodil leaves poked out from the earth like long green fingers pointing up to the sky, their vibrant flowers hanging down like large golden bells.

The big old tree awoke from its slumber, to find the world bursting with life once again. The sun was up and its glorious rays were warming and energising everything they touched, it was a wonderful day and the tree felt blessed to be alive. Birds were singing happily from its branches, squirrels darted playfully around on the ground below, and away in the distance, nodding sheep grazed nonchalantly on the green grass.

Then, the most astonishing and wonderful thing happened - the tree noticed something on the ground, close by. Coming up from the earth was a tiny shoot, and from its one solitary leaf the tree could tell that it was the same as it was - the shoot would grow to become a big oak tree just like itself! The tree was filled with joy, it now had its very own companion and would never feel lonely again. The special feeling had answered its prayers after all, and the big old tree was so happy.

Standing proud, bathed in glorious sunshine, it said a

big thank you, because it knew that at that very moment the special feeling was right there, sharing the special moment. And it all made sense now, the storm had been a blessing and had happened for a reason. The strong wind was needed to blow the fruit from the branch at just the right time, the heavy rain had softened the ground so that the acorn could nestle itself into the soil, and the warmth of the sun had done the rest, so that a new life would be born and the big old tree would always have a companion.

It was the magic of nature. Life truly is amazing, and it has a remarkable way of giving us exactly what we need just when we need it most. It may not always seem that way, but if we trust, and have patience, then things will come to us in their own time. And yes, when we are able to connect with the special feeling - it does listen.

Umpiddipompus

Nabih's journey would be a long one: a four-hour coach trip to Dunstable Heath to spend a few days with his grandparents. He had visited several times before, always with his parents, but now he was old enough to travel the considerable distance by himself.

He was pleased that the journey was going to take some time, and there was a reason for that - because Nabih loved books. He liked to read about strange things, the stranger the better, and it so happened that on this particular morning he had in his possession one of the strangest books he had ever seen.

He'd discovered the item the previous day in his favourite secondhand bookstore. This quaint little shop, tucked away down a side-alley, had been there as far back as Nabih could remember, and he would always go there whenever he got the chance. The shopkeeper seemed to have a knack of getting the most interesting and unusual books, the weird and wonderful things that you wouldn't find anywhere else.

The books in the store weren't categorised or put in any order as such, they were pretty much scattered about all over the place, stacked on shelves or chairs, and even piled up on the floor. Many of them were old, some were very rare, and others were so bizarre that you would never believe they existed unless you saw them with your own eyes.

Nabih had learnt that the best thing to do was to scour the dusty old shelves at the back of the shop, because that's where all the interesting stuff was, and it was whilst doing this that he came upon his latest find; as soon as he spotted it he knew that he'd found something special.

He'd reached up and took the book from the shelf, then wiped the dust off with a swipe of his arm so that he could see the front cover clearly. The title immediately stood out, in gold embossed letters it read: *Amazing Creatures of Legend and Folklore*, and underneath, an impressive looking illustration of an extraordinary beast with three eyes.

He'd sat himself down immediately on a nearby stool, eager to find out more, and opened up the book excitedly to turn over the pages. To his delight, he discovered that each page was devoted to a different creature, the top half of the page showed a depiction of the beast and the bottom half had some written information about it. The text was brief, but it did give some important facts, such as the colour and size, its habitat, what food it liked to eat, and it also stated whether the being was friendly or not. Nabih was fascinated, it was a fantastic discovery, so without further ado he had taken *Amazing Creatures of Legend and Folklore* to the counter and bought it, not even bothering to ask how much it was - he was going to buy it regardless.

* * *

Now, sitting on the coach by himself, Nabih would be able to have a close look at his new discovery for the first time, at each and every one of the creatures in detail. So as soon as the coach was on its way, he began flicking through the pages, and he was immediately absorbed, the book was even more fascinating than he'd expected. He discovered many interesting facts, like the Bigfoot and the Sasquatch are in fact the same thing, as are the Yeti and the Abominable Snowman, they are just different names depending on the area where they are seen.

There were creatures within the pages that Nabih had

heard of, such as the Loch Ness Monster, a Changeling and a Giant. But there were many that were totally new to him and some of these were quite bizarre, like a flying jellyfish, a nine-foot-tall purple alien with a triangular head, and a spider-like thing called a Cryptid.

All of the creatures were fantastic, in one way or another, and they were fascinating to read about, but there was one that got his attention more than any other. About two-thirds of the way through the book, sandwiched between the Ogo Pogo and the Mothman, was something called an Umpiddipompus. The illustration showed it to be a blob-like being, with a pinkish-coloured gelatinous body which appeared as though it would wobble whenever it moved; it reminded him of the globule of wax that a lava lamp creates when it gets hot. However, it was neither the peculiar appearance nor the unusual name that had sparked his interest, it was because of what was written in the text below:

Size: Approx. 4-5 feet
Colour: Pink
Habitat: Forests
Food: Acorns
Friendliness: Friendly, but very shy and elusive.
Location: Dunstable Heath

Nabih could not believe his eyes. Did it really say Dunstable Heath, the very place where he was heading, he had to read it several times over to believe it. It was true, he was not mistaken, it seemed that this bizarre creature with an equally bizarre name was from his grandparent's hometown, where he would be arriving at in a few hours' time.

* * *

Nabih made it to his grandparent's house by late afternoon, and he was pleased to see them both again. He always had a good time whenever he went there, he loved his grandmother's cooking and he and his grandfather did lots of interesting things together. He was even more excited this time however, because he couldn't wait to show them his recent discovery. So, after unpacking and settling in, Nabih wasted no time in showing off his new book.

They were very impressed when they saw it, and told him that he had done well to find such a rare and interesting artefact - but when his grandfather turned over the page and saw the umpiddipompus, his eyes lit up. He informed his grandson that he was aware of such a thing, and that many of the locals had heard rumours of a strange creature that lived in the woods, but he was surprised that it was known of outside of the town.

"Such stories have been around for many years," he said, "some believe them to be true, others say that they are just stories, made-up tales told by parents to embellish a child's imagination at bedtime."

Nabih asked him if he believed the rumours to be true or not, whether he thought the umpiddipompus was real. His grandfather said that he did, and told him the reason why. A neighbour, who was also a good friend, had told him that he had seen the creature on more than one occasion, and the man was someone whom he trusted.

"If Harry tells me he has seen something then I tend to believe him," he said.

His neighbour reckoned the creature to be nocturnal, because it had always been nighttime when he had seen it. This was information that was not included in the book, so

Nabih made a mental note that when he got home he would try to contact the author to let him know.

* * *

That night, as Nabih lay in bed, thoughts about the umpiddipompus went around in his head. If it were nocturnal then it would make sense, he reasoned. The book did say that the beings were shy and elusive, which would explain why they would only come out at night when humans are sleeping, and also why so few people had ever seen one.

He was finding the whole thing fascinating, and when he switched off his bedside lamp he could see the stars in the night sky through his bedroom window. The window faced out onto the garden, which backed onto the forest, and as Nabih snuggled up to sleep, the thought that there might be a strange creature roaming around just outside was very exciting.

* * *

The following morning, Nabih was up bright and early. Whenever he came to stay, he and his grandfather would often go for long walks into the woods: they enjoyed spending time in nature, being amongst trees and spotting the different animals. He was more eager than ever this time however, because of what he'd found out may be living there - and he had an idea which he wanted to put to his grandfather.

The plan was, to lure the umpiddipompus into the garden with acorns, which according to the book was its favourite food. They could create an acorn trail from the edge of the wood, all the way to the garden, and then make a pile of them to be collected. When he heard his grandson's plan, Nabih's grandfather said that it was a good idea that was certainly worth trying, and knowing the woods so well, he knew exactly where there was a big old oak tree that was over two-hundred years old; it was bound to be full of acorns at that time of year.

So the pair set off into the woods, and it wasn't long before they came upon the oak tree, and just as they had hoped it was ripe with fruit. Nabih was an excellent climber, he ascended the tree with ease and proceeded to pick acorns off from the branches one by one, which he then threw down to the forest floor. His grandfather stood below, bagging them all up, apart from a few that were taken by an opportunistic Jay before he'd had a chance to collect them.

It was a great system, and it wasn't long before they had a bagful of umpiddipompus-tempting treats. So, just as planned, when they reached the edge of the wood they began laying down a trail. Methodically, one acorn after another, they made a line that led from the forest edge all the way to the garden, and whatever acorns remained were used to make an enticing pile in the middle of the lawn - everything was now in place.

* * *

As evening approached, Nabih could feel the anticipation welling up inside. He couldn't wait for the night to come, but his grandfather told him not to expect too much, the book did state that umpiddipompus were very shy and elusive, and besides, they didn't even know for sure if they really existed or not.

When darkness eventually fell, the pair camped down in the lounge. Nabih's grandfather turned off the lights and pulled the curtains wide open, so that they had a panoramic view of the garden. They could keep a lookout throughout the night, so if anything did happen they wouldn't miss it.

They had chosen the perfect night, the sky was clear and a three-quarter moon gave off a subdued light, just enough for them to see the whole garden. Nabih lay on the sofa with a blanket over himself, facing the window, and his grandfather sat in his recliner armchair looking toward the same direction. A log fire was lit beside them, not only would it keep them warm during the night, but it would also provide a bit more light to see - although not so much that it would deter anything from venturing into the garden.

They were well prepared with a selection of snacks to last them through the night, and Nabih's grandfather would make hot cinnamon cocoa which they both loved. Everything was set and Nabih was now very excited, because although he was safe and warm and snuggled up on the sofa, the possibility of spotting a rare and bizarre creature for real made it seem like he was having a great outdoor adventure. With the log fire glowing beside them, the pair chatted as they waited for something to stir outside - his grandfather recounted some of the adventures that he'd had and Nabih loved to hear these.

Time soon passed, and they conversed well into the night, but unfortunately there was no sign of the animal that they'd attempted to lure in, although there had been some interesting visitors: a fox, a badger, and a hedgehog. Nabih discovered that a lot happened during the night as people slept in their beds, totally unaware of all the activity that was going on outside.

The lateness eventually got the better of them and the pair began to feel very sleepy, neither could keep their eyes open any longer, and they both dropped off to sleep.

* * *

In the middle of the night, Nabih was awoken from his slumber by a shuffling sound. Sitting upright, he rubbed his eyes and looked around. The subdued light from the moon was emanating in from outside, and the room remained warm as a few embers continued to glow in the fireplace.

Glancing over, he saw that his grandfather was sleeping soundly in his armchair. He must have been the one who made the shuffling noise, Nabih concluded, as he'd turned in his chair. But he heard the sound again, and realised that it was coming from outside. When he peered through the window into the garden, he could not believe his eyes - it was an umpiddipompus, standing in full view.

The creature looked exactly as it was depicted in his book. It was about four feet tall, pale pink in colour, and somewhat plump in build. It moved very slowly, and just as Nabih had suspected, its body wobbled when it did. He watched in silence as the amazing animal bent down to collect acorns from the pile that they had left in the middle of the garden, picking them up with one hand and transferring them for collection to the other hand. He figured that the visitor had probably eaten all the acorns along the trail and was now full, so was gathering up the rest to take away.

As he watched from the window, Nabih became aware that there was something curious about the creature's hands. They were large in proportion to the rest of its body, and he also noticed that the fingers on the hand that collected the acorns were stretched thin, ideally suited for picking up small fruit, but the fingers on the hand that accumulated the acorns were wide and seemingly moulded together, so that the hand was shaped like a bowl - perfect for containing things without dropping them. He concluded that an umpiddipompus must be able to morph its body, to change its shape for different purposes, which would explain their somewhat jelly-like appearance.

As he sat watching, keeping as still as he could, it dawned on him that his grandfather was missing everything. He wanted to wake him, but couldn't speak loudly otherwise he might scare away their visitor.

"Grandad, wake up," he whispered.

But his grandfather remained fast asleep in his chair, missing the extraordinary event that was taking place just outside.

In the moonlight, out in the garden, the fascinating being gathered up the last of the acorns, Nabih was certain that it would leave as soon as they had run out. He was desperate for his grandfather to awaken, not only did he want him to see the amazing spectacle for himself, but he also needed him to be a witness, so that when morning came he would know that it had not been just a dream.

"Grandad, you have to wake up." But his grandfather did not stir.

The umpiddipompus had now gathered up the last of the acorns. Remarkably, it then turned its head towards the house, walked slowly up to the window and peered in. Nabih froze, it was looking straight at him. Their eyes met but he wasn't afraid, the creature had a friendly face, and as it looked at him, he could tell that it knew that *he* was friendly too: even perhaps that he had been the one who had left out the food. With its big eyes looking in, the being seemed to give a slight smile before turning to walk slowly away.

"Grandad please, you must wake up."

This time, his grandfather heard him, he stirred in his chair, then opened his eyes.

"Grandad look, look outside, do you see it?"

His grandfather's eyes became wide, "Yes, I see it," he said, 'it's incredible."

Together, they sat and watched as the umpiddipompus

retreated slowly down the garden before disappearing into the night.

* * *

When Nabih awoke in the morning, he immediately remembered what had happened in the middle of the night - but did it really happen, had he really seen an umpiddipompus? He looked over to his grandfather's chair: it was empty. Maybe his grandfather had gone upstairs to bed after he'd fallen asleep, perhaps the whole thing was just something that he'd dreamt whilst sleeping alone on the sofa. But at that very moment, the door opened and his grandfather entered the room with a pot of tea and biscuits, and before Nabih could say anything his grandfather pre-empted him.

"Yes I did see it," he said, with a big smile on his face, "it wasn't a dream."

* * *

Before he left Dunstable Heath, to return home on the coach, Nabih went out into the garden one last time. It was a beautiful autumn morning and he felt good. He noticed that all the acorns were gone, and when he looked closely at the grass he saw that there were large, unusual footprints across the lawn - it was further confirmation that the events in the night had truly happened.

On the journey back home, he sat with his book once again, but it felt different this time. Perhaps because, as he looked through the *Amazing Creatures of Legend and Folklore*, he knew that he was one of the very few people to have seen one of them for real.

Reunion in the Night

She awoke in the middle of the night, to find a ball of golden light hovering in the centre of her room. She was intrigued, but not frightened, quite the opposite in fact, the light gave off a feeling of warmth and love - but she had no idea what it was or why it was there. Sitting upright in her bed, she watched as the light slowly expanded, until it filled a large area of the bedroom. Looking deep into it, she saw that the light shimmered and sparkled - it was quite beautiful.

As she continued to stare at this strange phenomenon that was happening right before her eyes, she became aware that something was beginning to form within, taking shape in the centre of the sphere. After watching it closely for a while, as it slowly manifested, she realised what it was - it was her pet dog from many years ago, from when she was a young child. Although it had been such a long time ago, there was no mistaking it. The sweet friendly face, the big brown eyes, and she could feel the animal's energy too, which she instantly recognised: it was definitely her dog. She was amazed, yet perplexed. How could this possibly be, how could her dear friend from the past be standing there in front of her. The realisation then came to her - it had come back to see her.

She slipped slowly out from the bed, and was now standing in front of the golden sphere. The figure emerged out from the light, to stand before her, and it was now much clearer to see. She had loved her pet very much, so seeing it once again, looking healthy and so full of life, made her heart rejoice. She wanted to bend down and hug her dear old friend, but the dog began to run around her in circles, excitedly. She remembered that this is exactly what it used to do all those years ago, and she knew precisely what it meant. Her dog was asking her to go somewhere, to follow it, just as it used to do when it wanted to go out to play in the park. So she followed her companion, and could hear its enthusiastic barks inside her mind, it was telling her to hurry up. Together, they entered the ball of light.

*   *   *

Stepping inside the golden sphere, something fantastic happened. Instantly, the pair rose up from the floor and were shooting upwards at an incredible speed towards the sky. It felt amazing, and she wondered how it was possible, but then realised that she was no longer in her physical body, which was lying still in the bed - she was leaving it behind as her spiritual body sped upwards.

Up and up they both went, like rockets leaving the earth. Her dog turned its head around to look at her as she followed, and she could sense the joy and happiness coming from her canine friend. The higher they went the faster they seemed to go, they were now whizzing through space and time. She could sense that the earth was a long way down, that they'd gone way beyond the clouds and the sky and even the moon, and were now in another realm altogether. Different colours streaked by as they accelerated upwards, passing stars and galaxies as they went, it was exhilarating. She somehow understood that her dog was leading the way, and that it knew exactly where it was going.

*   *   *

As the pair soared through space, they eventually came

upon a huge expanse of silvery-white haze - it was extremely beautiful. When they entered the haze, it tingled and sparkled all around them, and as her dog led her into the centre she felt suddenly loved, and safe and protected - she was cocooned in a living, loving presence. The energy was alive, and it knew her, she could feel it. It knew everything about her, her thoughts and desires, all of her memories and experiences. It was aware of everything that she had been through in her life, the happy and sad times, plus all the trials and tribulations.

The presence began to heal her. It penetrated deep within, healing her very soul. She basked in its powerful yet gentle energy, and as she did, buried emotions began to stir from deep inside. Not just from this life, but from other lives too, a thousand lifetimes, memories from aeons ago, unlocked, reawakened, revealing themselves fleetingly before returning to whence they came. When the healing was done, she felt wonderful, as if reborn. Her dog beckoned her to follow it once more, it wanted to take her somewhere else - to show her something.

* * *

She could not believe her eyes. Panning out in front of her was a magnificent land of rolling green fields, and as she touched down with her dearest friend, it was the softest, most luxurious grass she'd ever felt. The colours that surrounded her were stunning, more vibrant than she'd ever known, and each colour seemed to have its own energy, to be alive.

The sweet aroma of freshly cut grass filled the air, unlocking memories from her childhood, of summer days out with her dog, throwing a stick or ball and her companion charging off enthusiastically to fetch it. She wondered how she had allowed herself to forget such wonderful times, those precious moments that she had once experienced.

She collected a stick from the ground and threw it through the air, then watched as her dog bounded off excitedly before returning to drop it at her feet. She picked up the stick and threw it once more, then again and again, it was so much fun. She laughed, and could sense that her dog was laughing too. It was just like all those years ago, she had forgotten how happy she had once been, when she was younger and life was so much simpler.

* * *

When the game was over, her dog encouraged her to follow as it ran up a hill. As they were reaching the top, the animal began to communicate to her, through her mind, it was telling her that this was its home.

It was then that she had the most wonderful surprise, because waiting for her at the top of the hill were all the pets that she had known throughout her life. They were all there to greet her, every single one of them. She had loved her animals so much, so seeing them all again brought tears of joy. At that very moment, she knew that the bonds of love that she once shared with her pets remained, that they had never been severed, and they felt stronger than ever.

Her dogs were barking with joy to see her, but it wasn't only her dogs, all the other animals were there too. The wise old cat that had lived with them in the country house, purred enthusiastically, and she saw her pet budgie, her mouse, her rabbit, and even the little tortoise that they'd once had, they were all there to greet her. It was the most wonderful experience, she was overjoyed to see her beloved companions once again, and to know that they were happy and living in such a beautiful place.

*   *   *

It was a magical reunion, and she hugged and kissed each and every one of her adorable animals. As she stood with her old friends once again, they communicated to her, telepathically. They told her that this is where they live, a paradise where animals come when they leave the earth, and any ailments or health concerns they once had were left behind. We are perfect here and feel wonderful, we can run and play whenever we want and for as long as we want, and at the end of it we have the most blissful sleep that you could ever imagine. Some of us will return to Earth again one day, perhaps to share another life with the same owner, but only when both are ready and the time is right. We never forget the people who once took care of us, just as they never forget us, our love for each other always remains. We brought you here to show you the reality of how things are, and so that you know that we are all fine. But unfortunately, this can only be a brief encounter, it is time for you to return, but please always remember - a bond of love is eternal.

Almost instantly, she felt herself back in her physical body, lying in her bed once again. She opened her eyes. Deep inside, she knew that what she'd experienced was more than just a dream, that she'd really been visited by the spirit of her beloved dog, and had met all of her pets. And from that day on, she knew that all the animals that she had once loved and cherished, and who'd shared part of her life with her, were happy, and that one day she would see them all again.

Quark Strangeness

Davis slumped in his chair, then let out a deep sigh. He felt strange somewhat, as if in a dream, one from which he would suddenly awaken then wonder how his mind could have concocted such a thing. But this was no dream, bizarre as it all seemed, the events of that day were real, they had actually happened, and as head of the SQS Project, the inventor of the Sub-Quark Scope, it had been his job to make the announcement to the world.

For almost ten years, Professor Davis and his team had worked tirelessly on the project; it had become their life's work. They were devoted to the 'Superscope', as it was more commonly called, which was to bring about the next big breakthrough in science, and open up a new frontier of knowledge and understanding.

The SQS was the pinnacle of twenty-first century technology, a work of craftsmanship, and the pride and joy of the Southern State Research Centre. Consisting of over forty-thousand moving parts, an amalgamation of tubes, chambers, condensers, crystals, lenses and filaments, meticulously primed to work in conjunction with lasers, x-rays and electrons, all synchronised with the most advanced software. The result - a microscope with a magnification power over a million times greater than anything that had preceded it.

As he relaxed his body into the chair, the head scientist tried to calm his mind, but it was difficult. The events of that morning and afternoon played over and over in his head, like a set of movie clips on repeat. It was the correct thing to do, the natural course, he told himself, what else would we have chosen to look at, and if not us then someone would have done it sooner or later. It's human nature, we are seekers, always looking further, deeper, pushing the boundaries, it's the way it's always been and always will be.

The tiny coms device on his chest flashed.

"Yes," he said.

A calm, self-assured female voice responded, it was Clara Thompson, his head assistant.

"Reporting current status, Professor. The scope is stable sir, it's functioning smoothly. We did have a slight instability issue with the cryofixation plate but adjustments have been made and it's now in perfect alignment, so all good."

"And the image, is it the same?" he asked.

"The same, but clearer. It sure is vast. We are running computer scans now and we'll process the data."

"So no mistakes then, it is what is it?"

"Without doubt Professor."

"Okay, thank you, keep me informed."

*   *   *

When the team had made the decision, as to what would be the first thing to be observed through their new state-of-the-art equipment, the choice of human DNA was an obvious one. When they disclosed this to the scientific community and the outside world, it was met with a positive response. People were not only intrigued that science now had a machine that could actually do this, they were also eager to find out what it would reveal.

At 7:15 that morning, the project team had gathered enthusiastically in their lab. A DNA sample, extracted from Robert Davis himself, was placed on the plate of the SQS and the Superscope was fired up. The small group of scientists had waited a long time for this day, and now, after so many years of work, their goal would be realised - they would discover what lay deep within each and every human being.

All eyes would be on the large screen sited on the laboratory wall. Throughout the day, the SQS would transmit its image directly onto it, and as it probed deeper and deeper into the strand of DNA, its secrets would be revealed.

* * *

There was great excitement when the first image appeared, although it was something they had seen countless times before; the Watson-Crick double helix, as seen through standard electron microscopes. But this was just the beginning of course, as the day progressed the SQS would be going much further than a standard electron microscope and as it did, outside the Southern State Research Centre, the whole world would be waiting for news of their findings.

At approximately 8:25, just forty minutes after it had revealed its first image, the SQS was powerful enough to penetrate the outer wall of the strand of DNA. The highly developed machine followed its preprogrammed course, delving deeper, searching for the target area. As time passed, the watching team observed the image go from molecular to atomic, and then subatomic. Throughout the morning, the eyes of the scientists were glued to the screen as the instrument's coded software took it down through the nucleus, the nucleon, and then, at 11:08 hours, the Superscope entered the quark. Davis and his team looked on with bated breath, intrigued, as they were about to see something that no human had ever seen before.

But the image showed nothing, just empty space. Time

passed by without any change, as they looked up at the screen on the wall, the small group of scientists saw nothing but a void. There were some who had predicted this, sceptics who were opposed to the project and the financial cost. They argued that physically we had already gone as far as we could, that we had discovered our smallest particle and there was nothing more to see - the answer they professed, lay in metaphysics. If this were the case, then at least if nothing else, the SQS would confirm it. But many others, including Professor Davis and his team, did not go along with this view, they were sure that there was something more, after all, isn't that always the case. Whether searching within the human body or exploring the vastness of outer space, the further we look we always find something. Davis held this belief firmly, which is why he had devoted his life to the project.

*   *   *

Two more hours elapsed, and despite the scope increasing its magnification with each second that went by, the image on the wall remained the same: it continued to show nothing, just endless empty space. At 13:22, however, something happened - a minute dot appeared on the screen.

The eyes of the scientists were fixed on the image, and as they watched, the tiny dot on the screen grew. Soon more dots appeared, and then substantially so, as time passed, with the scope delving deeper and deeper, hundreds of tiny specks of light became thousands, which turned into seemingly millions, filling up the whole screen on the laboratory wall. There was great excitement amongst the watching scientists - what could these tiny points of light possibly be?

By the time that the SQS had reached sixty per cent of its capabilities, the lights had become much larger. Some of them were noticeably brighter too, and others were different shapes. The project team were transfixed as they watched the image unfold, conscious of the fact that they were discovering something new. When the scope reached eighty per cent, the image on the screen was substantially sharper, the shapes now had clear definition, revealing themselves to be orbs, stars, discs and spirals. The black background, which had initially appeared to be empty space, began showing areas of shade and colour also, it wasn't a void after all - there was something there too.

The team were absorbed in what they were being shown - but something was not right. Something was niggling away inside all of them, and as time passed, it gradually dawned on them what it was - they had seen the image before. But what was unfolding before their very eyes was so extraordinary, so shocking, that to begin with none of them would accept it. They tried to dismiss it from their minds, as coincidence or imagination, for what they were seeing was surely impossible. But eventually they had to accept it, it was there on the screen in front of them, becoming more evident over time - and it couldn't be denied.

It was Clara Thompson who mentioned it first. "It's incredible," she commented, "it's like looking into outer space."

"Absolutely," said one of her colleagues, "like superclusters of galaxies."

Then Davis said it outright. "Not like galaxies," he uttered, "they are galaxies. Those are stars, and I can make out black holes and supernovas. . . it's all there, we all know what they are."

"But that's inside us, in our DNA, how can that be?" asked another of the scientists.

But no one had an answer, they just looked on in silence,

trying to come to terms with what they had discovered.

"I will need to make an announcement," was all that Davis could respond with.

"What will you tell them professor?" Thompson asked.

"I'll just tell them the truth."

* * *

Davis was pleased to find a bit of quiet time in his office. Less than an hour ago, he'd informed the world that there were galaxies of stars and planets inside each and every one of us.

No doubt it was already global news, and almost every person on the planet would be talking about it. At some point he would have to face the media, soon, he knew that, with the bombardment of questions, many of which he would not have an answer to. But he wasn't ready for that just yet, right now he needed peace and quiet, to clear his head and gather his thoughts.

As he sat alone, questions churned over in his mind. What would the implications be? How would this discovery affect humankind? Would it mean a whole new perspective, or maybe things wouldn't change so much after all? He became tired of thinking, so he closed his eyes.

* * *

A beeping and flashing from Davis's coms device startled him - he had fallen asleep.

"Professor sir, it's Thompson, the scope has reached its maximum capacity."

He detected a slight apprehension in her voice. "What is it," he said, "is everything okay?"

"Yes sir, it's fine."

"Has the image changed?"

"No, not exactly."

"Then what is it, what's up?"

"Robert, you should come and see this for yourself."

Moments later, he entered the lab, to find his team standing together in front of the large screen on the wall. When he walked over to join them, each one turned to look at him, somewhat sheepishly he noticed, and no one spoke. They look as exhausted as I feel, Davis thought to himself, they should get some rest.

Looking up at the screen, the inventor of the Superscope could see that his colleagues had zoomed-in and enlarged one particular galaxy. He addressed them.

"It makes sense," he said, "it's what we should expect to see I guess. Magnificent isn't it, I've always thought of galaxies as the most beautiful things, and now, seeing this one, knowing that this incredible creation is inside all of us makes it even more beautiful.

"But Professor, it's a bit more . . ." Thompson tried to say something, but Davis hadn't finished speaking.

"Incredible, truly amazing," He concluded.

"Sir, Professor, there is something you need to know."

He picked up the seriousness in Thompson's voice, so stopped and looked at her.

"What is it? he said, "tell me."

She looked at him intently. "The galaxy on the screen, it isn't just another galaxy, it's our galaxy."

Davis was puzzled, what could she mean by such a remark.

"What are you saying?" he asked, "That this galaxy inside our body is the same as the one in which we exist?"

"Not the same as, it *is* our galaxy," she replied. "We had the computer run a scan, just out of curiosity really, to see if there was anything within the SQS image that matched our own external galaxy, and it found it."

Thompson highlighted a small area of the image.

"Look, there is our solar system. We've done tests, it's been confirmed, it's the same image that we see through our telescopes, it all matches, every star, every planet, it's identical."

His colleague was right, he could see it clearly. As he stood staring up at the wall, trying to come to terms with what he was being shown, his assistant pushed some buttons on the control panel beneath the screen. It mapped out the image into gridded sections, and she zoomed-in to enlarge one of them. It showed our very own solar system, large and clear, and plain to see. Davis could see the sun, and all the planets - and our very own planet Earth.

Thompson continued. "The location of the planets, their current positions, they correspond exactly as they do right now in our solar system. The movement, the orbits, they are identical, the space inside our DNA is the same space that we are simultaneously living in, what is happening outside us is also happening inside us, at each and every moment, to each and every one of us, they are one and the same."

Davis looked at Thompson, and at everyone else standing before him, then uttered the words:

"As above, so below, as within, so without."

The Ox and the Oxpecker

This is a tale about two very good friends, an ox and an oxpecker. Actually, they were more than very good friends, they were the bestest of friends. They were not family, not in any sense at all, as this would have been impossible - what with the ox being a huge cow-like animal with horns and the oxpecker being a small brown bird with a bright red beak. Their bond was so strong however, and their love for each other so genuine, that they certainly were like kith and kin.

* * *

The pair were a familiar, if not slightly comical sight to all the other animals who shared the vast open plains of Africa. The huge ox weighed as much as five-hundred sacks of potatoes, whereas the oxpecker was as heavy as one Brussels sprout. Together, they roamed the big expansive fields, one on top of the other. That is, the oxpecker on top of the ox - the other way around would have been silly.

They had what is known as a symbiotic relationship, which is where two different things live together for the benefit of each other. In this case, the oxpecker would dine on all the plump juicy insects that would land on the big animal's back, so would never go hungry, and the ox in return would have its own personal cleaner to get rid of all the bugs, which meant that it would never be itchy.

* * *

The two animals spent a lot of time in each other's company. As soon as the sun came up on the horizon the oxpecker would wake up its friend, so that they could start a brand-new day together. The little bird was so reliable in doing this, it was like the ox had its very own personal alarm clock. Each morning without fail, the big ox with eyes still closed, would feel the gentle pitter-patter of tiny feet on its back - and that's when he knew that it was time to get up. He was always happy to see his feathered friend, so would start each day with a big smile on his face.

All day long they would walk the plain, in their own time of course, nice and slow. The big beast would occasionally stop to graze on some nice fresh grass, or take a dip in a waterhole to cool down in the midday sun.

"Don't forget to splash me," the bird would say, "I'm hot too you know."

As they strolled around together they would chat. The pair would talk about anything and everything, like the weather for instance, or politics or economics, and sometimes deep philosophical things such as what the world would be like if holes did not exist. They would sing songs too, as well as tell jokes to make each other laugh, and if either had any exciting news to share then the other one would be the first to know. Like when the ox revealed the fantastic news that he was going to be a father. The oxpecker was so happy for his friend and congratulated him on the wonderful news. Needless to say, a few more songs than usual were sung on that day.

* * *

Early one morning, out on the vast African plain, something out of the ordinary happened. As the ox lay with his eyes closed, the sun appeared on the horizon. The crickets stirred in the brush and the birds began to sing - but the oxpecker did not arrive, no pitter-patter of tiny feet. That is strange, the ox thought to himself when he awoke much later than usual, I do hope my friend is okay.

He reassured himself that it was nothing to worry about, and that the little bird would be back all the earlier the next morning. But when the next day came, the same thing happened. The sun appeared on the horizon, the crickets stirred in the brush and the birds began to sing, but no oxpecker. The same thing happened the next day too, and the following one, and the days turned into weeks, with no sign of the little bird.

* * *

The ox carried on with his daily business, he had no choice really, besides, he had responsibilities now, what with becoming a father and all. But it's fair to say that the big beast was slightly sad, he missed his friend dearly. He missed the conversations that they had, and the songs that they sung, but most of all he missed the companionship - and on top of all that he was starting to itch.

The ox would smile to himself when he remembered a joke that the little bird had told him, or when he recalled something funny that had happened to them, but then he would get sad when he thought that he might not see his dear friend again. It was a shame also, that the oxpecker never got to meet the ox's newborn son, the little ox, who now walked the fields alongside him.

* * *

One morning, as the ox lay with his eyes closed, the sun appeared on the horizon. The crickets stirred in the brush and the birds began to sing . . . and he felt the pitter-patter of tiny feet on his back. The ox leapt up with joy, he knew those feet anywhere - his friend had returned! It was the most wonderful surprise for the animal and he was overjoyed.

The big beast was just about to ask the bird where he'd been all this time, when he noticed something that took him totally by surprise, and it was something quite wonderful. As he glanced over at his son, the little ox, he saw that perched on top of him was a tiny little oxpecker, a miniature version of his friend. He then knew where his companion had been all this while, he had taken some time off to have a little one of his own, so that the little ox would have his very own little oxpecker.

The four of them became a familiar, and even more comical sight to all the other animals with whom they shared the vast open plains. The big ox, with the oxpecker on his back, and alongside them, the little ox - with the tiny little oxpecker perched on top.

Train Journey in the Fog

Amelia stood at the station booth. An elderly man, wearing a suit that had obviously seen many years, smiled gently at her as he slid the ticket underneath the glass screen. Collecting it up and smiling back, she thanked him, then walked casually off towards the steps that led down to the platform.

It was all quiet, there were just a few mundane figures waiting along the platform: one couple and two lone people. Nighttime was arriving and darkness had fallen on the little town of Nethybridge, a few street lamps dotted around lit up the old railway station; their radiance revealed that a fog was coming in.

Amelia didn't have long to wait, just five or ten minutes of standing alone dealing with trivial mind-chatter, when a big old steam engine rumbled noisily in to shatter the stillness. She was surprised to see that these icons from a bygone age were still in use, but it kind of figured, she was in the back and beyond.

In a way, she was pleased that her conveyance was going to be a steam train - it was a throwback to the past and made her feel nostalgic, a reminder of her childhood days when everything in the world was much simpler and not so crazy. There's something about old steam locomotives that makes you feel warm and cosy inside, she thought to herself, as she watched the smoke from the chimney spread around the platform before rising up to blend with the fog.

* * *

It may have been old, but it was certainly impressive. One

hundred tons of solid iron, big and powerful. A brass plaque welded to the front revealed that it had a name - *Misty*. Somewhat appropriate for the evening, she thought to herself.

Boarding the train, she placed her luggage on the top railing before settling into her seat. It would be a straightforward journey, a direct route from Nethybridge to Dungoon with no stops in between. The duration would be exactly two hours, of which she intended to spend a large amount of sleeping.

With a hoot and a whistle, and a shout from a railwayman standing on the platform, Misty chugged forward on its way. Amelia immediately discovered that the seats were extremely comfortable, and after a short while, the train's rhythmic ch-ch-ch-ch, ch-ch-ch-ch, had sent her into a deep sleep.

* * *

Amelia was awoken sharply by a hissing and screeching as the train ground to a halt. She was puzzled, surely we can't be in Dungoon already, she thought to herself. Glancing down at her watch, she saw that she was right, it had only been about an hour since they'd left Nethybridge so they were only halfway to their destination - but the journey is a direct route, the train should not have stopped. She concluded that it must have done so to pick up some goods or freight, or perhaps a mailbag to drop off when they arrived at the other end, so she decided to sit it out and wait, expecting that they'd soon be on their way.

Several minutes passed however, and nothing happened. As Amelia sat, pondering as to what to do next, there was a knock on the carriage door and the glass window was pulled down from outside. A man's head poked through.

"Apologies Miss, but the train has had to stop for a while,

a slight engine problem that's all. We'll have to remain here for a time, once its all sorted we'll be back on our way."

As the man spoke, she couldn't help but notice how strange he looked. He appeared very old, perhaps a hundred years, and his neck seemed unnaturally long as it stretched in through the open window to converse with her. He had large round eyes, and the little holes of his nostrils were too high on his face. The railwayman had no hair whatsoever, not even eyebrows, and both his neck and face were extremely wrinkled. She couldn't help thinking that the man looked remarkably like a tortoise.

"Oh I see," she managed to say, "well thank you for letting me know. How long do you expect us to be here?"

"It will take an hour Miss, so if you want to get out and stretch your legs then feel free to do so. The village is just outside the station and there's a nice little tearoom that's always open if you fancy a cuppa. Or if you're feeling peckish, they do a lovely salad sandwich," he added as an afterthought. The curious man then slid the window back up and disappeared along the platform.

Reclining back in her seat, Amelia contemplated the encounter. He must be the stationmaster, she assumed, although amongst the dark and the haze she couldn't possibly make out a uniform. She closed her eyes, perhaps she could go back to sleep and pass the time that way. But she soon realised that it wasn't going to happen, without Misty's hypnotic sound to lull her it was impossible, so she gave up trying. An hour would be a long wait, she thought, then considered the tearoom that the stationmaster had told her about. It wasn't such a bad idea after all, she could stretch her legs and get some fresh air, and perhaps a cup of tea would freshen her up a bit.

* * *

Stepping out from the train, Amelia looked around her. The fog had thickened, she was able to see only partway along the platform. She saw no life whatsoever, but through the mist could just make out the exit up ahead, lit up by an old-fashioned street lamp. As she walked towards it, Amelia became aware of how eerily silent it was, and there seemed to be a strange, almost otherworldly feeling in the air. On the way out, she spotted an old wooden sign hanging on the brick wall - in worn out painted letters it read, *Wicken Station.*

Outside, the station had the same unworldly feeling as inside, accentuated even more by the now heavy fog that lay across the cobbled street like a ghostly white veil. Up ahead were the hazy lights of the village that the man had told her about. As she stood looking over at them, wondering where the tearoom might be, a voice close by spoke.

"Good evening Ma'am," it said, and a figure stepped out from within the mist.

It was a policeman, but not how she was used to seeing them. His uniform seemed very dated, as if from another time. He wore a heavy-looking overcoat with large round buttons, which was belted up around the waist. On his chest was a shiny, silver-coloured seven pointed badge, and a rounded hat sat on top of a somewhat hairy face: a beard, moustache, and thick black hair. It was a friendly, welcoming face though, and it smiled at her warmly.

"Can I help you at all Miss? I haven't seen you around these parts before, are you looking for someone?"

As he spoke, she became aware of how gruff-sounding his voice was, and couldn't help noticing that he seemed to have an extra-large tongue, so much so that he appeared to struggle very slightly to keep it in his mouth when he talked.

"Oh good evening Officer," she replied, "I've just come from the station. My train has had to stop for a while and I was informed that there was a tearoom close by, so I thought I might get myself a hot drink to pass the time."

"Yes of course, I understand. It's just over there," the policeman said, then turned his head quickly to face the outline of a small building whose windows were lit up. He stared motionless at it for several seconds before returning his gaze to Amelia, who couldn't help but notice this peculiar mannerism.

"You'll find it open," he eventually said, "it always is, a lot of folk around here are nocturnal you see."

"Really?" she replied, finding that a bit odd too. "Well thank you very much."

"My pleasure, have a nice evening," he concluded, as she walked away in the direction of the building. The policeman had reminded her of something, but she couldn't quite figure out what it was.

* * *

Pulling down on an old brass handle, she pushed open the wooden door and entered the building. Glancing around, she liked what she saw - the tearoom was small and quaint, cosy and inviting. A little old lady wearing a floral apron and hat stood behind the counter, oddly munching on a carrot, she noticed.

"Good evening, I'd like a cup of tea please," Amelia said politely.

"Certainly, what type of tea would you like?" The lady was soft spoken, timid, with a slightly nervous disposition.

"Oh, an Earl Grey please."

"One Earl Grey tea it is."

There was something unusual about this person too,

Amelia realised. She had a small face, but her ears appeared enormous in comparison, and her round eyes were positioned too much to the side of her head. And there was an oddness about her behaviour also, every now and then she would stop what she was doing, wiggle her nose slightly, and then continue. As Amelia watched the lady preparing the tea, it suddenly dawned on her what it was - she was like a rabbit.

What a strange place this is, she thought to herself, first the man at the train station, then the policeman in the street, and now the tea-lady in the cafe.

"Would you like anything to eat?" the lady asked her nicely, as she placed a teapot and cup and saucer onto a tray. "We have a delicious carrot cake."

"Oh not at the moment, thank you," Amelia replied, "the tea will be just fine."

She handed over some money and thanked her, then took a seat at a small round table by a window. When she was comfortably seated, she glanced around the room. There were others sitting at tables too, eating and drinking or simply chatting to each other. As she sipped her tea, Amelia examined them all closely one at a time, and that's when she noticed that there was something a little peculiar about all of them.

The man in the corner for instance, with the bow tie, sitting alone reading a newspaper, he looked remarkably like a bulldog. His physique was strong and sturdy, his face, round with baggy skin, and he had an upturned nose. At another table, a couple of elderly ladies sat busily eating, they must have been related as they looked very similar. Both had tiny eyes and beakish noses, and they were eating from bowls of what appeared to be mixed seeds. Sitting opposite were a group of ladies with tiny facial features, that included small pointed ears and little round eyes: they were eating sardines. Each one had their own teapot and cup, but when they poured their tea however, she noticed that instead of tea coming out from the spout it was milk. The ladies sat together chatting to themselves, whilst consuming their fish and drinking their cups of milk. When she listened closely, Amelia was sure that she could hear faint purring sounds between their words.

She sat at her table quietly drinking, discreetly watching the curious characters around her. After she'd finished her second cup, she reasoned that she must have been away from the station for about forty or forty-five minutes - it was time to return.

Walking back through the mist, Amelia felt refreshed, the exercise and hot drink had done her good. The village is certainly an odd place, she thought to herself, but she liked it, and although the locals were strange they all seemed very nice, and besides, it was a lovely cup of tea.

When she arrived back at the station it looked exactly the same as when she'd left it: silent and eerie, with the big steam train sitting mysteriously in the fog. She opened the door and stepped up into the carriage, then settled down in her seat once again. About ten minutes later, the engine roared back to life and Misty was on her way once more. She felt much better after her little walk and refreshment, and feeling contented, she snuggled up in her cosy seat and went back to sleep.

* * *

Amelia awoke as the steam train pulled into the station: they had arrived at their destination. She adjusted her eyes to the surroundings, then glanced down at her watch to check the time. But something was wrong, her watch told her that only two hours had passed since they had left Nethybridge, which didn't make sense. It doesn't add up, she thought, the journey from Nethybridge to Dungoon takes two hours, but the train had stopped for an hour for repairs. Perhaps her watch had stopped, she wondered, so she checked: it was still working - it could be slow, she supposed.

The passengers disembarked from the train and began walking along the platform towards the exit; the fog was a lot thinner here, she noticed. She was the last one to pass through the station, and as she did, a sweet elderly man was waiting to collect her ticket.

"Thank you Madam," he said sprightly, as she handed him her stub, "I hope you had a pleasant journey."

"Yes it was very nice, thank you."

"Excellent. Goodnight Miss," he concluded.

Amelia started to walk away, but then halted.

"Excuse me, there is one thing. My watch, it seems to be slow, could you tell me the correct time please?"

"Certainly."

Removing a brass fob watch from his breast pocket, the man looked at it closely.

"It's 21:34 precisely." It was the same time as on Amelia's watch.

"21:34," she replied, somewhat puzzled, "are you sure?"

"Positive Madam, this old fob watch is as reliable as they come."

"But I don't understand," said Amelia, now looking confused. "The journey from Nethybridge to Dungoon, it takes two hours does it not?"

"It certainly does."

"And we left on time, at 19:30?"

"That's correct Miss. The train left a 19:30, and a two hour journey means it arrived at approximately 21:30."

"But . . but what about the stop?"

"The stop Miss?" the ticket collector asked, looking somewhat perplexed.

"Yes, when we stopped at the station for repairs."

"The train didn't stop Miss, besides, there are no other stations along the line between Nethybridge and Dungoon where it could have stopped."

Amelia was shocked to hear this. "No stations at all?"

"None whatsoever."

"But what about . . . . ." She remembered the old sign that she'd seen on the wall. "What about, Wicken Station?"

The man looked at her with a puzzled expression on his face.

"Did you say Wicken Station, Miss?"

"Yes I did."

"Well, there was a Wicken Station once, but that was a long time ago, before the war in fact. It doesn't exist anymore, there's nothing left of it nor the village, they were both flattened during the Blitz."

"Are you sure?"

"Positive, there wouldn't be any need to have a station there now, it's just empty wasteland. I'm afraid the only thing that remains of the village of Wicken is the old fable."

"The fable?" inquired Amelia.

"Yes, folk still talk about it even to this day, it's all very interesting but nonsense of course. The fable says that during the war, government intelligence had received a tip-off that the village was about to be bombed, and the locals had just minutes to evacuate before their homes were destroyed. It has it that for some strange reason, none of their pets would go with them, they either ran off or refused to budge. It seemed they loved the place so much that they didn't want to leave, so the people of the village had no option but to go without them. Apparently, some say that the spirits of the animals transformed themselves into humans, so that they could keep the village going just as before. There are still some of the older folk around who believe this, and they say that a Wicken village does still exist, but not in our world as such, in a twilight world which we cannot see. It's absurd of course, just an old wive's tale, although I have to say there have been some strange incidents reported, I've even had passengers tell me that they've seen things from out of the train window, as they've passed through where the old village used to be."

"I see," said Amelia, slowly and softly, not really knowing how to reply.

"Well thank you, and goodnight," was all that she could say, before walking away into the night, deep in thought. I wonder what would have happened if I'd stayed too long in the tearoom and missed the train, she thought to herself.

Haya - Composer of the Stars

Haya lived with her parents in a small house upon a hill. From where she was, she could look down on the whole village below, and when she did, she could make out all the different people going about their daily lives. It was amusing to see, although it did sadden her sometimes to think about them, because she could tell that they were no longer happy. Life had almost become a burden for them, they were so bogged down with worries and problems that they spent most of their time complaining and bickering with each other, or not saying anything at all.

Sitting on the hill, away from everything, Haya was content, but she often wondered if there was something she could do to make the people in the village below feel better. They have lost their sense of wonder with the world, she thought to herself, and when this happens to a person they are left hollow and become sad. Being so high up, it made her feel special in a strange sort of way. Little did she know, but she was special - very special indeed.

* * *

Although looking down at the village was something Haya liked to do, it wasn't her most favourite thing, there was something much better than looking down - and that was looking up. Because, from where she sat on her little wooden bench, she had fantastic views of the night sky. Gazing out on clear nights, she would become transfixed by the magnificence of it all: the enormous open space, the immense numbers of stars, and the all-pervading silence.

She would sometimes become so totally absorbed in fact, that she'd be unaware of anything else around her. She would lose herself, it would be just her and the vast expanse of the universe.

Looking up at the night sky, Haya would try to spot other things besides the stars. There was the moon of course, if it were out, but she could often make out planets too, like Venus, Mars and Jupiter, and she knew all of them when she saw them. Occasionally, a satellite would pass across the heavens on its lonely trajectory. Clear summertime skies were the best, when she could see the milky way, billions upon trillions of tiny dots of light out in space. Haya knew these to be suns and planets and whole new worlds.

* * *

She loved living where she did, in her little thatched cottage with its surrounding flower garden. A pathway led from the front door of the house to an iron gate at the end of the garden, opening the gate and stepping down a few stone steps and she was at the start of a natural pathway. Following the pathway took her to her favourite spot - the wooden bench where she could do her skywatching. So, quite often, and just before nightfall, Haya would make her way to the bench and sit quietly as the sky overhead gradually darkened. Stars would begin to appear, one by one, like tiny lights being switched on by some invisible hand. Occasionally, if it were totally quiet, she was sure that she could hear a faint 'ping' sound, as a star suddenly appeared.

She would often sit by herself until the whole sky was filled with thousands upon thousands of tiny points of light, it always felt magical to her no matter how many times she experienced it. Haya had always felt a connection to the stars, as though somehow, in some strange way, she and the stars knew each other.

Sometimes, from amongst the multitude that were above her head, she would pick out one single star and then imagine what it would be like to be standing on it at that very moment in time. And then, she would wonder if the star, millions of miles out in space, was aware that a girl on a faraway distant planet was looking up and thinking about it.

* * *

There came a time when Haya, being of a rather curious and playful nature, decided to test if there really was a connection between herself and the stars. So one summer's evening, as she looked up at the thousands of lights above her, she selected one single star. She focused her mind on it, and when it felt as though she'd made a connection, she sent out a thought - if you are aware that I am thinking about you, blink off and on to let me know. Now just as she was about to tell herself off for being so silly, something quite extraordinary happened - the star blinked off and on. Haya was amazed, did that really happen, she thought. Of course not, she told herself, it's just my imagination. So she tried again . . . . and lo and behold, the same thing occurred - the star flashed off and on.

She was now intrigued, and couldn't quite believe what was happening. So, she decided to test it out for good, she chose a different star this time, a distance one, one of the farthest stars that she could make out. She focused her mind as before, sent out her request, and waited . . . . . . and the very distant star blinked off and on. Haya then realised that she really did have a connection with the stars.

So from that night onwards, Haya's stargazing took on a whole new meaning. She would sit on her bench as accustomed, but now, instead of just looking at the stars, she would interact with them. Over time, and with practice, she became skilled at communicating and discovered that she could get her celestial friends to do all sorts of things. They flashed on and off for her, they changed colour and sparkled, and she could even get several stars to do different things at the same time. Her favourite trick of all was to create a shooting star. If she focused intently, and concentrated really hard, she could send it racing across the sky in a glorious streak of light. Haya was now a composer of the stars - and they danced to her tune.

* * *

The people in the village were so preoccupied with everyday matters that they never notice the amazing things that were happening right above their heads. They are so wrapped up in their daily lives that they never stop to look at the natural world any more, Haya realised, such as the birds and animals, the flowers and the trees, and certainly not the sky above them. They have forgotten that they used to be happy, she thought to herself, and that once upon a time the village was a pleasant place to live, where people smiled and conversed. It was then that she had an idea, she knew of a way where she could put the magic back into their lives, and get them talking to each other once again.

One morning, the people of the village awoke to find that a note had been posted through their letterbox:

'Look up tonight at 9pm - there is magic in the sky!'

The villagers were intrigued. Who could have written such a strange message? And what did it mean? No one knew, but they intended to find out.

So that evening, as the time approached, the villagers prepared to do as they had been instructed. Some peeked out from windows, some chose to sit in their gardens with lanterns, whilst others decided to stand together as a group in the street - all of them totally unaware that up on the hill, sat Haya.

* * *

It was a lovely clear night, perfect for stargazing, and when 9pm approached everyone looked to the sky. A few commented on how lovely the stars were.

"It's been a long time since I've looked up at the night sky," someone said, "I'd forgotten how beautiful it is."

But others weren't so impressed.

"It's all very nice," someone uttered, "but I wouldn't quite call it magic in the air."

Minutes passed but nothing happened, and some amongst those who were standing outside were beginning to think about returning home. However, one of the group spotted something and pointed upwards.

"Look at that star over there, it seems to be blinking off and on."

Everyone searched for it with their eyes.

"Yes I see it," someone replied.

"Me too," said another. "It's flashing."

Voices began to echo around the group.

"Yes I see it too."

"It's that one just there."

"How peculiar."

Eventually, everyone could see the flashing star, the group that stood in the street, the ones that had chosen to watch the sky from their gardens, and those who peered out from the windows of their homes. And just as they were all trying to figure it out, another star started to do exactly the same thing, and then another, then more and more stars joined in.

As the villagers looked up at the night sky, stars were

flashing off and on right above their heads. They were astonished, how on earth could this be happening? Stars started to flash more quickly, others changed colour, and some began to sparkle then dance around each other. It was turning into some great cosmic firework display put on especially for them.

The light show went on for several minutes, while the villagers looked up in awe. They were witnessing something quite incredible, and talked excitedly to each other about what they were seeing. As they did, a magnificent shooting star shot right over their heads, lighting everything up in a deep purple colour. It was followed by an orange shooting star, then a blue one, a yellow one, and then all different-coloured shooting stars were whizzing across the sky at the same time, leaving trails of twinkling lights behind them. It was the most amazing thing to see, and the spectators were spellbound. Haya and the stars had given their best performance ever.

* * *

The next morning, the whole village was talking about the light show of the previous evening, and the fantastic spectacle they had witnessed. Haya's plan had worked, not only were the people of the village talking to each other again, but the spark inside them had been reignited.

The villagers began to enjoy life once more, and once again, seemed to know what was and what wasn't important. And from that day on, the people never lost their sense of wonder with the natural world that was all around them, and they always found time to look up at the beautiful night sky. The village was a happy place once again, the magic was back, and it was all thanks to Haya - composer of the stars.

A Time Before Humans

On Earth, two million years ago, there were no humans, they were a long way off from being invented. But there were lifeforms, all over the planet, like velusians, huvas and langoonids, and many other creatures that no longer exist today. Some of the species were weird and wonderful, extraordinary-looking things, and some were magnificent, such as the enormous aquasaurs that swam in the deep oceans, some the size of tower blocks.

There were many animals that roamed this primordial land, some had long legs, some had long necks, and others had long heads. Also, during that time, there were winged-creatures that flew through the air, some of them very large. There were birdlike varieties as well as insectoids, and it's fair to say that planet Earth was a lot different then to how it is today.

Amongst the multitude of bizarre creations however, there *was* something that resembled a human being - they were 'trogmongols,' and they lived in caves. Although not human, they did have similarities to modern-day man; they walked upright on two legs, and had two arms and only one head. But there were differences too. Trogmongol bodies were thinner, what we would now call lanky, and they were taller with long arms and fingers, and they had greyish, slightly wrinkled skin. Their faces were somewhat different also. Their chins were long and pointed, and their noses were longer too, with hairs growing out from them. In all honesty, they were not the prettiest of sights, although they did have mesmerisingly beautiful eyes. Trogmongol eyes were much smaller than our human eyes, but when you looked into them it was like looking into a gemstone. The eye colour of the males of the species was always hazel and gold, whilst the females were blue-green turquoise.

* * *

The trogmongols lived in small groups, with each family having their own cave. They were by far the most developed species on earth at the time, and even had speech, albeit somewhat limited, and we would never be able to understand the language today. They had also developed a primitive form of currency, called a dobla, which they used as tokens for trading. Doblas were actually small metal ingots that were mined in just a few locations over the planet, then polished up ready for use.

There was one particular family of trogmongols that lived in a cave next to the sea - they were known as the Nag clan. They consisted of two elders, Bonk and Dogleggy, with their five offspring: Guff, Bash, Gunny, Thekla and Poy.

Now every trogmongol family had a trade, and the Nag family were no exception. Their lineage was in net making, which they were able to do by using fibres which they gathered in from the sea. They'd been very successful in doing this, for a long time, but in the space of a generation it came to an end. The flying huvas, for which the nets were used, were over-hunted, eventually to extinction, and no more huvas meant no need for nets - which meant no business for the Nag clan. But luckily, Bonk the elder in his younger days was a pretty shrewd chap, and he created another way of making a living.

At that time, the climate on Earth was hot and dry, water was in short supply as rain would fall only occasionally. But one trogmongol's curse is another one's blessing, as they used to say in their own language, and the arid conditions provided the Nag family with an even more lucrative trade than crafting nets. Because, they lived right next to the sea, and Bonk invented a way of extracting the salt from seawater - thus converting saltwater into drinking water. None of the other clans knew how to do this, so the family guarded the secret with their lives.

As a result of this skill and knowledge, the Nag were very comfortably off, and the pile of doblas in their cave was a good size. So for a while, trading drinking water gave the family everything that they could possibly need. But all good things must come to an end, as they also used to say in their own language, and one day things took a rather sudden change, which made this newly devised business obsolete also - Planet X came to visit.

* * *

Now some of you may know about Planet X, but others not, so for those who don't, let me fill you in. Planet X is a rogue planet, not like the other planetary bodies in our solar system, it likes to do things in its own way, somewhat differently.

To begin with, the planet goes around the sun clockwise, in the opposite direction to Earth and Saturn and Jupiter and most of the other planets. It also has an extremely wide orbit, whose trajectory takes it way out into deepest space, to areas that even today our telescopes can barely reach, and because of this, Planet X passes by the earth only once every twenty-thousand years. However, when it does happen to pass by, it comes very close, so much so that it messes with the Earth's gravitational pull and causes havoc. Happenstance had it, that this twenty-thousand year cycle came around when the Nag trogmongols were on Earth, trading in drinking water.

As the rogue planet approached Earth from the deepest depths of space, it became visible in the heavens. No one, and no thing, noticed it to begin with, because it looked just like any other of the thousands of points of light in the night sky. However, as the weeks and months went by, it got bigger and bigger, so much so that it began to stand out, and that's when the trogmongols and all the other life forms that walked the earth became aware of it - and they could see that it was gradually getting closer. When it appeared larger in the night sky than the moon, there was concern.

It so happened that the inhabitants of Earth at the time were actually quite fortunate, because although Planet X did indeed arrive, and cause major upheavals to the Earth's surface, it did not collide - which is what happened with our unfortunate neighbouring planet twenty-thousand years before, and wiped out nearly all the life forms on Mars. But it did pass by very close, so much so that it appeared as though one could almost jump from one planetary surface to the next, and as it passed, it caused significant changes to Earth's gravity. This reshaping altered the sea levels and climate for good, and in doing so destroyed the Nag family's livelihood, because from that time on, Earth was much wetter, and the nights much colder, pretty much as it is today. Planet Earth now received regular rainfall, which meant that there was plenty of fresh drinking water to go around, and no longer any need to purchase saltless seawater.

* * *

So the Nag clan, once again, found themselves without a business. But apart from net making and water conversion, they knew no other trade, and it wasn't long before their impressive stack of doblas began to dwindle. The beautiful

Nag family home inside the cave by the sea became somewhat dilapidated, they were becoming desolate, and in desperate need of an income. All that they had to their name was an old wooden boat, a clapped-out net making contraption, an obsolete saltwater filtration system, and a huge pile of empty buckets which were once used for selling water.

Luckily for the Nag, all was not lost, because Guff had inherited the family genius and would save them from their plight. One night, under the stars, as he sat atop their cave looking out at the vast sea beyond, Guff was in one of his thinking moods. The sudden change in climate meant that obtaining drinking water was no longer a problem for trogmongols, he thought to himself, but as the nights were now much colder, obtaining heat was; there was clearly no future in water, but there was in warmth.

Another change brought about by the passing of Planet X was that, at the time of each full moon, meteors would rain down from the sky in their hundreds. It was something to do with gravity, although no one understood this at the time. Guff had noticed that the meteors always crashed down in the same area out at sea, and whilst gazing out at them on this full moon night, he had an idea. His family had their old wooden boat, and plenty of buckets, and having grown up next to the sea they were seafarers all; they knew how to navigate across water. So he decided, that on the next full moon, they should set sail to where the fire rains down from the sky, and attempt to catch the meteors in their buckets. If they were able to do this and return them to land, in the current climate, the hot stones would sell like hot cakes.

* * *

One evening, under a starry sky and the light of a full moon, an old wooden sailboat set off from land to make its way across the sea. Lanterns lit up the vessel as it sailed forth, and it could be seen from far, far away. The occupants of the craft were tall and skinny, with long chins and noses, they were trogmongols, the Nag clan, and they were on a mission - heading out to the distant horizon.

The crew consisted of Bonk, Dogleggy, Guff, Bash, Gunny, Thekla and Poy - all family members. They had also recruited another of their species, one by the name of Cromagnon. He was known to be skilled at catching, and was therefore regarded as an asset to their mission.

With eight bodies on board plus supplies, including two-hundred buckets, space was limited, but despite the cramped conditions the crew were content. Confidence was high. Guff and Bash were superb sailors, and Bonk, the old sea-dog, was a master navigator. The evening was a pleasant one too. The sea was calm and the full moon provided enough light for them to see their way, enabling the mariners to head out to the precise patch of sea where fiery rocks fell from the sky. They were mindful not to make too much noise though, which might have attracted the attention of the gigantic aquasaurs that swam beneath them in the deep waters.

Sailing along in the twilight was all very romantic, which was ideal for Cromagnon, who was smitten with the young Poy. She was certainly beautiful. Her eyes sparkled like diamonds, her chin was as pointed as a spearhead, and her nose hairs swayed gently in the breeze. He spent the outward voyage flirting with her, she had bowled him over with her beauty. He tried every trick in the yet to be invented book: flattery, humour, educated conversation, and halfway across the sea he even produced a musical instrument which he softly played as they cruised along. As Cromagnon blew on his flute, it made a sweet gentle sound that drifted out across the water. Their new companion certainly knew how to play, he was clearly a trogmongol of many talents, but alas, even this couldn't win Poy's heart, it seemed he wasn't her type. He may have had the Y factor and the Z factor, but he was lacking the X.

* * *

It was a long but pleasant journey, and the motley crew eventually arrived at their destination on the horizon of the sea. When everything was in place, they waited patiently for the meteor shower to start, and when the rocks of fire began to fall from the sky, they scurried around trying to catch them in the buckets. There were many misses, and the crooked old boat shook with the impact from the deluge of rocks. It was Gunny and Thekla's task to, as quickly as possible, remove any red-hot balls that hadn't been caught and had landed on the deck of the boat, before they had a chance to set the craft alight. It was a risky strategy, but they were able to succeed by using the boat's oars to whack any missed meteors out to sea in spectacular fashion. Dogleggy stood by with buckets of water, to put out any small fires that had started.

Everyone did a great job, but the star of the night was most definitely Cromagnon who clearly proved his worth, he rushed around like a blue-bottomed huva and his hits were numerous. As soon as he captured one hot meteor in a bucket, he immediately stacked it in the corner and was ready with another bucket in his hand. There were even occasions when he caught two fireballs simultaneously - he was, in the zone, as they used to say in their own language. It was impressive to witness, especially for young Poy, Cromagnon's skill and athleticism had won her over.

When the meteor shower had finished, the crew set off to return to land, exhausted but over the moon. The plan had worked, and to celebrate they opened up a few bottles of fermented ant juice on the way. In the twilight, on the gentle sea, they gazed up at the stars and sang songs. The crew were happy and contented. Cromagnon's hand held the flute to his lips as he played, and his other held the hand of Poy's. Despite the noise from the singing, the aquasaurs were not a danger, they were repelled by the huge piles of buckets at both ends of the boat which were brimming with fiery rocks.

* * *

Back on land, the hot balls did indeed sell like hot cakes. They sold for quite a price, with the larger ones fetching ten times as much as the Nag would get for a bucket of saltless drinking water during boom-time, and the family had plenty of ideas to make the venture even more popular. They ran a deposit scheme on the buckets for instance, whereby a customer could make a dobla down payment on one, and when their meteor died out they could return it for a refill, without having to pay for another bucket. It encouraged customer loyalty, as well as being good for the environment. They sold bargain buckets too, which were larger, family-sized, with several balls of fire in them, enough for a whole group of trogmongols to keep warm in a large cave. It worked out cheaper than buying lots of individual meteors and they were a huge success.

The Nag had discovered a pretty lucrative business, so on the night of every full moon they would set sail on their old wooden boat for the distant horizon of the sea, to the patch where fire falls from the sky. The other trogmongol clans were happy that they were doing this, for they now had glorious buckets of heat to keep them warm and cosy through the cold nights. The Nag clan, of Bonk, Dogleggy, Guff, Bash, Gunny, Thekla, Poy, and Cromagnon, who was now one of the family, lived a happy and prosperous life. All thanks to Planet X, and a little ingenuity.

Extraordinary Occurrence in Takayama

Takayama, many years ago, was a typical Japanese village of its time. There were no modern contraptions in those days, so it was a simple and natural existence for those who lived there. The people of the village went from place to place either by rickshaw or on horseback, or simply by walking, which was absolutely fine, because the pace of life at that time was a lot slower and much more relaxed than it is today.

There was no electricity either all those years ago, so when nighttime came, darkness fell upon everyone and everything. Torches were carried to see the way and lanterns were used for lighting up the narrow streets, and both were perfect for such functions. The lanterns also made everything look rather wonderful at night, because the lake that ran alongside the little village reflected their illumination, which made Takayama appear almost magical.

There was no need for lanterns during the day of course, throughout which time the place was generally bathed in sunshine. The villagers would awake each morning at sunrise to have their breakfast, usually porridge and green tea, and afterwards they would set out for their daily routine. The children would go to the local school and the adults would go off to work, ploughing and sowing the fields, planting crops like rice and sweet potatoes.

At the end of each day, the workers would set down their tools and return home for a hearty meal, and as the sun began to set the lanterns would be lit for the evening. This was a time for rest and relaxation, and also enjoyment, when family and friends might visit. Discussions would be had and games would be played, and those who wanted some peace and quiet would take a stroll beside the beautiful lake.

And this is how things were, each and every day for the people of the village, they lived their lives around the cycles of the sun and the moon and they liked it that way. They didn't want it to change, and they never expected it to. However, there came a time when it did change, because something happened one morning that was totally unexpected - the sun did not rise.

* * *

The inhabitants of the village awoke from their night's sleep, the same as always, but when they did, they found themselves in total darkness. Everyone was puzzled of course, wondering how this could be. Perhaps something had awoken them all in the middle of the night, and they had mistakenly thought that morning had arrived; it was the only explanation they could think of. Fortunately, there was something they could do to test this theory. The water-clock in the centre of the village was always reliable, so they could go check its time, to see if morning really had arrived or if they were still in the midst of night - which is exactly what they did.

The villagers gathered up their lanterns and torches and went out in the dark, to the centre of the village to see what time it was. The clock confirmed it, although it was still pitch black, it was indeed morning, and no one could understand it. Perhaps the clock is broken, they wondered, or maybe the water had run dry, causing it to give an incorrect reading. So, under the artificial light, they carefully examined the water-clock. They discovered that the mechanism was working just as it should, and there was also plenty of water running through it; the clock was functioning perfectly as always. There was now no denying it, morning had arrived - but where was the sun?

That first day in darkness felt strange for the residents of Takayama all those years ago. They went about their business as best they could, but with no sunlight to gauge the time they had to rely solely on the water-clock to tell them how the day was progressing. Many candles were placed around the timepiece, so that it was permanently lit up for everyone to see. In the centre of the village square, the large clock shone in the darkness like a beacon.

* * *

Now if one day in darkness wasn't peculiar enough, then things were about to get even more so, because the following day the same thing happened - the sun did not rise on the village once again. Things were now getting serious, so with lanterns in hand, the villagers gathered themselves together by the side of the lake to discuss the situation. As the group stood, debating how they could best get by in these unusual times, it's fair to say that many cast their eyes toward the horizon, but more in hope than expectation, that the sun might suddenly appear and their lives return to normal. But it never did, eight o'clock came - no sun, nine o'clock came - still no sun, by ten o'clock the villagers were resigned to the fact that the sun was not going to rise on them that day as well - so the lanterns would continue to burn.

The sun did not show on the following day either, nor the next, nor the day after - it appeared to have forgotten them altogether. The people were now very concerned, worried that they may never see the sun again. What would life be like? How would they survive? The rice and sweet potatoes would not grow in the fields, and the fruit would not ripen on the trees. The oil supplies for their lanterns would eventually run dry, meaning the streets and homes would be in total darkness, and on top of all that, when winter came they would be very cold.

The villagers urgently needed a plan, so they met once again by the side of the lake. After much thought and discussion, they came up with one, it was a long shot, they knew that, but it was all that they had. Although there was no sun, they did still have the moon, and appreciated it more than ever during these dark times. But maybe the moon could help them even more, perhaps it could shed some light on the reason for the sun's absence - so they decided they would ask.

* * *

When the moon next appeared, it was like a big shiny coin in the night sky. The villagers gathered themselves together by the water's edge, and looked up at their celestial companion shining brightly above their heads - and then they addressed it.

"Please tell us dear friend, the Moon, have you any idea why the sun is no longer visiting us?" they asked.

There was silence, as the hopeful group stood huddled together gazing upwards, waiting to receive an answer. They waited . . and they waited . . and then, finally, the big old moon stirred. It slowly opened one of its eyes, then the other, and looked down upon the assembly below.

"Good people of Takayama, I hear you," it said, "and I understand your concerns. The absence of our great solar friend is indeed a botheration to us all, a matter of the utmost importance, one in need of consideration, one worthy of deliberation, one demanding of elucidation. . ."

And with that, the moon closed its eyes and fell silent.

The villagers were slightly perplexed, and not quite sure what to do next. They were obviously delighted that the moon had responded by speaking to them, but disappointed that it hadn't given them a solution. But then, just as a conversation had started as to what they should do, the moon stirred once more. It slowly opened one of its eyes, then the other, and looked down upon the gathering once again.

"Good people of Takayama, you will be pleased to know that I may have the answer to your question." Relief came upon the illuminated faces of the watching group, then a look of expectancy as they gazed upwards.

"You see," said the moon, "consider this for one moment. Each and every morning, the sun comes up to send forth its rays, which give sustenance to the land and to each and every one of you. It gives you light so that you can see, heat to keep your bodies warm, and it provides energy so that your food will grow. It does this every single day, day-in-and-day-out, without fail, and it has done so since the beginning of time - yet none of you has ever shown any appreciation."

With that said, the moon stopped speaking and closed its eyes. The realisation dawned on the residents of the village, their celestial friend was right, for all that the sun did for them they had never shown any gratitude.

* * *

When the time for the next sunrise came around, the people gathered themselves together once more by the lake. In darkness, they placed their lanterns on the ground then looked over in the direction of the horizon, to the location where the sun was supposed to rise. Everyone that was present sent out thoughts of appreciation and gratitude to their absent friend, then stood and waited.

For a while nothing happened, but then, above the outline of a far distant mountain range, appeared a tiny speck of light. The speck turned into an arc, which became wider and wider, until an orange ball of light could be seen rising above the mountain top - the sun had returned! It was soon shining down in all its golden glory, and to the eyes of everyone in the village, it looked even more magnificent than ever. There was cheering and celebration, Takayama rejoiced - life had returned to normal at last.

"Thank You," they said, "thank you so much for getting up on this fine morning and blessing us with your wonderful presence," and they meant it.

Two big eyes opened up on the face of the sun, and then a smile appeared. "The pleasure is all mine," it said.

* * *

When someone does something for us all of the time, it can easily be taken for granted, and often we don't even notice anymore that they are doing it. Sometimes, all it takes is a thank you, to let them know that you do notice, and that you do appreciate it.

It took an extraordinary event all those years ago for the people of Takayama to learn this, but it was a lesson that they never forgot. So from that day on, each and every one of them never took anyone or anything for granted again. They said thank you to each other, and they said thank you to all the animals, to the flowers and the insects, to the birds that sang in the trees, to the water in the lake and to the sky above their heads, and to the very air that they breathed. They said thank you to it all, and they always said a special thank you each morning to the sun, and to the moon in the evening whenever it came out.

*   *   *

So that is the tale of Takayama, and the extraordinary occurrence that took place there. Now you may not know this, but there are things that happen in our world today because of what happened in that little village all those years ago. For instance, in the Eastern practice of yoga, they will often begin with an exercise known as the Salutation to the Sun. This is to honour and give reverence to, and to show appreciation for all that it does for us. And another thing, from that day on, because of the heartfelt warmth and gratitude it receives from the people of Takayama, the sun always visits them first. Which is why the sun rises in the east, and why Japan is known as the place of the rising sun.

The Stream from the Otherworld

At some time in their life, every person will be witness to an event or happening, which reveals to them that there is more to life than they can perceive with their mere five senses. When for some reason or another, a veil is lifted, and they are able to see things otherwise invisible. Some may experience more than one such occasion, perhaps even several, but everyone will have at least one such moment. The reason I say this, is because I am about to relate a series of events, when I myself was privileged to a glimpse of . . . . something more.

*   *   *

I remember the days of my childhood well: my friends, my family, the small group of houses where we lived with the vast woods behind them - you could venture out as far as you could and you wouldn't see anyone. My mates and I spent a lot of our time 'out the back', playing in the fields, climbing trees and exploring. We knew the local part of the woods like the backs of our hands, since we spent so much time there, but on occasions we would go farther out, into unknown territory, and when we did it always felt like we were going on a mission of discovery.

It was on one of these forays into the unfamiliar that we encountered the place that we called the *Stream from the Otherworld*, so named because anyone who saw it knew that it was not from here - it was from a totally different place altogether. To this day, I still don't know for sure what it actually was or where it was from, but I reckon that the name it was given wasn't too far from the truth. If I had to guess, I would say that the Stream from the Otherworld was some kind of connection between two different dimensions, that had somehow crossed our own, and that the curious entities that we saw there were probably going from one world that we don't know of to another.

I was fortunate to have found the stream more than once, although found isn't perhaps the right word to use, stumbled upon might be more appropriate, because everyone knew that if you went looking for the stream you would never find it - it found you, and usually when least expected. It also appeared at different locations each time, so you couldn't exactly go looking for it anyway. I don't know the reason why some managed to see it and others didn't, whether destiny or divine intervention, or simply a matter of luck. If it were down to luck then I was certainly fortunate, because I saw the Stream from the Otherworld three times - many never saw it at all.

* * *

Even before the first of my encounters, I knew of the stream, all of us kids did. We'd heard the rumours about this mysterious place that was supposed to exist, where strange things happened. Some thought that the stories were made up, but those who claimed to have seen it swore that it was real, and their accounts always matched so I tended to believe them. Like a lot of things, I guess you have to see it for yourself to totally believe it, which I did, the first time when I was just ten years old.

As I recall, my friends and I had been out all that morning, the three of us, just walking mostly, although we had stopped a few times to play a game or to take a rest. It was afternoon when we came upon the phenomenon, which seemed to appear out of nowhere. We immediately knew that there was something odd about it, I suppose it just felt different, we had discovered streams before on our long walks but nothing like this. When we first came upon it, we did wonder if it might be the place that we had heard about.

The stream emerged out from some trees, then meandered its way through a clearing. Its beauty immediately struck us, it was wonderful, enchanting almost. The water was crystal clear, I distinctly remember how it sparkled mesmerisingly in the sunlight, and there were occasional patches of mist that floated above the surface. I can also recall how soft and green the surrounding grass was, and noticing a multitude of interesting tiny coloured flowers dotted along the bank.

There was a little wooden bridge where we stood, which arched over from one side to the other, making it possible to cross. The three of us had walked over the bridge and stopped halfway across, to look down at the water below; if you gazed into it too long it made you feel slightly heady. When we got to the other side, we made our way slowly down the bank to the water. One of my friends rolled up their sleeve and dipped in their hand, then said how amazing it felt, so my other friend and I did the same. They was right, I had never felt water so soft - it made our skin tingle.

What happened next made us realise that we definitely were at the mysterious place that we'd heard about, because the previous day I had grazed my arm climbing a tree, but when I took my arm out from the water the graze had completely disappeared. My friend had cut their finger that very morning, and that was totally healed too. We really had found the Stream from the Otherworld, and were very excited because we'd heard so much about it - and now we were there ourselves.

The brother of my friend had already had an encounter some time before, and he'd told us what we should do if we ever found ourselves there. He said that the best thing to do was to be patient, to sit down on the bank and wait - so this is exactly what we did. The three of us sat on the grass by the water's edge, chatting quietly to ourselves, but keeping an eye on the stream at the same time - and after about one hour, something happened.

Some shapes appeared in the distance, they were floating down the water towards us. We soon realised that it was a small group of boats, there were three of them, and as they came closer we could make them out in much more detail. The craft were small, semicircular in shape, and they were very unusual: they were not like any boats we'd seen before.

As they got near, we were able see inside them, which was the strangest thing of all - because standing in the boats were the most extraordinary beings we had ever seen. We later referred to them as stickmen, because their bodies were thin, and upright and rigid like poles, with the topmost part having a small face. The beings were quite bizarre, and they floated by in their boats without appearing to notice us, seemingly totally unaware that we were even there. The stickmen had appeared quite content as they drifted along on the water, some even seemed to be smiling. We all agreed later that it seemed as though they were communicating with each other, because we could make out soft clicking sounds as they passed. It really was quite surreal, and an image that none of us will ever forget.

Whatever those strange beings were, they gave me the impression that they were heading to a certain destination, as if the watercourse was taking them somewhere in particular. We had watched, transfixed, for several minutes, as the boats slowly passed us before eventually disappearing from view.

My friends and I stayed a little while after by the side of

the water, in hope that some more boats might come along, but they never did so we made our way home. That was my first experience with the stream, and it wasn't until two years later that my friends and I encountered it again. This time, having seen it before, we knew immediately what it was.

* * *

It happened around autumn time. We'd been out collecting conkers when, just like before, the stream appeared as if out from nowhere. But on this occasion we didn't have to wait for something to happen, we had arrived at just the right time, for there was already a boat floating along on the water.

The little wooden bridge was there once again, and we quickly ran onto it so that we could watch the boat from above as it passed underneath us. It was just one boat this time, but much bigger than the semicircular boats that we had seen two years before. As the craft approached, we could see that it was a sailboat, and that it had all different shapes and tubes sticking out from it, it really was peculiar looking. The mainsail was up, catching the gentle breeze that carried it along, and projecting out from the stern was a long pipe emitting puffs of smoke.

As curious as the boat itself was, it wasn't the oddest thing about our experience - that was the man who happened to be sailing the boat, as well as his companion. The man must have been at least a hundred years old. He had a white moustache and beard that went all the way down to his feet. There were little round glasses on his face that hooked over pointed ears, and his chin was unusually long. We all got a clear view of him as we looked down from the bridge, he was sitting hunched-up grasping the wooden steering arm, smiling and singing quietly to himself.

The man in the boat was certainly strange-looking, and just as odd was the cat-like animal that accompanied him, sitting on the edge of the boat looking out. It sounds incredible to say, but it too was wearing glasses. My friends and I watched, intrigued, as the two extraordinary occupants passed underneath us then carried on down the stream, eventually to disappear out of view. Just like before, with the stickmen, the man in the boat appeared to not even notice us - the cat-like entity however, seemed to sense our presence.

Only a few had ever encountered this mysterious place, so my friends and I knew how fortunate we were to have been there twice. Little did I know at the time, but I would see the stream once more.

* * *

My third and final encounter with the Stream from the Otherworld was in the middle of a long hot summer, and this time I was all alone. I remember it well, I'd been out scrumping and had just finished picking some apples and plums from an orchard. I was looking for a place to sit and rest for a bit, somewhere that offered shade from the midday sun, so I headed in the direction of a thicket that was nearby. As I was coming towards it, I became aware of the faint sound of running water. My first thought was that it might be a gentle flowing river, or even a small waterfall, either would make an ideal place to rest for a while.

As I went toward the source of the sound it got louder, and it did cross my mind at the time that it might be the stream, although I passed this off as wishful thinking. But when I walked in amongst the trees, to my amazement, I found myself there once again. I knew immediately where I was, and I was thrilled.

The place appeared even more magical than ever this time. The water gave off a pinkish glow, and made tinkling sounds as it gently flowed along. I could feel a vibrant energy from it too, which as I remember seemed to affect me deep inside - it made me feel so alive and invigorated, yet serene at the same time.

It was very quiet and peaceful, so I sat myself down on the bank to take in the beautiful surroundings, and I laid back on the soft grass to listen to the gentle sound of the running water. The peace and tranquility must have overcome me, because I fell asleep.

I've no idea how long I'd slept, but when I awoke from my slumber, I couldn't quite believe my eyes. What looked like wisps of smoke were floating above the water, all over, as far as my eyes could see. My initial thought was that it was mist rising up from the stream, caused perhaps by the sun as it shone down upon the water, but when I looked closer, I noticed that the wisps of smoke had faces - they were living entities.

The mist beings, as I called them, were floating between two and four feet from the surface, yet were moving along with the current, so although they were not touching the water, it was like they were connected to it in some way. It was astonishing to see, and something that I will never forget. I sat there alone, marvelling at this spectacle for what must have been thirty or forty minutes, and in that time hundreds of mist beings passed slowly along the water before my eyes. They never saw me, it was as if I was privileged to glimpse momentarily into their world, but they couldn't see into mine.

Needless to say, as soon as I arrived back home I told my two friends all about my experience. They were fascinated to hear about the mist beings, and delighted that I'd had another encounter; although they both confessed that they were a little disappointed not to have been there with me. That was the last time that I ever saw the place, although I did hear that some others had managed to see it after this occurrence.

* * *

Not long after the last of my encounters, my family and I moved away, but I have never forgotten this mysterious place, nor the experiences that I had there. They were rare and precious moments, when a veil was lifted and I was able to glimpse briefly into another world.

I have sometimes thought of returning, to search for the stream once again, but I know that I would never find it. I do wonder if it is still revealing itself, appearing out of nowhere to astound and enchant some unexpected person; I think that it probably is. I also believe that there are other places, just like the one that my friends and I experienced, where for some unknown reason other realities briefly appear in our world, to be witnessed by someone who happens to be in the right place at the right time. Everyone should be aware of this, because it could happen to anyone at any time - including you.

The Gift

This is a story from a land far away, where an emperor once lived in a beautiful palace. He was liked and respected by all the people, whom he regarded as friends, and they were happy, peaceful times for everyone. But a change was imminent, the emperor was getting old and had no offspring to succeed him. The people of the land were beginning to wonder - who was going to take his place in the palace.

The time came when the emperor was about to reach the grand age of one-hundred years. An announcement was issued from the palace, that in honour of his special birthday, there would be a celebration - and everyone was invited. The news was met with excitement, the doors of the palace would be open to them all and they would see the splendours within.

It was stated in the announcement, that the emperor wished to express his gratitude to all the people for their loyal service over the years, he thanked them for everything that they had done for him and wished for them another one-hundred years of peace and prosperity. The announcer then went on to inform the people that the emperor's days were coming to an end, and that someone would be needed to replace him. He declared that on the day of the celebration, there would be a competition. The competition would be open to all, and whoever won would become the new emperor, and take their rightful place in the palace. The winner would be the one who could prove their worth by presenting the emperor with the most impressive gift that he had ever received.

The thought of becoming the new emperor and living in the magnificent palace filled the people with excitement. Winning would not be easy though, everyone, from all over, was sure to enter, and it would have to be something quite spectacular to take the prize. But how do you impress a man who has everything?

* * *

Over the months that followed, everyone got to work. The master cook decided to create the most delectable dish ever made, it would contain the finest ingredients and spices from far and wide and it would be cooked to perfection. The emperor will love my dish so much, he told himself, that I will surely be his successor.

The carriage-maker decided to make the most elaborate and decorative carriage possible. He used the best quality wood, and got his staff to work day and night to mould and produce the grandest carriage in the land. When it was built, he decorated it in glorious layered gold.

"I will surely be the next emperor," he said, "how could anyone not be impressed by such a magnificent piece of craftsmanship."

The perfumer put together the most exquisite scent imaginable, containing over one thousand different oils from far off places, the aroma was delightful.

"The emperor will be in heaven when he smells it, he will certainly hand his palace to me."

And so it was throughout the land. The bookbinder made the biggest, most elaborate book ever produced, the tailor made a suit of purest silk, and the artist painted a masterpiece. Everything was made with the most expensive materials, and everyone put their skills and expertise to use - everyone that was apart from the local peasant boy, who made nothing. He had no craftsmanship to bring to hand, and no means with which to buy materials, so he just looked on as those around him busied themselves creating their finest works.

* * *

The big day arrived. People flocked to the palace from far and wide to marvel at its splendour. A delicious banquet was enjoyed by all, in honour of the emperor's one-hundredth birthday. Music and dancing followed, and then came the moment that everyone had been waiting for - the giving of the gifts.

The emperor took his place in the Grand Hall. He sat patiently as one by one the people presented him with their offerings. There were gasps as he was handed the most magnificent presents: elaborate carvings, intricate jewellery, costumes of exquisite materials, and delicious foods. Everything had been created with the utmost skill and craftsmanship, and the emperor thanked each and every one of them for their wonderful gifts. But alas, it seemed that no one had impressed or amazed him enough to be worthy of becoming his successor. Having lived a life of luxury, surrounded by the most precious things that money could buy, it seemed there was nothing that could truly move him.

There was one person however, who had not yet presented a gift - it was the peasant boy. As he stepped up and walked towards the emperor, who sat regally on his chair, it appeared that he carried nothing with him.

"What on earth could he have to offer?" someone remarked, "he is merely a farmhand."

A hush fell upon the palace as the boy came face to face with the emperor.

"Greetings," he said, "and what do you have for me

today?"

The peasant boy put his hand deep into his pocket, removed it, then held out a lightly clenched fist. As the emperor looked at the boy's hand, he opened it, to reveal a freshly picked ear of wheat. There was silence around the hall, followed by an uproar of laughter as the crowd realised what the peasant boy had offered.

"Silence please," said the emperor, before giving his attention to the boy. "You offer me this as a gift?" He asked.

"I do," replied the boy, "and I ask just one thing. That you take this ear of wheat from my hand and examine it, but really look at it, look at it like you have never looked at it before, see it for what it truly is."

The emperor took the ear of wheat from the boy's hand and gazed at it closely.

"Notice the precise symmetry," the boy said, "yet no gauge was used to measure it. Notice its impeccable construction, yet no tools were used to cut it, and no human hand was needed to carve the perfect shape of each grain. Now take it to your nose and inhale the scent, have you ever smelled anything so glorious and heartwarming? Within this ear of wheat is so much wholesome goodness that it can sustain the life of a human being. It is perfection, and it is a gift from God. What you have in your hand is a miracle, it is the work of nature, and there are a million such miracles all around, if you only took time to see them - and as gifts, they cannot be bettered."

A smile appeared on the emperor's face. A hundred times had he looked upon such a thing, but a hundred times had he never truly seen it for what it was.

He stood up from his seat. "My people," he said, "here is your new emperor, he has given me the greatest gift of all - at last I understand."

A Space Story

The Comas Sola drifted slowly through the dark infinity of space, with just distant stars for company. As the space station floated gracefully along, it made no sound - a lonely capsule in a silent world.

* * *

Safety checks were being made to Yuri's spacesuit; he was preparing to leave the relative safety of the craft to go outside. There was a problem with one of the propulsion tubes, nothing too serious but something that needed to be sorted, besides, the routine external inspection was due so he could 'kill two birds with one stone.' Petra, his companion, gave him the all clear. The pair had been in space now for almost two years - in eight months time they would be going home.

The air-lock chamber door slid slowly open and Yuri floated outside. He had done the spacewalk many times before, but still found it a strange experience. It was the sheer vastness that affected him the most - outside, being alone amongst the stars, made him realise how insignificant he was.

The cosmonaut knew that he was safe, he could propel himself in any direction he wanted to by using the keypad located on the sleeve of his left arm, which was connected to the jetpack on his back. It had never failed anyone, and even if it did, as a safety measure he was firmly tethered to the ship by his C Cord.

* * *

The routine inspection went very well, completed in record time. One-hundred and seventeen minutes, under two hours, Yuri was pleased with himself. All was fine with the external body of the craft, there were no concerns there, which just left the issue with the propulsion tube to address before he returned.

The fault had been discovered twelve hours earlier. Ground Control had instructed the crew to adjust their position slightly, and when they had done so the ship had not moved as smoothly as it should have. The main computer alerted them to a fault with one of the propulsion tubes, and a further diagnostic check revealed a blockage in propulsion tube number five. Yuri and Petra were puzzled as to what it might be, and Ground Control could offer no explanation either. There had been no meteor shower for several months, and the last comet that had passed by the space station was over four years ago. There was nothing in that area of space that could have caused a blockage, but the ship's computer system had told them there was - and it was never wrong.

* * *

Yuri examined the silver metal tube that was PT5; it looked fine. He shook it to check if something was loose, but nothing was. He commed-in to Petra, informing her that he was going to remove the outer casing to take a look inside. From out of his toolkit, the cosmonaut took a small screwdriver, the same one that he used all of the time; every screw on the outer body of the space station was exactly the same. One by one, he loosened the twelve magnetic screws that held the metal cover in place, then secured the cover to his body with a line before disengaging it: the inside of the propulsion tube was revealed.

With the cover floating beside him, Yuri carefully

returned the screwdriver to the bag, before switching on a tiny torchlight that was attached to the cuff of his spacesuit, shining it down into the tube. The diagnostic check was correct, there was something lodged inside, he could see it. Whatever it was, was about the length of his hand, maybe slightly longer. He was puzzled. There was nothing from the ship that could have found its way in there, and there was nothing floating around outside that could have been sucked in either. His instinct advised caution, he was in unknown territory. Was it a new phenomenon that they had never encountered before, perhaps some strange life form that they didn't know of. He needed to take care.

From his toolkit, he took out a small stick about six inches long. By twisting the stick, it extended to become a rod, two feet in length. If it were some bizarre life form, then it would likely react to being prodded. Somewhat nervously, he poked gently and cautiously at whatever it was; there was no response. He poked again, it seemed hard, lifeless. He prodded one last time, much harder, but nothing happened. He was relieved, convinced that whatever it was that was lodged in the tube was a solid inanimate object, not organic, so he reduced the rod back to a small stick before returning it to his toolkit.

Putting his arm down into the tube, Yuri was able to reach the object. Gripping his hand around it, he pulled, but it didn't budge. He tried again, still no luck, it was jammed inside. With one last effort, pulling as hard as he could, the object finally became dislodged and Yuri removed it. He was now holding the mystery object in his hand. It was solid, bottle-shaped, black and heavily charred. At that moment in time he could do no more, he needed to get whatever it was into the ship to take a closer look. So, after placing the object into his bag, he screwed back the cover of the propulsion tube and informed Petra that he was coming in.

* * *

Inside the space station, the two occupants studied the object. Testing revealed that it was hollow, but an effort to chip a piece off with a small hammer was unsuccessful, the material was too tough. They attempted to drill into it but the bit would not penetrate, the object was so heavily carbonised that it was rock hard. But its hollow tubular shape told them that this was not a piece of space rock, and close examination revealed it to be constructed of a glass-like material - constructed being the keyword, meaning that someone, or some thing, had made it.

Yuri and Petra surmised that the emissions from the propulsion tube had thickly coated the object in carbon, which explained its rock-like texture; intense heat had then converted some of the carbon to glass. That was all that they could come up with, and all that they could do. A proper examination would have to take place down on Earth, the tiny lab facilities of the space station were primitive in comparison to what was available on Terra. So both the object and the cosmonauts' report were sent down to Earth via a controlled dispersal capsule. Once recovered, the object would be properly examined using the latest scientific equipment.

* * *

Almost five months after being shot from the Comas Sola space station, the dispersal capsule came into Earth's orbit, where it was gathered in and taken to the Nations Alliance of Space Exploration laboratory. The NASE had been eagerly awaiting the shipment, whatever it was that the space station had inadvertently picked up it was going to be interesting. The capsule was taken to their headquarters in Hawaii and opened up. As a careful examination of the artefact got underway, the accompanying report was read by all the scientists and technicians at the facility. There was one paragraph in the cosmonaut's conclusion that immediately created a stir:

'Considering the fact that the object is hollow and symmetrical in shape, points to it being not of natural origin, but intelligent made. If we further take into account the environment and location of Comas Sola when it was found, we can only assume that the object is of alien origin.'

The space team were intrigued by this inference, and somewhat stunned by its implication. Some were adamant that Yuri and Petra were wrong in their conclusion, confident that they would immediately find a rational explanation for the puzzle. But nevertheless, news of the report leaked and spread around the globe. Everyone was talking about the discovery from far out in space, it became the story of the time. Had we really discovered an alien artefact? Was this the evidence that mankind had been waiting for, proof that we are not alone in the universe? People wanted to know more, and the NASE laboratory became the centre of the world's attention.

* * *

Because the matter was clearly of global interest, perhaps the most important discovery in human history, the centre announced that it would exercise total transparency throughout their investigation, and would keep the world updated with any developments. They were as good as their word, just forty-eight hours later a statement was issued:

'We would like to make a brief announcement concerning the initial findings of our study into the origins of the mysterious object. Firstly, we can state with confidence that the object is not the result of natural phenomena, and therefore concur with the two cosmonauts aboard the space station that the object is intelligent made. We have also ascertained that the piece did not originate from any part of the Comas Sola. Considering these facts, and taking into account the unequivocal circumstances regarding the locale of where the artefact was discovered, we can only assume that the object is extraterrestrial in nature.'

The announcement shocked the world. It was confirmation that we are not alone in the universe, and that other, intelligent lifeforms are either in or around our very solar system. Following this disclosure, the item was no longer called the mysterious object, but was now referred to as *the alien artefact*. Just twenty-four hours after the first statement was made, the NASE Centre issued a second announcement - it turned out to be even more explosive than the first:

'We would like to announce that we have made further, very important discoveries regarding the alien artefact. Firstly, we can confirm that the object is cylindrical in shape, hollow in nature, and is made from a glass-like substance. Secondly, thanks to our latest state-of-the-art technology, we have detected that the outer shell has some kind of inscription embossed onto the surface, beneath the layer of carbon. Lastly, and most exciting of all, we have reason to believe that a piece of folded parchment is contained within the object, upon which is written a message. It will not be possible to decipher or decode the alien message until the parchment has been completely removed from the centre of the hollow, glass-like container, which our team are working on as we speak.

These are unprecedented times in human history, and we understand that you are all eager to discover the meaning of the message from deepest space, just as we are. We appreciate your patience. You can rest assured that we will be working around the clock to discover the secret of this phenomenon as soon as we can. We fully expect to have removed all of the remaining carbon deposits covering the artefact within the next forty-eight hours. This will make it possible to both read the inscription on the outside of the object, as well as to remove the parchment contained within. We have already gathered together the best cryptographers in the world, who are waiting to begin deciphering and decoding ET's message. We will make a full announcement in due course'.

* * *

Things were now getting very interesting, the whole world was absorbed in the mystery of the artefact from space. What message did the extra-terrestrials have for mankind? Were they friend or foe? Was it a welcome or a warning? What would this communication mean for the human race? Everyone was asking questions, and waiting expectantly for answers, to find out the meaning of the alien message. They had to wait just two days. The Nations Alliance of Space Exploration laboratory issued to the waiting world, what they stressed would be their final statement on the matter.

'Thank you once again for your patience. We are pleased to announce that we have concluded our examination of the mysterious object and are able to reveal its true identity. We have been successful in reading both the inscription embossed on the outside of the glass cylinder, as well as the written message on the folded parchment contained within.

The first thing to state is that none of our expert decipherers and decoders were required, the reason being that both the outer inscription and the message contained within were written in the standard English language. We are not at this present time prepared to make any further comments regarding the findings, other than that which follows in this statement. The inscription embossed on the outside of the container, which we now know to be a glass bottle, reads: Burke & Burge's Best. A full transcription of the message contained within reads as follows:'

Hello out there. My name is Albert Hubble. If you are reading this then my plan has worked and you have discovered my message-in-a-bottle. It was sent from an asteroid somewhere out in space, my new home, but I'm not sure where that is exactly. Using natural materials found on my rock, I was able to construct a launcher to hurtle the bottle out into space, it's what I do you see, I'm an inventor. I calculated that the odds of my message ever being discovered to be a million-to-one, but you never know, I remember reading once about a man who had been struck by lightning twelve times. I was once from planet Earth, I'm struggling to remember the name of the place exactly as I've been here for such a long time now and the air has affected my mind slightly. I think it was called Noke Stewington, or something like that. I ended up where I am now after one of my experiments went slightly wrong. What happened exactly I'm not too sure, all I know is that when I materialised on my asteroid I was so clean that I didn't have to wash for a very long time. I just want to let everyone know that I'm fine. There's plenty of room here, it's not polluted and congested like Earth, it's just me and the small creatures. It's nice and quiet here too, there's no screaming children or noisy neighbours to disturb you, in fact, it's unearthly quiet. The silence seemed strange at first, but it's lovely once you get used to it. I do occasionally hear weird noises coming from far out in space, whistles, bells, twinkles and gurgles, etc. I hear all sorts of things, I'm not sure what they are. The atmosphere is different here, it makes you feel kind of spacey. Anyway, I won't go on for too long, there is so much I could tell you about this place and what has happened to me since I arrived but messages in a bottle are supposed to be short, so I'll just conclude by saying that I am safe and well. I have a pet, it's a strange thing but very friendly, I've named it Kenneth. I have plenty of food (the space cacti are delicious), and there is liquid here that resembles water. I've even managed to invent a contraption that converts it into something that tastes remarkably like cream soda, so I have everything I need.

All the best, Albert

Ps: say hello to Mum for me

The Shmungen

Away from the towns and cities where people live, is a very secluded place that few know of. It is quiet here, and clean, with tall trees and green fields, and a gentle flowing river too, and air that is so pure that each breath makes you feel alive.

This beautiful location is home to a mere handful of people, just six cottages in all are dotted over the area, which is good for many of the other lifeforms, because they don't like places where there are lots of humans. Some people that have stumbled upon this idyllic location, whilst out exploring, or when they have strayed from their intended path, and those that have done so have been enchanted by its natural beauty.

* * *

One of the six cottages is a small one, nestled by the side of the river, and it's home to an elderly couple who have resided there for a long time. For them, it's the perfect place to live. The river supplies fresh clean water whenever they want it, and the forest provides a varied selection of fruits and berries - as well as being home to many animals whom they adore.

The further you go into the forest, the stranger the animals become. If someone were to venture deep within, they may come upon such creatures as a spectacled badger, a singing sloth, or the upside-down bear. At night, the forest echoes with the sound of hooting owls calling from branches and holes within tree trunks.

The sparkling river that runs through the centre of this magical land is home to many interesting specimens too, such as frogs, water-boatmen and diving-beetles. Fish of all colours and sizes swim freely beneath the surface, whilst freshwater muscles and crabs live out their lives on the riverbed. Above the water, majestic dragonflies and damselflies of striking blues and pinks hang in the air during the summer months. Water nymphs occasionally frequent the riverside, but are so secretive that they are seldom seen.

The flower meadow that lies adjacent to the forest is a delightful patch of land, especially in springtime, when it comes alive with fragrance and colour. Certain areas are transformed into swathes of striking oranges, reds, and yellows, whilst the part that blends with the woodland is carpeted in bluebells. There are taller flowers here too, such as campion, foxgloves and hollyhocks; bees, ladybirds and butterflies buzz and flutter around these in the summertime. If you look closely, and if you are very lucky, you might see a fairy or two, for they whisper to each other and play games amongst the flowers. Not that fairies can be seen by all humans, only those whose ancestors once communicated with them in days of old can do so.

In the surrounding fields, rabbits graze at dawn, and at nighttime there are hares, with their long ears and heads tilted backwards, - they sit motionless gazing up at the moon.

* * *

Along the forest edge, where the trees meet the fields, grow mushrooms of all shapes and sizes. Small ones and tall ones, thin ones and fat ones, white ones, browns ones, some with spots and some without. Some of these fungi are quite unusual and there is one that is extremely rare, it is so rare in fact that this is the only place in the world where they can be found. It is known by the locals as a dotted-purple, so called because its white bell-shaped cap is covered in purple spots. But there is something much strange than it's appearance however, something that no one knows of, because tucked underneath the cap of this striking mushroom, curled up and usually sleeping, nestles a little creature - a little creature called a shmungen.

A shmungen, when curled up, is about the size of a table-tennis ball. It has stripy cream and yellow fur that covers its whole body, apart from its tiny pink feet. It has a very small mouth, little white nose, pointed ears and big round eyes, and it has a long tail that for most of the time is kept rolled up.

Shmungen nestle underneath the cap of the dotted-purple, holding on to its stem by wrapping their tail around it then curling up into a little ball and going to sleep, and this is where it spends most of its time. In fact, the only occasion that these tiny animals come out is when there is a full moon, and at midnight, when all the shmungen emerge at the same time to nibble on grass and drink from the river before returning once again to their hiding place. This behaviour makes them the most secretive creatures in the world, so secretive in fact, that no human being had ever set eyes on one. Until that was, the time that two children came to stay at their grandparent's cottage, the little one nestled by the side of the river.

* * *

George and Sophie were delighted when they saw the cottage for the first time; they would be spending a few days there with their grandparents. Being from the city, the two children had never seen such green fields and tall trees, and breathed in air that was so fresh - to them, the place seemed enchanting. They were very happy with where they found themselves, and immediately decided that they would spend much of their time exploring, trying to discover new things that they had never seen before.

One afternoon, whilst out investigating the forest edge, the children came upon something that they found especially interesting - they were large mushrooms with purple spots. They had never seen mushrooms quite like it before, and thought them extraordinary. Sophie found them so fascinating in fact, that she decided to pick one and take it home with her.

When the children arrived back at the cottage, they told their grandparents all about the exciting day they'd had and all the different animals and plants they'd seen. Sophie showed her grandfather the mushroom that she'd picked. He smiled when he saw it, he knew exactly what it was. The dotted-purple, he informed her, was one of his favourites. He went on to tell them something remarkable about the specimen - that the purple dots glow in the dark. To prove it, he closed all the curtains and switched off the lights, and the dots on the mushroom lit up like purple Christmas tree lights. The children found this astonishing, so when the demonstration had finished, Sophie took the mushroom up to her bedroom and placed it on her bedside table - tonight she would have purple lights beside her bed whilst she slept.

When evening approached, Sophie and George's grandmother said that she had some good news to tell them. She explained that they were very fortunate to have visited at this time, because tonight there would be a full moon.

"It's a special time in these parts," she said, "because remarkable things can sometimes happen."

The children looked at each other and smiled, they were excited to hear this, and even more so when she told them that if they got themselves ready for bed and into their pyjamas, they could stay up late and sit outside on the porch to see the moon.

"We never miss it," said their grandfather, "because you never know what you might see."

For sure, the children were going to be ready.

* * *

The sun was setting behind the trees in the far distance, and darkness was beginning to fall over the land. Sophie and George sat on the porch with their grandparents, on old wooden chairs with comfortable cushions. Everyone had blankets to cover themselves with, not that it was cold for it was a warm summer night, the blankets were simply to make them feel cosy. Lanterns had been hung at either end of the porch, and the family sat drinking hot chocolate and chatting whilst waiting for the moon to show.

It wasn't long before it did. As soon as the sky had become dark, millions of twinkling stars appeared, followed by a large, luminous, silvery-pink moon which bathed everything in a warm, gentle glow. To the children, it was magical, and there was a strange, dreamlike feeling in the air too, which didn't go unnoticed by either of them - so it really did seem as though anything could happen. Their grandparents were right, the children thought to themselves, it really is a special time around here.

With the moon shining brightly, everyone spoke in hushed tones, not wanting to frighten anything away that may be close by. As they sat together, the quietness of the surroundings was sporadically broken by the sound of hooting owls echoing out from the forest, as well as the shuffling of nocturnal animals emerging out for the night. Most of the creatures were not seen, only heard, but as time went by some of them did show themselves: a busy vixen doing her rounds, rabbits nibbling on the grass, and an impressive looking stag emerged from the trees before realising it was being watched and heading back under cover. A tiny wood mouse was oblivious to their presence however, as it scuttled busily past the feet of everyone who was sitting on the porch.

*   *   *

It had been a wonderful experience, one that the children enjoyed very much, but it was now getting late and their grandfather was saying that perhaps they should all be thinking about turning in for the night. But then, all of a sudden, he stopped talking in mid-sentence. He put his finger to his lips and emitted a gentle "shhh," to indicate silence. He pointed slowly over to the river, and when the children looked they could not believe their eyes - emerging out from the cover of the trees was a unicorn.

Time appeared to stand still, as everyone watched, captivated, while the magnificent beast walked slowly over to the river. With its pure white body glowing in the moonlight, and legendary spiralled horn atop its head, the unicorn bent down without a sound to drink from the water. It then lifted its head, sniffed the air as if to check its surroundings, then quietly trotted back into the cover of the greenery. The moment seemed to last an eternity, but in reality, the whole process probably took no more than a few minutes. It was a special moment, one that would forever remain in the memories of everyone who witnessed it. The children's grandparents said that they were very lucky to have seen such a thing.

*   *   *

It was now very late, and time for sleeping, so Sophie and George said goodnight and tucked themselves into their beds. As she nestled her head into the soft pillow, Sophie thought about the unicorn, the image as it drank from the river went over and over in her mind, she couldn't quite believe what she had seen.

Because of all the excitement, she had forgotten about the mushroom that she'd picked earlier that day - until that was, she leant over and switched off the night lamp on her bedside table and purple dots lit up beside her. As the moonlight shone in through her open window, it cast a gentle light over the room, and a warm summer-night's breeze flowed gently in. It was the perfect ending to an incredible day, but Sophie's amazing experience was not over just yet, because the wonderful day and fantastic evening were about to be followed by an incredible night.

* * *

Inside the cottages that were scattered around the land, humans were snuggled up in their beds. They were totally unaware that outside, an area along the forest edge was coming alive, lighting up with the purple glow of mushrooms twinkling their lights.

All was quiet, but when midnight approached something stirred. Emerging out from beneath one of the mushrooms was a tiny creature - it was the first of the shmungen to appear. The little animal climbed slowly down the stem of the mushroom, stretched out its body on the short grass and yawned. Another soon followed, then another, then many more, until hundreds of shmungen were emerging out from the clusters of mushrooms. It certainly was a spectacle to be seen, had anyone been there to see it.

At the same time, back at the cottage, as she lay in bed,

Sophie felt the sensation of tiny feet walking over her legs. She stirred briefly with eyes shut tight, then told herself to stop imagining things and to go to sleep. But she felt the footsteps again, and this time she also heard a very faint shuffling sound - there was no mistaking it, something was walking across her bed. Sitting upright, she forced her eyes open, and that's when she beheld the most incredible sight. There on her bed, was the most amazing little creature she had ever seen. It was small and furry, with a sticky-out nose and pointed ears, and it was looking up at her with big round eyes. It was the strangest yet cutest thing ever.

Sophie pinched herself to see if she was dreaming, "Ouch," she said, she wasn't. She stared at the little creature for several seconds without moving or making a sound, but then she decided to talk to it, gently, to reassure it and to let it know that she was friendly. The tiny animal seemed to listen, it didn't reply back, but it did appear to understand her somehow. Sophie leaned over and cupped the little shmungen into her hands, then began stroking it softly. How strange it is, she thought to herself, she'd never seen anything like it in any of her schoolbooks. What on earth could it be, she wondered.

* * *

Outside in the moonlight, along the forest edge, mushrooms were twinkling their purple dots and shmungen were scattered all around, feeding on the grass and drinking from the river. But something was wrong, and it didn't take them long to realise what it was - someone was missing. So, as usual in such situations, it was immediately reported to the owls, and when they heard the news they promptly sent out the owl call. The low, quivering sound of hooting owls echoed around in the stillness of the night, and on hearing the call, the other animals and creatures knew what it meant. They immediately gathered themselves together in a secret location by the forest, to find out what had happened.

Now there is something that people do not know, which is this - whenever a human walks in nature, there is never a time when they are not being watched. This could be from a hedge or a tree, from down low amongst the grass or from high up in the sky, but wherever they are, and wherever they go, a pair of eyes will always be observing them, and this indeed was the case with Sophie and George that day when they were out exploring.

The squirrels announced to the gathering that they had seen two children in the afternoon, walking along the forest edge examining the flowers and plants. This was confirmed by the badgers, and a field mouse stated that it had seen them too. A group of rabbits added to this, informing everyone that one of the children, the girl, had in fact picked one of the mushrooms and taken it away with her. Some magpies then addressed the meeting, reporting that the children had walked back along the forest edge and across the flower meadow. A sharp-eyed kestrel fitted the final piece to the puzzle, informing all present that whilst hovering up high in the sky around late afternoon, she had observed two children entering the little cottage by the river.

The events of the day had been pieced together, and the mystery of their friend's disappearance had been solved. All they had to do now was to get them back, and there was no time to waste. So, a plan was quickly hatched, and a search and recovery party was assembled and dispatched.

* * *

Sophie had been sitting up in bed, chatting to her new friend. She assumed that the creature didn't understand a word that she had said, but it did seem to like the sound of her voice and had sat quietly listening to her for some time, before eventually returning back under the mushroom on the bedside table.

As she lay, pondering as to what she should do with it, her eyes were drawn to the bedroom window - there was something moving outside. Looking over and focussing her eyes, she could just make them out, and couldn't quite believe what she was seeing. Standing outside on the window ledge, was the strangest group of beings she had ever seen.

There were six figures all in a line, and each one was totally different to the next. The one at the front, who seemed to be the leader of the gang, was holding a lantern, presumedly to light their way. As she watched, one by one and keeping in line, they entered in though the open window until they all stood on the inside window ledge looking over at her. She could see them very clearly now, and what a bizarre bunch they were.

The head of the party, the one holding the lantern, Sophie immediately recognised. Having read many books that contained pictures, she knew exactly what it was - it was a gnome. He had a portly figure, and a jolly face with a long white beard. He wore a blue jacket, secured around the waist by a brown belt with a shiny metal buckle. Covering his legs were black trousers, and on his feet, big black boots that came all the way up to his knees.

Her eyes panned slowly along the line, to each of the other members of the group, one-by-one. She recognised the second figure also - it was clearly a fairy.

"So fairies are real too," Sophie said softly to herself, and they were even prettier than she had thought.

This one had long flowing hair with a ring of flowers around her head, and she wore a yellow dress with matching slippers. A pair of wings protruded out from just below her shoulders, and if Sophie looked closely, she could just make out a secondary, much smaller pair below them. The wings lit up from the light of the lantern, and when they moved they shimmered the colours of gold, purple and blue.

If the fairy was beautiful, then the figure standing next to her was contrastingly comical - it was a funny looking fellow dressed all in green. He had a long pointed hat, wore tights on his legs with brown boots, and had large ears and a big grin on his face. This must be what they call a pixie, Sophie thought to herself.

Fourth in line was something that she definitely did not know. It was a splendid looking animal that stood upright on two legs, it had silky silver fur and reminded her of a fox. The face was certainly like a fox's face, with large yellow eyes and a pointed snout, and the tail was foxlike too, being long and bushy. Like the rest of its body, the tail was silver in colour, but the animal did have dark stripes running down its back.

Sophie had no idea what the next creature was either, it was something quite bizarre. Standing about six inches high, with long thin arms and legs, it had a round belly and face. The creature's colour was a mixture of different shades of greens and browns. It had hairy, bat-like ears that protruded out from the sides of its face, but the most incredible thing about it was that it had three eyes. From the look of it, she guessed that it probably spent its time camouflaged amongst the leaves on the forest floor, which would pretty much make it unnoticeable.

Bringing up the rear of this odd assemblage was a large black bird, which she'd noticed had been looking at her curiously the whole time, tilting its head from side to side as if trying to work her out. She definitely knew what this was, she had seen these before many times in both the city and in the country, it was unmistakably a crow. But there was something very different and rather peculiar about this one - because on its face, it wore a pair of round spectacles.

* * *

Sophie thought the group of characters standing on her window ledge to be a most curious bunch, but wondered why on earth they had come to visit her in the middle of the night. She was startled when the gnome began to speak.

"Warm greetings, you must be Sophie," it said, "it's a pleasure to meet you. I am Mingus Widebottom and these are my friends." With that, he gestured his hand towards the odd-looking bunch standing in line behind him, and collectively they nodded their heads in acknowledgement.

"But how do you know my name?" Sophie asked.

"We are nature creatures, from the forests, meadows and fields. We tend to distance ourselves from people, but if ever we do encounter a human being, meet them face to face as we are now, we immediately know everything about them, including their name."

"How interesting," Sophie replied.

She then went on. "So if you avoid people," she asked, "then why have you come to see me?"

"Well," said the gnome, "that is a very good question, to which we have a very good answer. You see, we are here on a mission, and a rather important one at that. We have lost one of our friends, and we are led to believe that you may have taken him."

"Taken one of your friends, I would never do such a thing!" Sophie exclaimed.

"Oh by mistake of course," the gnome quickly interjected, "and if we are not mistaken, our little friend is curled up inside that mushroom over there, the one that is lying beside you on your bedside table."

Sophie immediately knew who they were talking about, and realised what had happened. "Yes of course," she said, "now I understand."

Mingus Widebottom continued to speak. "You see, the mushroom is what is known as a dotted-purple, and it so happens that this particular specimen was picked by your kind self whilst out walking today, naturally oblivious to the fact that it was also the abode of our dear companion."

"The little creature," Sophie replied. "Yes it's here, I've seen it, it came out and went back in. I'm sorry I didn't realise, I liked the mushrooms so much that I took one home, I had no idea that the . . . ."

"The shmungen," said the gnome.

"The shmungen, so that's what it's called, what a delightful name. I had no idea that the little shmungen was inside."

"Of course not," said Mingus, "an understandable mistake for sure. But now it must return with us from whence it came."

"Of course," said Sophie, "it should return immediately."

So she said goodbye to the extraordinary search and recovery party, and wished them all the best. They told her that it was a genuine mistake and no harm was done, and that it had been a pleasure to meet her.

"Likewise," was her reply.

They thanked her for keeping their friend safe, and she was happy that it would be returning to its true home. She watched on, as the unlikely gang lifted up the mushroom stalk, rested it on their shoulders, and with the gnome's lantern lighting the way, they marched through the open window and out into the night.

* * *

When Sophie awoke the next morning, she saw that the dotted-purple mushroom was no longer beside her on the bedside table. She smiled to herself, happy in the knowing that the little creature was now with its family and friends. She thought about the incredible night that she'd had, and she was delighted that she had seen a shmungen, and a unicorn, as well as a real-life fairy, a pixie, and the foxlike being, plus the bizarre leaf creature and a crow who wears glasses. And not forgetting of course, Mingus Widebottom the friendly gnome - and that was all in one night!

Event on Strumpshaw Common

This is the account of an event that took place in the year of 1972. It occurred in an area of south-east Canada, close to the U.S border, at a place that is known as Strumpshaw Common. Exactly what happened there all those years ago is not certain, and it's still debated even to this day.

* * *

It was in the midst of a long hot summer, when the Morris family decided to pack their bags and head into the country to spend a few days at their lodge retreat, just as they had done many times before. There were ten in all that set off early one morning for the short vacation: four adults, five children, and one dog, and when they arrived at the cabin later in the day they unpacked their vehicles and settled in.

At the start of their stay, everything was as it always was for the family group. They spent the first few days relaxing, hiking, spending some time by the lake and so forth, just normal stuff. However, when evening approached on the third day, things took a turn for the not so normal.

* * *

It had been a hot balmy day, and as the sun was beginning to set, the whole family were back at the lodge. The adults were sitting out on the porch having a cool drink. Some of the children were outside too, and the remainder were indoors. It was one of the children that first noticed something up in the sky, and had pointed it out to the rest. According to later testimonies from the parents, when they saw what young

Billy Morris was pointing at they immediately got up from their chairs. They'd all stood on the porch watching, as an unusual bright object crossed the sky above them.

It was apparently travelling from the northeast, heading in a southwesterly direction, all of them saw it, but no one had any idea what it was that they were looking at. It was described by the family as being egg-shaped, and some of them claimed that it gave off a humming sound as it passed overhead. They had all seen planes and helicopters before, and it was neither of those. The colour of the object was a mixture of reds, oranges and yellows, and it travelled at a reasonable speed. From the statements that we have, one of the adults claimed that they saw bits of fire dripping from it, and one of the children said that flames were coming out from the back. At the time of the occurrence, someone in the party was heard to have shouted, "Look, it's a spaceship!"

Whatever it was, it apparently either came down to land or crashed, depending on what family member's testimony you go with. The claim that the object came to earth was also backed up by a local farmer, who was the only other person apart from the family to have seen it that evening. He was less than a mile away from the Morris lodge, and stated that he saw a ball of light travelling across the sky before coming down in Strumpshaw Common. It's worth mentioning also, that throughout the weeks preceding the incident, there had been numerous reports of strange sightings in the sky around the area.

Immediately after witnessing the event, the family began to discuss what they had seen. Most of the group managed to convince themselves that they had witnessed nothing more than a meteor crashing to earth; although not all of them were sure.

The excited children wanted to investigate, to go to

the common which wasn't far away. The parents told them that they would not be allowed to go on their own, but as they were all so desperate, Mary Morris, one of the parents, said that she would take them. She later admitted that she'd opted to go not only to please the children, but also because she wanted to see for herself. "I was convinced that what I saw was no meteor," she told reporters.

* * *

A party of five set off in the direction of Strumpshaw Common - one adult, Mary Morris, and four children: Charlie Morris, the eldest of the kids at 14 years old; his sister Olivia, 13; and their relatives: Adam Jacobs, also 13; and Theo Jacobs, the youngest of the group at just 11 years old. One of the children was too frightened to go, so stayed back at the lodge with the rest of the adults. Accompanying the group was the family dog, Hoss. They were wise enough to realise that it would soon be getting dark and torches would be needed, especially for when they returned. Two torches were kept at the cabin at all times, so they gathered these up.

The group headed off in the direction of where they thought that the object had landed, which happened to be the common. The children were familiar with the area and knew the quickest way to get there, using shortcuts through farmers' fields. On the way, they bumped into another child whom they knew; his name was Scott Parish and he would also go on to witness the event and write a statement. He had been heading in the opposite direction, returning home, and upon meeting the group had told them that he had not seen anything, but when they told him what had happened he became interested and asked if he could join them. So the group now consisted of one adult, five children, and one dog.

* * *

Getting to the common the quick way involved crossing fields and climbing some fences, the first of which was not easy to surmount. It resulted in the youngest of the group, Theo, returning home, leaving the others to go on; Hoss the dog was able to squeeze underneath the fence. So the remainder continued on, towards where they had suspected that the mysterious object had landed, and as they did so it was just starting to get dark.

They walked down a country lane that led to a pasture, and when they reached it they were now getting close. The common could be made out up ahead, the group simply needed to follow a dirt track up a gentle slope to get to it. It was then that they spotted something in one of the fields, it appeared to be an object of some kind and was lit up with lights that pulsated on and off. They were intrigued by this - was the object in the field the same thing that they had seen soar across the sky?

All of them made their way up the dirt track, steadily walking whilst keeping an eye between the spaces in the bushes and trees at the lights in the field. It was now slightly dark, so they switched on both of their torches. As they neared the common, the flashing lights in the field suddenly went out and they could no longer see anything there, but the group pressed on nonetheless; they'd come this far and didn't want to return without some kind of investigation. As they did so, they became aware of a strange odour in the air, which the witnesses now describe as having smelled like sulphur. At the same time, a faint mist appeared, floating all around them, a few feet above the ground but not any higher; this seemed odd as it wasn't there before. Was the mist natural, just rising up from the fields as they cooled down from the midday heat, or was it coming from whatever it was that was in the field?

As the group neared the top of the track, the odour became very strong, so much so that it affected some of the kids. The most affected by it was young Scott Parish whose eyes had begun to water, so he told the others that he wasn't going to go any further, he would retreat out of the mist and watch on from the lane. So five went on, Mary Morris, Charlie Morris, Olivia Morris, Adam Jacobs, and Hoss the dog.

* * *

They were now very close, and they could hear a strange noise coming from the direction of where the object was sighted in the field. It was at this point that Hoss seemed to detect something and shot off ahead as fast as he could. It is claimed that the dog had suddenly stopped at the top of the track and was heard barking frantically. Then, after what was estimated to be about half a minute, the canine stopped barking and began whining. It apparently passed them all just moments later, running as fast as it could in the opposite direction towards home. The reports from those that were back at the cabin state that when the dog returned, he had uncharacteristically gone straight to his basket where he'd stayed until late the next afternoon - something had clearly spooked him.

* * *

The group decided to carry on regardless, determined to find out something about the mystery. It was now totally dark. They soon reached the top of the slope, at the start of the common, but as they proceeded up the last bit of track, one of the torchlights caught something amongst the trees - there was something there.

When they shone both lights in the direction, everyone saw it. According to the statements that Mrs. Morris and the children made, the thing was either sitting or standing amongst the trees. The parent and one of the children claimed that it was on a branch, but another child stated that it was actually hovering in the air; the remaining youngster said that she wasn't sure either way. As they stood huddled together in the dark, looking up at whatever it was, the creature was staring back at them - and then its eyes lit up. Mary said that at the time, she'd wondered if they weren't looking at some kind of nocturnal animal. But no animal she knew of was like that, and what happened next suggests that whatever it was, was not from this earth.

The thing let out an eerie screeching call that echoed around the common. It apparently then glided out from the trees towards them, stopped and hovered in mid-air about thirty feet away. As both torches shone directly at it, the creature floated closer.

'It was goblin-like, with large pointed ears, and its eyes were bright yellow,' wrote Charlie Morris in his report.

As it came towards them, it was said to have waved its long thin arms in the air. One of the children, Olivia Morris, claims that she got a good look at the hands, which were wrinkled with long claws. When the children had seen the creature in full torchlight they turned and ran, and Mary Morris followed.

* * *

When the group reached the bottom of the lane, they were breathless and had to stop for a rest. When they looked behind, they were relieved to see that the thing was not following them. They stood for a while, trying to regain both their breath and their composure, wondering what on earth they had seen. As they did so, a light appeared up in the sky, and they wondered if it might have been the same object that had been sitting in the field. The light flew around in the air for several minutes, then shot off at an incredible speed. Many years later, when the children had become adults, they stated that there is nothing from this world even now that can move at the speed that they witnessed that night.

The following day, two of the adults went back to the common to take a look around. There was no evidence of any creature or spacecraft, although they did admit that they could detect a faint smell of sulphur in the air. Mrs. Morris, all of the children and the dog, were no worse for wear, and everyone around was talking about the extraordinary incident of the previous evening - and they still talk about it to this day.

* * *

So that is the event that supposedly happened on Strumpshaw Common. Today, opinions are divided. Sceptics say that it was just the wild imaginings of a bunch of excited kids, and that Mary Morris had egged them on for fun, but others claim that there are just too many witnesses for it not to have been real. The children have now grown up, and all of them stand by their testimonies, saying that it happened exactly as they have said. It's just a shame that Hoss wasn't able to tell us his version of the event.

The Great Dig in the Earth

Sam Scud was bored with his life. He had very little to do, each and every day of the week. He did not even need to work, on account of a mysterious discovery in his house one day, of a shining lump of gold, which meant that he was financially sound - for the time being anyway. The unexpected windfall was great of course, but not having to go out and do a day's work did leave a void in Sam's life that he was struggling to fill.

He lived alone, on a reasonably-sized patch of land that he'd inherited from his parents. He had good friends, and nice neighbours with whom he spoke regularly, so it wasn't as if he had no one to talk to. What he really missed was digging, because that was his job, before the gold nugget had seemingly appeared out of nowhere to place itself in the pocket of his old donkey jacket. He loved to dig holes for people, and he was great at it, if anyone needed a hole dug then Sam was your man, the best there was, when it came to digging a hole no one could do it faster or better than he could. But now, there was no need for him to do it, and no reason for him to do anything much at all really.

Then one day, Sam had an idea - why not dig the deepest hole that anyone had ever dug. To start digging and not to stop, to keep going down and down to where no one had ever been before. It had never been done, so no one had any idea what was down there. If anyone could do it, he could, he used to dig so fast that his work colleagues had nicknamed him 'the Mole'. The project would give him a purpose in life, it would focus his mind and add some much needed excitement to his daily routine - and it would also be a great adventure. It was a fantastic idea, so fantastic in fact that Sam wondered why he hadn't thought of it before.

* * *

One bright morning, with torch-helmet on head, spade in hand, pick-axe over his shoulder and trowel in his pocket, Sam Scud started to dig - and it felt great.

He was soon burrowing down through the earth at a rapid rate, and it wasn't long before he made his first discovery - a drinks bottle made of thick glass. The bottle had a marble rattling about inside, which he concluded must have been used as a stopper, and it looked old, nineteenth century perhaps. Strange to think that someone hundreds of years ago held the very same bottle in their hand as they drank a fizzy drink, he thought to himself.

He continued on, down through the subsoil, and the next thing he came upon was a small metal disc. After cleaning away the dirt that was stuck to it, Sam was able to see it much better. It was a silver coin, and there were images on either side. The obverse depicted a man's head, he looked like a Roman, and on the reverse, an impressive looking eagle. There were some letters inscribed around the edge of the coin, but the writing was tiny and the words were in Latin, so Sam had no idea what they said.

For a while after that, pretty much all that Sam saw was mud, lots and lots of it, it varied in texture and wetness but it was still mud. Occasionally, something would break up the monotony of the brown sticky stuff, a startled rabbit for instance as its tunnel was disturbed, and a mole with big teeth and a wet nose, but basically it was just mud, and at one point Sam wondered if this was all that he was going to see. He pressed on nevertheless, eagerly, day and night, stopping only for brief rests and sleep breaks, or to take in food or water.

He was now entering new territory, reaching depths where no one had ever been, and the thought of this excited him. Anything could happen now, he told himself, and it did, because it wasn't long before he discovered something else - a new species of animal. It was a hairless ball of a creature, with a shovel-like nose and long fingers and toes. It must spend its whole life underground, Sam concluded, living in tunnels so deep down that no one even knows of its existence. It dawned on him that, as he was the one who discovered the little critter, it was his responsibility to give it a name. So he named it the Scuddler - after himself of course.

* * *

One day, as Sam was merrily digging away, his spade struck something hard and metallic that was embedded deep within the earth. After scraping around the object with his trowel, he was able to release it from the mud - it was a metal box. He spent some time cleaning away the soil that was stuck to the surface. This definitely looks like something interesting, he thought to himself.

The rectangular box was about a foot long, and it was made from a kind of metal that he had never seen before. It had not rusted at all, despite having been underground for so long, which was puzzling, and how had it gotten to be buried there in the first place, so deep in the earth. When Sam shook the mysterious box he could tell that there was something inside. He initially tried opening the lid with his hands, but time had sealed it so tightly that he was unable to do so. By using the blade of his trowel, however, and with plenty of effort, he was able to prize the lid open. Looking inside, he investigated the contents, and that's when he realised that he'd discovered a time capsule - but from whom, and from how long ago?

There were two small figurines inside the box, carved from stone. Holding both in his hands, he examined them closely. They were human in form, but slightly different, with elongated heads. One was holding a strange object that he didn't recognise, the other was depicted as wearing a necklace and carrying some kind of bag. Sam also noticed that they were both carved to have only four fingers on each hand.

There were other items in the container too, and it was all very interesting: an ornate broach with different coloured stones embedded into it, something that appeared to be a small hand-tool, and a thin slab of stone with an unusual pictogram etched into it. Last but not least, Sam found a piece of rolled-up parchment, similar to, but not paper. He got the impression that the material was indestructible, which would explain how it had remained so well preserved after all these years. There was writing on the scroll, but writing that he didn't recognise, it appeared to be more like Egyptian hieroglyphics than letters. After having a good look at all the contents, Sam decided to return them to the box, reseal the lid and then place the container back into the earth. Leaving the time capsule for someone else to discover in the far future.

Since the start of his dig, Sam had found some great items, and it got him thinking about all the interesting things that must be hidden in the ground all over the world. People are walking about on the earth every day, he thought to himself, totally oblivious to what is lying just beneath their feet. There must be all kinds of strange and wonderful artefacts and relics from all different ages, just waiting to be discovered.

*   *   *

Sam was now really enjoying his adventure, he was finding it fascinating and wasn't about to stop just yet. He would go further, even if it took him to the centre of the Earth. So he continued to dig both day and night, deeper and deeper into the depths, down and down into the darkness, with the torch-helmet lighting his way.

As he went on, the earthly material that he encountered started to become less and less like mud and more and more like stones. Just ordinary stones to begin with, plain colours and regular shapes, but the further he went the more interesting the stones became, and the deeper he went the more curious he got, wondering what he would find. There were no diamonds unfortunately, but some of the stones that he came upon were very beautiful, and all different colours too, from jade greens and cobalt blues to ruby reds and jet blacks - a stone collector would love some of these, he noted.

Then one day, Sam struck gold, literally, a big solid gold nugget. It reminded him of the piece that he had mysteriously found in his jacket pocket, and now, finding this one as well, he would have enough money to live comfortably for the rest of his life. Even if I were to stop now, Sam told himself, all of my effort would have been worth it. But he wasn't going to stop, he was enjoying himself too much, and besides, he wasn't doing it for money, he was doing it for the adventure - and this adventure was about to get even more interesting.

*   *   *

Over time, as Sam went deeper underground, the earth around him started to contain pockets of air, like honeycomb. The pockets of air became bigger and bigger, eventually forming holes, which themselves got larger and larger and began to connect to each other to produce spaces. As he continued on, the spaces got wider, becoming passageways and tunnels, eventually so large that he could stand up and walk along them without bending down. He appreciated the fact that he no longer needed to dig, that he could continue his journey simply by walking. As he made his way along the tunnels in the torchlight, it really did feel as though he had reached the centre of the Earth.

The dark tunnels through which he travelled eventually opened up into huge caverns, it seemed he had discovered a network of caves deep inside the planet. It was magnificent, as he shone his torch all around him, he saw stalagmites rising up from the ground and stalactites hanging down from above, and crystals sparkled in the light, glistening purples, golds and blues. Embedded in the rock were rose quartz, green malachite, yellow citrine and purple amethyst, crystals of all shapes, sizes and colours, sparkling brilliantly in the torchlight.

There was one crystal that was lying on the ground, and Sam had never seen the likes of it before. It was pure white in colour, and felt silky-smooth to touch, and it glistened when he held it in his hand and rotated it. The crystal appeared to be hollow inside, so Sam cracked it open - he discovered that the crystal contained a miniature pool of water, and the water shimmered with the colours of the rainbow.

Onwards and downwards Sam went, but as he did, something dawned on him - the caves were becoming less dark. Somewhere, somehow, a light source must be entering into the cavern, making it brighter. How could this be, he wondered, it was very strange, a mystery, and as he continued on his way it became so light that he no longer needed to use his torch. Where could this light be coming from so deep within the earth? he asked himself. It wasn't long before he found out, because at the end of the network of caves, he arrived at a huge opening, full of light.

* * *

Sam looked out beyond him, and he couldn't quite believe his eyes. There was an expanse so wide that he could see for miles, he could make out neither the end nor the sides, such was its vastness. The light source, he realised, was emanating from up above, but how he did not know, it was as if there was a sky, which was of course impossible so deep underground.

He stepped out into the vast opening, and the view that met him took his breath away. He was looking out at an underground city below him, so huge that it appeared as if it were out in the open, on the surface of the planet not deep within its core. Towering upwards were tall skyscrapers made from crystal, and smaller buildings were scattered around them in all shapes and sizes: rectangles, squares and domes. There was also a huge pyramid that appeared to be made of solid gold. Above the buildings, lights flashed on and off from various aircraft that flew overhead, it was like seeing a city from the future. Sam stood staring at the spectacle for several minutes, mesmerised, in awe of what he was witnessing.

* * *

As he gazed out upon the futuristic city, Sam became aware of thoughts that were entering his mind, from somewhere outside of his head, not his own. And at the same time, he sensed a presence, as if someone or something were watching him.

The thoughts in his head told him to look over to his right - so he did. There was someone standing there, looking straight at him, and he knew immediately that it was the source of the internal communication. The figure was humanlike, but not exactly human, it was tall and slender, beautiful, with blonde hair and big blue eyes. Sam was not afraid, the being gave off a peaceful and loving energy - he could tell that it was benign.

He walked slowly over towards the tall blonde being and held out his hand. The entity slowly raised its hand, and its long slender fingers connected with his. They were soft, and as they made contact they transmitted an energy of gentleness and compassion. The pair stood facing each other for a few seconds, and then the humanoid figure began to communicate again, telepathically, words appeared in Sam's head. "Hello Sam, it is good to see you," somehow the being knew his name. He realised that he could communicate back the same way, whatever he thought in his mind was picked up by the mind of the entity standing before him.

What followed can only be described as a mind conversation. The inner-earth being informed Sam that the underground city was the home of some of its people, but that they had originally come from the stars. "We have been here for a very long time," it told him, "before humans even existed on the surface of the planet." He was also told that the entities knew all about humans, their history and life above ground, and that they were trying to help the planet.

Sam was surprised to learn that the beings often came up from their hidden realm inside the earth and into the open, emerging out from our oceans and mountains. They travelled in craft, usually at night when they were less likely to be seen, but despite their caution, it was revealed that there had been many occasions when the flying ships had been spotted by people.

As they looked out upon the buildings and lights of the

city, the tall blonde figure pointed out some special places for its visitor: the Grand Hall of Mirrors, the Meeting Hall, and the Great Library. As they stood together, other beings passed them by, many looked the same as the entity with whom he telepathically conversed, but some looked different. There must be other species living down here too, Sam realised, or perhaps they were just visitors.

After a while, Sam was told that he would have to return to the surface, back from where he came, and he understood this. The inner-earth being informed Sam that he could return in one of their craft.

* * *

Sam was taken onto a large ship, a white tic-tac shaped craft. When he entered he was amazed, the ship was fantastic. It was futuristic, sparse and pristine, everything inside was pure white. It had sculptured seats positioned around the sides, and strange looking pictograms on the walls.

Through an opening, Sam could make out another room towards the centre of the craft. That must be the control room, he surmised, because he could see a large instrument panel with dials, and there were lots of flashing lights of all different colours. The whole ship was lit up in a gentle glow, although he could see no visible light source, it was as though the craft itself was emanating the light. A faint humming noise sounded as it started up, and a holographic image appeared in mid-air, showing what appeared to be a cross section of planet Earth.

* * *

It had felt as though the craft had hardly moved, so Sam was astonished when soon enough, a panel slid open to reveal the earth below him outside; he was back home already. The experience in the craft was short but incredible, one that he thought that he would never forget. Only he *would* forget, he would forget everything, because the inner-earth being told Sam that all he'd witnessed would have to be erased from his memory. The whole lot, from the first plunge of his spade into the soil in his garden, to the return journey on the ship - he would remember nothing. It was explained to him that he had seen things that humans were not yet ready to see, one day they would be, but the time was not right.

In an instant, Sam disappeared from within the ship and reappeared in his bed at home, fast asleep. The large hole in the garden was filled-in by a beam fired down from the craft, returning it to just as it was before the great dig, like nothing had ever happened there.

* * *

Sam Scud awoke in the morning. In the back of his mind was a vague semblance of a dream that he'd had, one that he couldn't recall but from which he still retained the strange feeling from. He paused for a moment, trying to delve deep into the depths of his subconscious to retrieve it, but was unable to do so, so he gave up trying.

He decided to get himself out of bed, to make some breakfast, and when he did, the leftover feeling from his apparent dream dissipated. But an event later that day made him wonder if there was perhaps more to the strange feeling that morning than he'd realised, because something happened that he found bewildering, and quite remarkable. In the pockets of his trousers, Sam found some items that were not there before - and he had no idea where they had come from. There was a silver coin, with an image of a man's head on one side and a depiction of an eagle on the other. But the other item that he found was astounding - it was a solid gold nugget! How on earth had it gotten there, he wondered. It was similar to the one that he'd mysteriously found in his jacket pocket a while back, and was probably just as valuable. For some inexplicable reason, another lump of gold had appeared out of nowhere. But Sam wasn't complaining, he was used to unusual things happening in his life, things that he could neither explain nor understand, and this was just another one of those.

"There is more to life than meets the eye," Sam would sometimes say to people, and he knew it. So he accepted life's anomalies and got on with things, besides, he would now be wealthy for the rest of his life, which meant of course that he would never have to work again for as long as he lived - two mysterious gold nuggets had seen to that.

* * *

Not ever having to work again was great for Sam Scud of course, it meant that he could have a life of relative ease, with no worries about making money or concerns with paying bills. But it did mean that he had lots of time on his hands, with very little to do, and after a while he became rather bored. He began to crave excitement in his life, to do something interesting.

Then one day, he had an idea. Why not dig the deepest hole that anyone had ever dug, to start digging and not stop, to keep going down and down to where no one had ever been. It had never been done before, and if anyone could do it he could. It would give him a purpose in life, focus his mind and add some much needed excitement - and would also be a great adventure. It was a fantastic idea, so fantastic in fact that he wondered why he hadn't thought of it before.

Carnival of the Cosmos

An impressive-looking sign arched over the entrance to the theme park: *Welcome to the Carnival of the Cosmos* in bright neon lights. A gathering of people stood outside, waiting to be the first ones to experience the newest, most fantastic amusement park ever built.

The complex had been several years in the making, despite containing just ten attractions, because apparently, each one of the rides was far superior to anything that had come before, offering a 'whole new experience.' None of the waiting guests would have expected to have been there, on account of the odds, but somehow their names had been randomly picked out from the many thousands who had entered the lucky draw. As of next week, the Carnival of the Cosmos would be open to the general public, but today was for the fortunate winners only.

* * *

The large gates swung slowly open, and smartly-dressed uniformed staff with friendly faces greeted the expectant group. First impressions are important, and as the visitors followed the attendants into the park they were met with pristine lawns and manicured trees, immaculate white stone pathways and elegant fountains, and grand statues positioned in carefully chosen locations.

Sliman scanned his surroundings, it looked magnificent. Above the line of trees he could make out the tops of some of the attractions: a huge spinning dome emitting coloured sparks, a network of tubes that twisted around itself like a giant ball of spaghetti, and in the distance, a tower so tall that it appeared to touch the sky. He wondered for a brief moment what it might be like to actually take those rides, and the thought excited him; no doubt the other attractions were scattered around the park too.

One by one the guests were attended to, and it wasn't long before a smiling lady wearing a uniform and name badge introduced herself. Tia was holding an electronic pad, and after the welcoming formalities she provided some general information about the theme park. Sliman discovered, amongst other things, that on account of it being so big, all visitors were given their own personal fully-automated vehicle for the day, called a transportation pod.

When the briefing was done, all that remained was for Sliman to choose his rides, and a list of ten options appeared on the pad for him to make his selections:

No 1: Moonwalk
No 2: Mystery Train Ride
No 3: Spaceship Voyage
No 4: The Human Body Experience
No 5: Kaleidoscope
No 6: Crystal Cavern
No 7: Fly like an Eagle
No 8: Supernova
No 9: Journey Around the World
No 10: The Enchanted Forest

The list was tantalising, Sliman wanted to select them all, but knew that he could choose just three. It wasn't easy, but after some careful thought and deliberation he made his selections and Tia entered them into the electronic pad. She attached a small tag to his wrist, and with a warm smile informed him that his transportation pod would be arriving shortly, then wished him good day.

* * *

Glancing around, Sliman saw that some of the guests were already boarding their pods, which then glided off in different directions along the white stone pathways that led through the bushes and trees. Shortly, a small driverless cart pulled up beside him and an electronic voice from within introduced itself as his personal transportation pod, before prompting him to take a seat.

The vehicle was very comfortable, minimalistic yet stylish and futuristic. He found himself facing a dashboard, with a large screen, a speaker grill, a small compartment and various buttons. The screen was green, but with a wave of his hand he could change its colour. He went through amber, scarlet, orange and mulberry, before opting for cornflower blue. The cart was open-topped which pleased him, he would have excellent views of the surroundings as he travelled around. As soon as he was settled, the pod's voice spoke again.

"Your chosen rides for today are: Spaceship Voyage, Kaleidoscope, Journey Around the World. Can you confirm please?"

"Yes that's correct," said Sliman.

"Thank you. Before we proceed, I would like to draw your attention to the food and drink compartment located in front of you. If you require anything, please press the blue button and then make your selection on the display screen. Are you happy to proceed to your first destination?"

"Yes, please do," he replied.

"Thank you. We will now proceed to attraction No 3: Spaceship Voyage. We will arrive in 8 minutes and 27 seconds."

The transportation pod accelerated gently, making barely a sound as it joined one of the pathways. The ride was extremely smooth, if he hadn't seen the wheels at the bottom of the cart the passenger might have assumed that the vehicle was hovering above the ground. On the way, he saw other pods taking other guests to their destinations, most were visitors but there appeared to be staff members too.

The transportation pods were all different colours and sizes, seemingly depending on how many people they contained. Sliman's was one of the smaller pods, white in colour, the largest were the silver-coloured ones that carried five or six passengers. As he went on his way, Sliman noticed that there were robots in the park too, busily going to and fro and carrying out specific tasks. His vehicle passed close-by to one of them that was picking up leaves from the path, and he laughed to himself at the bizarreness of it all. This place is remarkable, he thought to himself - and he hadn't even tried the rides yet.

* * *

An awesome-looking silver spaceship came into view. It was the classic flying saucer shape, smooth and rounded, with a panel at the front which Sliman reasoned must be a door. There were people already standing outside, waiting to board.

"We have arrived at our first destination, please depart," his vehicle announced in a pleasant tone. "You will find me in this location following the completion of your activity. Have a pleasant trip."

Sliman stepped out from his cart and joined the small group of visitors waiting eagerly for their ride. As he stood in line, other guests pulled up in their pods, set to take the ride with them.

It wasn't long before the panel at the front of the attraction slid slowly open, to reveal the inside of the spaceship and a flight crew standing ready to greet their passengers. They welcomed everyone on board, and when he saw the inside of the craft for the first time Sliman was amazed. A lit walkway of checkered, panelled flooring ran around the outer edge, and the whole ship was lit up by electric-blue lights. Corridors led into the centre, and there were rows of seats facing outwards. Some coloured lights were flashing on and off to one side, and he noticed an unusual looking pictogram etched into one of the walls. With everyone seated, the door closed and a voice sounded around the craft.

"This is the control centre speaking, a warm welcome to everyone on board, thank you for choosing to travel with us today. Your pilot and crew are located at the centre of the ship, you are seated in the outer section, this will enable you to have the very best views during our trip. We are about to embark on a voyage around the solar system, we will endeavour to get as close as we can to our neighbouring planets so that you can get excellent views of them, but please be aware that some of the planets have volatile environments which may affect how close we can get and how long we can stay. With that said, we are sure that you are all eager to get going, so without further ado, we would like to wish you all a pleasant journey."

As they sat in their seats, readying themselves for take-off, the excited passengers glanced around the ship and smiled at each other. As they did so, a faint humming noise started up from below their feet and a gentle vibration was felt. To everyone's amazement, the sides of the ship suddenly became transparent, transforming into one huge window. They could now see the outside, all around. The park was clearly visible, the pathway, the bushes and the trees, although there were no longer any people standing near the craft. Wherever it was the spaceship was taking them, the passengers were certainly going to get an excellent view.

A sudden whirring sound echoed around as the ship began to rise up. Looking out, they could see the whole park down below them, it was getting further and further away as the craft left the ground. The ship then suddenly accelerated and shot up at a high speed. Within moments they were passing through clouds, and it wasn't long before planet Earth was a long way off in the distance - looking like a blue, green and white marble.

* * *

The ship's velocity slowed, and a brief announcement was heard around the craft.

"We are about to do a complete circle around the Earth's moon. This will enable you to get a close look at our only orbiting satellite. Please enjoy the views."

At that very moment, the moon came into full view, so close that it took up the whole perspective through the window. Its surface could be clearly seen, the topography of the land, the hills and mountains, even the craters and boulders. Sliman could not believe his eyes.

As everyone on board was scanning the lunar landscape, it suddenly became dark, and the passengers realised that they had gone around to the far side of the moon, to the part that's impossible to see from Earth. Nevertheless, despite being dark, they were able to make out shapes and structures on the surface. There was actually more to see on the far side of the moon than there was on the near side; there were dome-shaped buildings, pyramids, towers, and even lights.

Sliman was finding the whole thing fascinating, so he was disappointed when the craft began to leave the location and head out into space. But he soon forgot all about the moon, because what followed was even more mind-blowing, as the spaceship took the passengers around the whole solar system - to each planet one by one.

Mercury was first, looking similar in many ways to the moon with its rocks and craters, but Mercury was more hilly and mountainous. Everyone was surprised at how much bigger the sun looked from where they were; a huge fiery ball, it was an awesome sight.

Planet Venus was next. As they approached, it first appeared as yellowish-white in colour, but after passing through a thick layer of cloud it became reddish-brown. Looking down through the haze, the passengers could make out the ground below, it was uneven with high ridges, blistered, dry and barren. For a while, the spaceship hovered above an active volcano that the crew had located on the surface, until the sky suddenly turned orange and lightning began to explode all around them, so they left for Mars.

The red planet was easily recognisable and as the ship approached, the dry dusty terrain could clearly be seen. There were valleys and canyons, and what appeared to be dried up lake beds. In some areas the environment was quiet, like a calm desert on Earth, but on other parts of the planet wild dust storms raged.

Visiting Jupiter was incredible, it was a swirling mass of different-coloured gasses. The ship passed through patches of blue, white and green, one contrasting misty layer after another. From what he saw, Sliman concluded that Jupiter may not have a solid surface at all, just various densities of gas.

As they neared Saturn, the craft had to take care, to

avoid the masses of floating rocks and lumps of ice that were drifting around in space; the passengers could see them clearly outside. The voice of the ship informed them that these are visible from down on Earth, as the rings that circle the planet. Saturn itself was shielded by brown and white clouds. When they passed through the clouds, they found themselves in darkness, and explosions of thunder could be heard, even from within the spaceship. All that was visible through the window of the craft were the red and white lines of lightning that streaked across the sky, it was fantastic to see, but when a warning alarm sounded the ship moved on.

Uranus was next, and the passengers discovered that it too had rings of floating rocks around it - black ones. The planet itself was covered in a blue haze, impossible to see through at first, but as they got closer the fog cleared and a massive ball of ice and gas became visible. Atmospheric bands of turquoise mist could be seen drifting across the surface of the planet, it was beautiful, a huge contrast to fiery Saturn. As was Neptune, everyone gasped when they saw the vivid blue world glowing in the twilight.

Having seen the gas planets, only the dwarf planet of Pluto remained. Mysterious and interesting, it too was surrounded by floating ice and rocks, but not as densely packed as Saturn. Blue and pink Pluto looked exotic and surreal with its ice mountains and falling snow. In the time that the onlookers observed it, Pluto changed colour several times, it was a spectacular and a perfect ending to an incredible voyage.

* * *

The tour of the solar system was over, the spaceship returned home at a rapid speed and it wasn't long before the familiar blue and white ball of Earth was visible through the window, becoming larger and larger before their eyes. In next to no time the craft had landed and the ship's voice was heard for the final time.

"We have arrived safely back on planet Earth, we do hope that you had a pleasant journey. On behalf of the control centre, I would like to wish you all a very nice day."

Sliman exited the craft with the other passengers, most of whom were speechless, seemingly stunned by what they had just experienced.

As he stood quietly on the soft green grass, he tried to reorient himself with where he was, to ground himself and return to reality. It was an amazing experience, incredible to believe that it was only an amusement ride, and that the craft had probably never even left the ground. He had no idea how they had done it, but if the other rides were as good as this one then he wanted to go on all of them. But he could only try three of course, and after spending a while sitting on a bench watching things go by, he was ready for the next one.

* * *

Sliman's transportation pod was exactly where he'd left it. "Hello Sliman," it said as he entered, in its now familiar artificial voice. "Did you have a nice trip?"

"Fantastic," he answered, knowing of course that he was talking to AI. He didn't care, he was having such a great time. Pushing the blue button on the dashboard brought up a food & drink menu on the screen, and he selected a sparkling water from the list. Almost instantly, a small compartment opened and the item appeared, just as requested.

"Would you like to go to your next destination?" the pod asked.

"Yes," Sliman replied, enthusiastically.

The vehicle passed by other transportation pods, carrying other guests to their rides. He noticed how excited everyone appeared, then realised that he probably looked just the same. After about ten minutes of pleasant meandering through the park, he arrived at his next destination, and his pod pulled up beside a gigantic, horizontal metal tube. Written along the side in large colourful letters was one word: *Kaleidoscope.*

* * *

Sliman stepped down from his cart, then walked over to the entrance to the Kaleidoscope ride; there were some visitors already waiting. Not long after joining them, an attendant ushered in the person at the front of the queue. A few minutes later the second was called, it seemed the riders were going in at short intervals - it would be his turn soon.

As he stood pondering what the ride might be like, he was gestured forward by a staff member who then gave out instructions as to what he should do. Sliman listened carefully to what he was told, then proceeded through a set of doors. He found himself in total darkness, apart from illuminated arrows which shone brightly along the floor. They were guiding his way, apparently to a launch point. Sliman did exactly as instructed and let the arrows lead him through, until he came to a luminous green bar that prevented him from going any further.

He was standing on a platform in the pitch black. A neon sign to the side read: *Please Wait.* He could feel the excitement in his stomach, what on earth was this crazy ride, he thought to himself. Moments later, the bar rose up and the *Please Wait* sign changed to *Jump Now.* Sliman took a leap of faith, and jumped off from the ledge.

For a brief moment he was in free fall, plunging down

through dark space, but then, the most astonishing thing happened, he suddenly stopped falling and began to float in mid-air, as if gravity had ceased to exist. It was the strangest, most bizarre thing ever.

As his eyes adjusted to the darkness, he was able to see all around him, he could make out the curved metallic sides of the construction and became aware that he was drifting along inside the giant tube. The beginning, where he'd entered, was very dim, but up ahead in the distance, the far end of the tube was lit up in an explosion of colour and light.

They were the brightest, most amazing colours he had ever seen. Purples, blues, whites, oranges, reds, yellows, greens, and more, every colour imaginable, sparkling and glistening like diamonds in bright sunlight - and something was guiding his body towards them. All around was silent, apart from the gentle tinkling sounds that were echoing out from the coloured pieces in the distance, as they changed their patterns. He laughed to himself, the sensation of weightlessness was weird yet amazing at the same time, he couldn't quite believe that he was floating inside a giant kaleidoscope.

As he drifted gently along, Sliman became entranced by the colours and shapes that he was heading towards. He could see them up ahead, getting gradually closer all the time. They were forming symmetrical patterns, just like the handheld kaleidoscopes that he'd once looked through as a kid. But this was no toy that he was peering through with one eye, he was actually inside, as though he'd been miniaturised to the size of a fruit fly. And just like the toy kaleidoscopes, this one too was dynamic. Intricate patterns of coloured shapes sat motionless for a few seconds before suddenly exploding, dispersing into a thousand pieces, only to reform once again into a new, totally different pattern, each one unique.

Sliman relaxed his body, savouring the sensation of drifting slowly through the space inside the giant tube, he had no idea how it was being done but he didn't care, it was such an incredible experience. He let the pull of the kaleidoscope take him along in its own time, he was in no hurry.

Ultimately, he arrived at the far end of the tube, where his body fell into the mass of colour and light. He found himself engulfed by all different colours and shapes, he could reach out and touch them. There were so many that he was unable to see beyond the shimmering and glistening of the diamonds, squares and circles that engulfed him. For several seconds his body turned and tumbled, as he disappeared amongst the swirls of colour, as though being consumed by a champagne supernova.

He eventually passed through the psychedelic mass, and came out the other side. When he did, gravity immediately returned and Sliman could feel himself falling. The next thing he knew, he'd landed on a huge inflatable pillow, he had come out at the other end of the tube and the experience was over. An attendant was there waiting for him, she asked if he'd enjoyed the ride but she already knew the answer, she could tell by the look on his face that he had.

* * *

The air in the park was warm with a pleasant gentle breeze, and Sliman had found a quiet place to sit on a bench under some trees. A songbird was singing from a nearby branch, and the sweet sound somehow helped him to adjust to the real world once again. What had happened inside the kaleidoscope ride was going around in his mind, it had been like some fantastic dream. He wanted another go, but he knew that he couldn't, and the thought disappointed him slightly. But he remembered that he still had one more ride to come, and at that very moment, as if on cue, his white transportation pod pulled up beside him and he entered inside.

He had been in the park for some time now, he was feeling peckish, so he sat for a while in his seat having some lunch, specially selected from the display screen, whilst watching the activity go by outside. Before he headed off towards his final ride, Sliman instructed his pod to take him to some shops and cafes that he had passed earlier, where he had seen several people congregating. He spent some time there, looking at all the interesting things in the shops, and he bought himself a scale model set-up of the theme park to take home with him as a reminder.

* * *

The ride to Sliman's final attraction took a little longer than usual, almost twenty minutes, but he didn't mind, he enjoyed looking around at the magnificent park as he glided through. Passing other pods, he could tell from the faces of the passengers that they were all having such a great time. Some of the visitors looked slightly astonished, he noticed, they were probably the ones that had just finished a ride, he concluded. He wondered if all the attractions were as awesome as the ones that he'd been on, he guessed that they probably were. A group of people in a blue transportation pod waved to him as they went by. Everyone seems so happy here, he thought to himself, as was he, even without having taken his final ride he'd already had the time of his life.

* * *

The electric cart pulled up in front of a huge glass dome, large letters above the entrance read: *Journey Around the World*. Getting out from his vehicle, Sliman walked over to the attraction and into the dome, to take his place in line. He watched as he waited. Those at the front were stepping forward one or two at a time, to be assisted into impressive looking transparent capsules. When the passengers were safely seated inside, the capsules edged forward into a huge clear tube then shot off at a high speed; as to where the capsules were going, no one had any idea.

After some time, a staff member gestured him forward; it was his turn. He stepped into the capsule and took his seat, it was futuristic and extremely comfortable. The vision through the Perspex shell was unbelievably clear, it was if there were nothing there, you could see out in every direction. The pod nudged forward, setting itself into position within the tube. He could feel the excitement welling up in his stomach as he rested back in the luxurious seat, wondering what lay ahead. Moments later, the capsule shot off down the tube and his ride began.

After only a few seconds, his capsule emerged out from the glass dome, and Sliman found himself travelling around the park inside the tube. He could see everything outside as he sailed over trees and weaved his way around the amusement park. Down below, different-coloured transportation pods were shuttling to and fro, and he could see people standing outside some of the other attractions. He caught a fleeting glimpse of the spaceship that he'd taken a ride on earlier in the day.

Suddenly, his capsule started to descend at a high speed, downwards towards the ground. Faster and faster it went, but it didn't crash, the tube in which he was travelling entered into the earth, he was going underground. For a few seconds there was total darkness, but then the capsule emerged out into a huge underground cave. It felt damp, musty, he could see the wetness on the rocks as they glistening and sparkling around him, and he could detect the faint smell of salt. Sliman marvelled at what he saw, as he passed by impressive looking stalactites and stalagmites as he went.

Eventually, the capsule came out from the cave and he found himself under the ocean - an unexpected and wonderful contrast of environments. From the comfort and safety of his transparent shell, Sliman could look out at the beautiful turquoise sea, watching the aquatic life all around him. A green turtle swam gracefully along, a large pink octopus sat motionless on the seabed, and a swarm of purple fluorescent jellyfish glided by. A curious shark came close up to take a look at him, and at one point he passed a magnificent blue whale, swimming nonchalantly within the watery depths. The capsule cruised along underwater for some time and Sliman enjoyed every moment, but in the end, it surfaced and he was travelling once more over land. The cave and ocean were amazing, but what followed was even more fantastic.

The Journey Around the World lived up to its name, and took him to many different places. It went through the heart of the jungle, weaving in and out of trees as it did, and Sliman caught glimpses of fantastic animals and brightly coloured birds. He also cruised above the ancient stone ruins of South America, gazing down upon Mayan temples and statues. He travelled from one incredible land to another, including a fiery island where he was taken into the heart of a volcano, his capsule entered in through one of the side vents before plunging deep into molten lava. Despite being surrounded by the red hot liquid, the cool temperature inside the capsule remained, it was very exciting. He eventually exited through the main vent of the volcano, to be ejected out at the top. After leaving the fiery island, Sliman travelled across a desert landscape, passing huge pyramids on the way. Looking out, he saw magnificent sand dunes, herds of camels, and Bedouin sitting around campfires as the sun set in the distance.

Wow, what an amazing adventure he'd had. But it wasn't over quite just yet, because the final destination on the tour was a visit to the North Pole, where Sliman found himself in a twilight landscape surrounded by a wilderness of snow as far as he could see. At one point, he passed a magnificent polar bear, which noticed him and looked over curiously as he went by. As he travelled over the arctic tundra, admiring the views, the sky above suddenly lit up - it was the spectacular aurora borealis!

Sliman had always wanted to see the Northern Lights, and they didn't disappoint. The sky above shimmered spectacularly with greens, blues and purples, producing a mesmeric and breathtaking light extravaganza, it was an incredible way to end his trip. He had no idea how long the ride had lasted, he'd been too absorbed in the experience to notice, but it had been the longest and the best one of all. He'd seen some incredible places around the world, all from the safety and comfort of his transparent capsule.

* * *

Sliman's time at the Carnival of the Cosmos had come to an end, the amusement park was closing, so he left along with the other fortunate visitors who'd had an unbelievable day. How they had managed to create such fantastic rides he had no idea, it was beyond his comprehension, all he knew was that they were all amazing.

Sliman had thoroughly enjoyed his adventure of a

lifetime, and that was just three of the attractions contained in the park. There were of course, seven other rides that he never got to take, so he told himself that he would return another day to try some more, which he did, but that's another story.

BRACHYURA ODYSSEY

Atticus was a small fellow, a tiny brook crab to be exact, with little legs and pincers; although the two eyes perched atop his head were rather big in comparison to the rest of his body. The brook where he lived was part of a gentle stream, that ran through the beautiful Welsh countryside.

The tiny crab lived a simple life, going about his daily routine without complaint, scuttling over rocks and stones and cleaning up as he went. If he needed to rest, he would sit at the bottom and watch everything go by beneath the water, or he would clamber up above the waterline and find a nice rock where he could sunbathe. The world above the water is totally different to the world below it, he often thought to himself.

Atticus was a likeable chap, friendly and polite, and he would always stop to acknowledge anyone that he met. Because of this he had many friends, and as crustaceans go, he was pretty content with his life. There came a time however, when the likeable crab started to feel restless, as though longing for a change. There was a strange feeling stirring inside him and it seemed to be urging him to do something, what exactly he wasn't sure, but as time went by the feeling became stronger and impossible to ignore. He eventually realised what it was, it was telling him to move on, that it was time to go somewhere and have some new experiences in his life. So early one morning, he said goodbye to his friends and to the brook, and to the rocks and stones that were so familiar to him, and set off downstream.

*   *   *

Along the way, he made many discoveries, and the two big eyes perched atop his head saw things that they had never seen before. There is a big wide world outside of the brook, he realised, that he never even knew existed. As he explored his new surroundings he grew, both physically and mentally, and it wasn't long before the tiny brook crab had become a little stream crab, who felt at home with the freshwater mussels and shrimps in the gentle flowing water. But the urge that had told him to leave the brook remained, and it was pushing him onwards, so day after day, the little stream crab continued on, clambering over small stones with ease and surmounting rocks with adventurous enthusiasm - he was on a voyage of discovery.

* * *

One day, Atticus came to the end of the stream, he saw that he could go no further for he had reached the river. It's been an interesting journey, he thought to himself, but this seems to be as far as it goes. He was thinking that perhaps it was time to settle down again, to take it easy once more, but the strange feeling inside him was still there and it didn't seem to agree - it was telling him to go on. But if he were to continue he would have to go into the river, which meant uncertainty, because he had never been in a river before.

The thought of entering was a bit daunting for him. To begin with, a river is far bigger than a stream, so the current would surely be much stronger. Also, being a stream crab, he had no idea what a river contained, or what would lay ahead should he decide to take the plunge. And last but not least, he knew that if he chose to enter the river there would be no turning back, because the current would almost certainly carry him away to somewhere else - to where he had no idea.

As he was trying to decide what to do, Atticus looked up and noticed a large rock protruding out from the water, between the stream and the river. He had learnt from his days in the brook that if ever he wasn't sure about something, the best thing to do was to find a comfortable rock to sit on and relax his mind. If he did this, and didn't try to think too hard, the solution would always come to him. So, using all of his ten legs, he clambered up onto the rock, sat himself down comfortably and relaxed.

Just as he had hoped, after a short while things became clear to him, and it was pretty simple really, even to a little stream crab like himself. He had two choices, he could stay, or he could go on. To stay would mean a relatively easy life, he was now comfortable with the ways of the stream and could take everything in his stride. If he decided to go on however, he would experience many new things and learn much more, but it would likely be challenging, with new obstacles to overcome and possible dangers, he would have to face the unknown and would need to adapt to survive. There was not a right or a wrong choice, whatever he decided was okay, but the feeling inside was telling him to go on - so Atticus leapt from the rock into the river below.

* * *

The current was even stronger than the little crab had expected, and he wasn't used to it. He found himself being tossed about all over the place. Out of control, he spun around in the depths of the water, turning left and right, sometimes he was upright, sometimes he was upside-down, and other times he didn't know which way he was. He had underestimated the force of the river and was hanging on for dear life, but as the river carried him along, he quickly learnt how to adjust his body so that it remained upright, nevertheless, he was still bobbing up and down in the water.

He struggled for what seemed like hours. At one point, Atticus thought that he'd regained control of his little body, but then became entangled in a branch which, like him, was being swept along by the force of the current. The branch had him trapped, it was impossible to free himself and he was repeatedly being bashed on the side of the bank as he went. He wrestled desperately to separate himself, but the effort of doing so was draining even more of his energy, he wasn't sure how much longer he could fight and was at the point of giving up. I took on too much, he told himself as he was carried along, it seems that I made the wrong decision. But then, just when all seemed lost, the branch that was holding him snagged on a rock and snapped in half. The breaking of the branch released him, he was free and was now able to regain control. He then managed to work out how to ride the current, how to angle his body so that he could move with the water.

He had somehow survived his ordeal and no longer needed to fear the force of the water, for he had mastered it. The little crab was able to guide himself to an area at the bottom of the river, where the flow of the water was calmer, and where he could take a much needed rest. But he was exhausted, the struggle had used up all of his energy, and he hadn't eaten for a long time.

* * *

Atticus sat at the bottom of the riverbed, a forlorn and dejected figure, but he was not ready to give up just yet, there was still hope and he could look for food. So, the battered and tired little crab began searching around on the stones and pebbles.

It appeared at first as though there was nothing for him

to eat, but then, mercifully, he came upon a clump of algae that was lodged between two stones; it was exactly what he needed. He was so hungry that he immediately began tearing pieces off with his pincer and putting them into his mouth as fast as he could - he was surviving. But when he'd finished eating, and just as it seemed that his troubles were over, he came face to face with a new challenge, in the form of a big black fish. It was much larger than the ones that he'd encountered in the stream, and it had spotted him with its large yellow eyes. It was hungry too, and the favourite food of big black fish is little olive-coloured crabs.

All Atticus saw was a huge open mouth and big white teeth lunging towards him. The poor crab was trapped in the fish's mouth. The fish shook its head repeatedly to disorientate and confuse him, then tried biting down, but Atticus had a hard protective shell, as well as a useful pincer which he knew how to use. The endangered crab stretched out his pincer and pinched the fish's nose as hard as he could, and it made the fish release him from its grip. He was free, but the big black fish was very hungry and very persistent, and it wasn't done yet. It chased the crab around the bottom of the river, through the weeds and over the stones, but the agile crustacean was evading the fish's lunges, keeping just out of reach. Until that was, he came face to face with a wall of rock and was trapped with nowhere to go, it seemed that the big black fish was finally going to have the little crab for lunch. But just when he needed it, Atticus had a stroke of luck, he spotted a gap between the rocks, big enough for him to squeeze through but too small for the fish to enter, so he scuttled hurriedly into the gap to safety.

He had survived once more, there was no way that the big black fish could get him if he stayed put. But his ordeal was not over just yet, for the fish knew that the crab would have to come out at some point for food, and was waiting for him.

* * *

Several hours passed, and Atticus could not come out from his safe place for he knew what was outside. Then nighttime arrived and darkness fell upon the river, and inside the gap in the rocks the moonlight could not penetrate, so the little crab clung to the wall in total blackness; it was a strange and unfamiliar place to be.

The situation seemed hopeless, he was battered and bruised, hungry and tired. He thought back to his life in the brook, how easy and trouble-free it was, it seemed such a long time ago now, almost like a different lifetime. Here, now, he felt lost, alone, and beaten, so he closed his eyes and surrendered. As soon as he did this, he was engulfed by a mysterious white light. It was warm, comforting, and seemed as though it had come to protect him. Atticus suddenly felt peaceful and serene, the light had appeared from out of nowhere and its warmth penetrated his whole body. It was reassuring him, telling him that everything was going to be alright, that he was going to be fine. With his eyes closed, in a blissful state, Atticus fell into a deep sleep. As he drifted off, he heard words in his head that seemed to be saying, "Don't worry, you will soon be a river crab."

* * *

Atticus awoke, and was relieved to see that morning had come. The sun's rays penetrated the water and lit up the riverbed, it was a wonderful sight and seemed like a totally different place to the one that he'd experienced during the night. A shaft of sunlight shone through the water and into the gap where he was hiding, as if purposely seeking him out, it warmed him through and through and it felt glorious.

The sunbeam gave him enough energy to walk, so the tired little crab picked himself up and took a look outside of the crevice, where he discovered that the big black fish had gone. He also noticed that the current of the river was much slower than the day before. He scrambled up out of the water and found a large rock where he could sunbathe. Clambering on top, he saw that an apple had fallen from the tree above, it was like a gift from the universe, just sitting there as if waiting especially for him. It was the tastiest apple he had ever eaten, he had never gotten so much pleasure from eating food before.

After devouring as much of the fruit as he could, Atticus rested in the warm sun, rejuvenated. He now felt invigorated, stronger than ever, and he knew deep down that something had changed inside him. He realised that everything that had happened to him had happened for a reason, and that things were exactly as they were meant to be.

He was now ready to continue on with his journey, and he knew that life would not be quite so hard for him anymore in the river. And this was true, the current didn't seem nearly as strong to him, even at its fastest it was no longer a problem because he knew how to handle it, and he was much tougher now, and much more adept.

Food was plentiful in the river too, and as the weeks and months went by Atticus grew bigger and stronger, and not only was he stronger, he was also much wiser. He had been through his struggles and had survived them all, and he wasn't afraid of big black fish any more, or any fish for that matter, because he knew what to do. He felt proud of what he had achieved, he had mastered the river.

One bright morning, as he sat above the waterline he

caught his reflection in the water; he looked impressive, bigger and stronger. He knew then that he was no longer a little stream crab, he was a river crab, just as the inner voice had told him he would be.

* * *

But the story wasn't over quite just yet for Atticus crab, there was more to come in the life of our friendly subject. Because he continued to follow the feeling inside him, the one that kept telling him to go on, and he had many more adventures and dealt with many new challenges - and he surmounted them all. On his way up the river, he had some great times and met some wonderful new friends, and each one of them had something to teach him - just as he had things to teach them.

Then one day, as he proudly made his way along the river, he suddenly beheld the most wonderful sight. The river opened up to reveal a magnificent expanse of water, so wide that he couldn't quite believe his eyes, he was looking out at a whole new world that he could never have dreamt of. It was the most fantastic water he had ever seen, the deepest blue, with a surface that glistened in the sunlight, and it appeared to have enormous depth.

Atticus looked on in awe, imagining all the amazing creatures that must live beneath the surface, and all the different shapes and colours that it must contain.

"It's called the sea," a voice spoke to him from close by.

His eyes turned, to see an impressive looking seagull standing right beside him. Perched proudly on the rock, the gull seemed to emanate freedom and wisdom, as though it had lived a long life of discovery, a life in which it had asked many questions, for which it now knew the answers.

"The sea," the crab said, "I'd heard stories, but I never

knew that it actually existed."

"It exists," replied the wise bird, "and it's there for all of us, for anyone who is brave enough to look for it."

"But I'm just a river crab," Atticus said.

"Nonsense," said the seagull, "look how much you have grown, look how strong you are and how wise you've become, you are not a river crab anymore - you're a big sea crab."

"I'm a sea crab," said Atticus, and with that, he leapt into the deep blue water.

THE GLASS SUBMARINE

Blackbonnie still stands today. That doesn't surprise me, although it was many years ago that I was there, I can still recall how strong and solid the building was. I was very young at the time, around eleven or twelve years old, and remember being impressed by the huge stone bricks. To a kid, the house appeared mountainesque in its strength. Someone once told me that the property had been there for over four-hundred years - it will probably be there for another four-hundred.

The big old house sits beside a lake, or loch as they say in Scotland. Despite its size, unless you were one of the locals you probably wouldn't even know that it was there, on account of it being so well-hidden amongst the tall pine trees. I know it's there of course, because I stayed there - for fourteen months.

It was during the war. When the bombs started to fall, my friends and I were told that we were to be moved to the country, just for a while until the conflict was over. We weren't told where we'd be going exactly, except that it would be far away from the city, somewhere safe. I was sent to the highlands of Scotland.

When I first arrived it was all a bit strange for me, not just being away from my parents for the first time, but also because everything was so different. Especially the house, with its gargoyles protruding out from the top of the building and smoke coming out from its several chimneys, it was nothing like back home and certainly took a bit of getting used to. But I soon settled in, and after a short while

I grew to love the place and became fond of the people who lived there, especially Gregor.

Gregor McTaggart was an elderly gentlemen and he was very interesting. During my time at Blackbonnie, he was always inventing or making something, and he also had plenty of stories to tell about his past. We spent a lot of time together. Apparently, in his younger days, he had worked on secret projects for the British government, and in a way, it was because of this that I had a most remarkable experience during my stay - one that I will never forget.

* * *

A pathway led all the way down from the house to an old shed that sat beside the loch. I'd been to the shed a couple of times, just to take a look around, but it wasn't possible to get inside on account of a large rusty padlock. Because of that, I never thought much more of it, until the time came when Gregor told me that it contained something very interesting, and asked me if I wanted to see it.

So the very next day, we made our way down the path to the shed. I remember Gregor pulling out a big metal key from his pocket, which he used to unlock the old padlock. The door was initially jammed, but with a bit of effort it came open and I followed him inside - and that's when I saw it for the first time.

Sitting in the middle of the shed, and taking up most of the space, was a large object hidden beneath a dust sheet. At first, because of its size, I assumed that it must be a motor vehicle of some kind, a car perhaps or an old tractor, but then realised that it was the wrong shape. Whatever this was, it was round, like a sphere, and the removal of the sheet revealed a huge glass ball.

Despite having been sitting there for many years, it was

surprisingly not dirty at all, due I guess to the fact that it had been covered up the whole time. There was just a fine layer of dust over the glass, and you could still see through it, and what I saw amazed me. Inside the glass ball, I could make out some seats, and there were knobs and controllers, and an instrument panel - it was clearly some kind of vehicle.

From one of the shelves that ran along the shed wall, Gregor took a bottle of cleaning spray and a cloth and began polishing the shell. As he did so, he told me all about the mysterious object. He revealed that it was in fact an underwater vessel, a sort of submarine. He and his colleague had designed and built it as part of a government project many years ago, and they had even successfully tested it in the loch. When the assignment was over, the vessel had been mothballed and placed covered-up in the shed, where it had remained to that day.

* * *

When the sphere had been cleaned it looked so impressive, the glass was gleaming and crystal clear. I could now see everything inside very clearly, the padded seats and shiny dashboard, all the workings. I was amazed, to a young kid at that time it looked like something that you would see in a fantastic adventure film. I remember standing in awe as Gregor released a latch on the outside of the door, and the dull clanking sound as it opened. Stepping inside, he had to duck as we entered, but I never needed to.

We sat down on the seats and I looked around, it was such a strange feeling being inside the glass ball. Through the glass, I could see the outside very clearly in all directions, not only the sides but above my head as well, and even beneath my feet. I remember the instrument panel opposite, with its many switches and knobs, some with numbers or writing on them. There were just two seats, one appeared to be the control seat as it had long levers either side which came up from the floor, the other seemed to be a passenger or companion seat. Apart from that there wasn't much else, just some storage areas underneath. Gregor bent down and took a small, yellowing booklet from underneath one of the seats. Written on the front in large black print were the words: *Operator's Manual.*

"Excellent," he said, "it's still there. Just in case I've forgotten anything."

He asked me what I thought of the submarine and I told him it was fantastic, and it was then that he stunned me with a revelation. He informed me that he was planning to take it back into the loch the next day, and asked me if I wanted to join him. He said that he would spend the rest of the day checking it over, and doing any minor repairs, and that by the end of the day it should be ready to take into the water. I said yes, of course.

That night, as I lay in bed, I could think of nothing else. The thought of going beneath the loch in a big glass bubble seemed awesome. What would it feel like? I wondered, and what would we see?

* * *

Breakfast the next morning was downed slightly quicker than usual, we were both eager to get on with our plan. When we stepped outside into the open, we saw that the morning was bright and warm, and the air was fresh and still with just a couple of solitary clouds in the sky. According to my companion it was the perfect conditions, as it meant calm water with good visibility.

We made our way down the pathway, and when we reached the shed we opened both the big wooden doors this time, as wide as they would go. Together, we pushed the sphere outside. Despite its size, it was surprisingly light and not hard to manoeuvre at all. Gregor and I rolled the big glass ball down the bank and into the lake.

The vessel looked peculiar and somewhat out of place as it sat in the shallow water beside the bank of the loch. The inventor opened the door and we clambered inside. I then watched as he closed the door firmly behind us, sealing it tightly with some extra clamps. We took our positions, he in the control seat and I beside him in the companion seat; our submersible was now safe and secure and ready to go.

* * *

The transparent sphere in which we sat bobbed gently up and down in the water. Looking out through the glass, we could see the whole loch stretching out before us. The pilot flicked a switch and pressed some buttons, then flicked some more switches and the control panel lit up, followed by a gentle humming noise that reverberated around us - the submarine was fired up. I remember Gregor looking at me with the biggest smile on his face, and he said something like, "Let's go exploring." I saw him push forward the big lever that was on his left side, and when he did we started moving along the top of the water. I could feel the excitement rising in my stomach.

"Here we go," he said, enthusiastically.

He pulled back the other lever, the one on his right side, and the water began to rise up around us, we were descending into the lake. I realised that the two levers were part of the steering system, one moved the vehicle forward and back, the other made it go up and down.

It was so exciting, the water level rose up around us, getting gradually higher and higher, and we were soon half below the surface and half above it. I remember it seeming quite bizarre, that I could see both under the water and above the water at the same time. We continued to go down, until we became totally submersed. As I can recall, there were lots of bits and pieces floating around in the loch when we first went under, like loose plants and pieces of wood. It was a strange sensation, we were under the lake yet we were totally dry.

To begin with, Gregor kept the submersible just a few feet below the surface, I guess that he was making sure that everything was okay before taking it down further. Then, after a short while, he manoeuvred it away from the side towards the centre of the lake where the water was deeper, and we descended. As we did so, the water became much clearer. Away from the surface there was none of the floating bits and pieces, so we could now see beyond us quite some distance. I remember looking up, I could see the top of the water from underneath, and could even make out where the sun was shining on its surface.

My pilot was excellent at controlling the submarine, and now confident that our vessel was absolutely fine, with an adjustment on the lever he took us even lower. That was when we started seeing fish for the first time, swimming around outside. Plain ones to begin with, brown or silver in colour, but as we descended the fish showed more colours and became more interesting. We saw fish with black spots, gold-coloured ones with pink spots, and tiny ones with fiery-red eyes. I remember spotting one particular fish that had big electric-blue eyes. It was fantastic to see all the fish so close-up, some didn't pay us any heed but others appeared to be intrigued, as if wondering who we were and what we were doing down there. Some came right up to the window to take a look inside; they were probably just as curious in us as we were in them.

I also remember when a playful otter came to investigate the unusual looking object in its territory, it came right up to the glass, touching it with its nose and whiskers, and peering inside before swimming off.

* * *

We travelled about in our transparent bubble for a while, watching the underwater world go by outside, it was quite remarkable. Then at some point, Gregor informed me that we had about twenty minutes left of air, just enough to take a look around at the bottom of the loch before going back; I thought that this was a good idea.

I felt the craft descend, down to the depths of the loch, and I remember seeing bubbles rise up around us as we sank quite fast. In less than no time we had hit the bottom and had settled on the lake bed, so that we could take a look at it before surfacing.

Things looked different down in the depths. I remember there were large rocks scattered amongst masses of green plants that gently swayed in the current. There were fewer fish down in the deep, but the ones that we did see were bizarre looking, and there were crustaceans too, interesting crabs and lobsters. Then, as we looked out from the comfort and protection of our big glass bubble - we both saw it.

It was the most incredible thing ever, and a sight that I will never forget. A huge head appeared outside of the submarine, so big that it covered the whole side of our craft. It came closer, and its nose almost touched the glass. We both sat transfixed, as two big eyes looked in at us. We noticed it blinking occasionally as we stared at it, we were speechless and in awe - and it was watching us too. But despite its size we were not afraid, because we knew that the huge leviathan was a gentle creature, it was harmless. We could tell that the beast was simply curious of the unusual craft that it had never seen before, with the two strange-looking occupants sitting inside.

With its large eyes looking in, the underwater beast scanned the inside of the submarine after looking at us. After a short while, the creature had obviously seen all that it had wanted to, because it turned to swim away. It was then that the rest of its body became visible, and we realised how huge it actually was. The thing was magnificent, its large head was on the end of a very long neck, and its body was massive, the size of a whale.

The gentle giant swam around for a bit, then, after giving us one last look-over, it swam away, causing our glass ball to rock in the turbulence. As it left us, we got a very good look at its body, and it's an image that I will always remember. We noticed that it had four fins, two smaller ones at the fore and two much larger ones at the rear, and it appeared to be using these to propel itself forward and for manoeuvring. As it retreated we saw its tail, paddle-shaped, swishing up and down in the water. We watched the creature disappear into the distance, then sat motionless for several seconds, just staring out from our glass ball without saying a word, coming to terms with what we had just witnessed. Gregor eventually spoke, and I can clearly remember what it was. He turned to me and said, "I think we should head back don't you - I guess we've seen everything now."

* * *

That evening, as we sat beside the log fire in the drawing room of the big house, we chatted about our remarkable experience, and my companion wrote a full report of the incident in his diary. He informed me that there had been reports of something in the lake for many years, some believed them to be true, others not. But we knew them to be true, because we had seen it with our very own eyes, and we also knew that whatever it was, it was a gentle creature, harmless, perhaps even friendly.

* * *

When I left Blackbonnie, Gregor and I kept in touch for a while. He did make a couple more trips in the glass submarine, but never saw the creature again; I guess we were just lucky on that particular day. It was certainly a day that I will never forget, and when I go to sleep at night I sometimes think of the gentle creature, and smile to myself when I realise that it's probably still out there, swimming around in the depths of Loch Ness.

Alumnia - The Invisible Island

Far out, in the middle of an ocean somewhere, is a small island, and like many small islands it is very beautiful, with golden beaches and lush greenery. There is something very different about this island however, because no one can see it - Alumnia is invisible. The island, and the people and the animals, do still exist, they are simply appearing in another place. How and why this happened is partly to do with the island itself, and partly to do with the people who lived there.

The Alumnians were peaceful people, never interested in squabbling or fighting, thus, many years ago, when wars raged around the globe, they kept themselves separate from all the chaos and turmoil that was going on around them.

They were gentle folk too, who lived in harmony with their environment. They felt blessed to live in such a charming place, and saw the beauty in the nature that surrounded them; in the animals and plants, the ocean, and the very earth itself. They loved all the creatures that lived alongside them, knowing that they had as much right to be there as they did. So the animals became their friends, and they came close and interacted with the humans in a way that was, and still is, unknown anywhere else. The people of the island looked up at the night sky with wonder, and felt an affinity with the moon and the stars, as well as with the sun during the day. To those who lived there, the island was alive, a living entity, and they cherished and preserved its natural beauty.

During that time, which was several hundred years ago now, Alumnia could be seen. It was clearly visible, as noticeable as any other piece of land out at sea. In fact, if you had in your possession one of those rare and old maps that still exist today, and looked at it very closely, you may well see the tiny island. However, around five-hundred years ago, the land ceased to appear on any maps - because it was no longer there.

* * *

Even in the days when Alumnia could be seen, it was different, and a bit special. To begin with, it was extremely beautiful, an enchanted isle surrounded by clear turquoise water. The land itself was made up of fifty per cent crystals, the energy from which made everyone feel uplifted and peaceful. And there were various locations scattered around Alumnia that had magical powers, and the islanders referred to these places as *mystical spots:* the Vision Tree for example, the Ring of Stones, the Ancient Pyramid and the Healing Waterfall. There were portals too, which could transport someone instantly from one place on the island to another.

It was a positive vibe that permeated Alumnia all those years ago, and due to the energy given off by the crystals, and the fact that the inhabitants had raised their consciousness somewhat, both the people and the island itself began to vibrate at a higher level. This made their world even more magical, and humans began to develop special gifts and abilities: like healing, premonitions, and telepathy. Their connection with the natural world became stronger, and they learnt how to communicate with both the animals and plants. Nature thrived even more, and the land became ever abundant with delicious fruits, colourful plants, and splendid animals and birds. In short, it became a paradise on earth - and there came a time when the magic of the island and the abilities of the people would save them both.

*   *   *

Among the mystical spots that were scattered around the island, there was one that was known as the Pool of Divination. It was a natural spring, whose water bubbled up from deep beneath the surface. Perhaps it was due to the rocks through which the water filtered that imbued it with special powers, for the Pool of Divination was able to foresee future events. The people, therefore, would sometimes visit this special place and gaze into it, to see if it had anything to show them - and one day it revealed the coming of a great tsunami.

The vision showed a huge wave that had formed out at sea, and as it travelled it grew, building up strength and power as it went, and the little island of Alumnia stood in its path. By the time the tidal wave would reach them, it would be so high as to appear to almost touch the sky. When the islanders discovered what was coming, they had to take action, but what could they do. Fortunately, they knew exactly who to ask - they would consult the Yeti of the Blue Mountain.

*   *   *

The Blue Mountain was the highest point on the land, taking two days to reach by foot, so without further ado, a party was assembled and set off post-haste. This small group made their way across the highlands, and after a couple of days they were in sight of the Blue Mountain and the cave of the yeti. Despite being a huge furry beast, the Yeti of the Blue Mountain was gentle and friendly, it had big kind eyes and spoke with a calm, deep voice; if ever the Alumnians needed help or advice about something they would always consult it, and they were never let down.

When they arrived at the cave, the beast was waiting for them; it somehow knew that they were coming. As the group stood beneath the immense figure before them, they spoke of the impending fate of the island. The gentle giant responded, and told them what they needed to do.

They must seek out and find the Shell of Time, and learn how to use it. They should then wait for when the time is right, and if they are attentive they will know when that is, it will be when the stillness follows the storm. One strong blow on the shell will freeze the tsunami, but only for a limited time, so whilst the great wave stands motionless they must gather themselves together, think positive thoughts, and imagine themselves as beings of light. Doing so will raise their vibration even higher, and that of the island and everything on it, so much so that Alumnia will momentarily shift from this dimension into another. When this begins to happen, as they are starting to fade, they must remember to give a second blow on the shell. It will reawaken the tsunami, so as the great wave passes through, Alumnia will not be there.

* * *

When the party returned from their quest, they recounted the instructions they'd received from the wise one. It had given them its words of wisdom, and although it had not told them where they could find the Shell of Time, it had told them what it looked like. So, the islanders searched, for several days, until successful. The shell was found lying on the sand inside a cave by the sea - as soon as they saw it they knew what it was.

Ariadne was a musician, who made instruments from the natural resources that she found on the forest floor or washed up on the beach; she would certainly know how to play the shell. So the instrument was handed to her, and it wasn't long before she was able to produce a haunting, melodic sound that echoed across the land. With further practice, she discovered how to use the instrument to stop time. She learnt that focussing all of her attention on something as she blew, would make it freeze, and a second blow would return it back to normal. The musician practiced for many days, and enjoyed it immensely, she found the object fascinating. She learnt how to stop and start the movement of fire, and she was able to throw fruit in the air and suspend it still. A cloud was stopped from drifting across the sky, a waterfall froze as if made of ice, and she could make birds and insects hang motionless in mid-air before returning them to their natural movement, totally unaware that anything had happened. Ariadne was ready.

* * *

When the day of the tsunami eventually transpired, it began like any other. The weather was initially mild and pleasant, all appeared normal, but by mid-afternoon a breeze had come up which soon turned into a strong wind, and the strong wind then became a wild storm, that blew across the whole island. For what seemed like hours, trees swayed to and fro and sand was tossed about in the air. But then, the wind abruptly stopped, the air became still without a hint of a breeze and an eerie silence came over the land. The islanders knew that the time had come - it was the stillness after the storm that the yeti had foreseen.

As they gazed out across the sea, the people of the island could make out the tsunami in the distance. The large wave was far away on the distant horizon, but it was moving closer all the time, and as it did it appeared to pick up speed. Ariadne prepared herself, she stood on the beach looking on, waiting patiently as the great wave grew in size.

Everyone watched, transfixed, as the tsunami became ever larger, getting nearer and nearer. The wave appeared to have a life of its own, to be a separate entity from that of the sea from which it was formed. By the time it reached them, the tsunami was a huge tower reaching up to the sky, and they saw the enormity of it. As she faced the great wave that was about to consume her and everything else, Ariadne took the shell to her lips and blew hard and long; the sound of the horn could just be heard amongst the roar of the sea. The great wave stopped, became motionless, and everything fell silent. The Shell of Time had worked - the tsunami had been tamed.

The sight of the immense tower of water cascading skywards was quite surreal. Frozen momentarily in time, seconds away from consuming everything in its path, the great tsunami was an awesome sight. The islanders felt insignificant as they stood beneath the giant structure, gazing up at its magnificence.

Immediately after the taming of the wave, no one spoke, they were speechless, coming to terms with what they had just witnessed. As soon as their senses had returned to normal, they cheered, and they smiled, and they laughed. Some swam out to the wave, and discovered that although it did not move, it was just like normal water. So, despite being motionless, they could swim inside it, then poke their heads out the side to take a breath and look down at others below. It was a bizarre thing to do, and very amusing, especially for the children. The fun time had to be brief however - for the Alumnians had something very important to do.

* * *

Just as their furry friend had instructed them, the people of the island gathered themselves together on the beach, beside the great wave. Taking deep breaths to relax themselves, everyone focused their minds and thought positive thoughts. They felt gratitude and appreciation for everything they had, for each other, for the animals and the nature, and for the Yeti of the Blue Mountain, and just as it had told them to do, they imagined themselves as beings of light.

As they did this, each one of them became aware of an energy stirring inside their body. It started as a tiny point of light, but soon grew larger into a ball, becoming bigger and stronger by the moment. They realised that this energy was their true selves, it was who they really were, their spirit. The light expanded, out beyond their physical bodies, until everyone was cocooned in a large ball of energy. All the separate energies then blended together, forming one great powerful sphere that covered them all. It spread out across the whole island, reaching the animals and plants, it touched the sky, it connected with the stars and planets, then the universe itself, everything was perfect in that moment, and it felt blissful.

It was then that their physical bodies started to fade, as did everything around them. They were shifting to somewhere else, just as the yeti had said would happen, the occasion had come for Ariadne to blow on the Shell of Time once more. This time, the haunting melody of the shell could clearly be heard all over the island, and it was followed by a sudden roar as the tsunami awoke, but to the islanders, the roar sounded distant somehow, as if from another place, because they were no longer there - the people and the island were somewhere else.

Everything was the same yet somehow different. The place where they found themselves was a new earth, where the consciousness of humans had evolved to a higher level.

It was a place of love, they could feel it, where people and nature coexisted in perfect harmony, and with Mother Earth, a living entity herself.

The islanders knew that they were experiencing the next level of human existence, where all humanity will transcend once it has shed the shackles of negative thought and behaviour that has enslaved it for thousands of years. It is the destiny of mankind, as each and every person raises their vibration, one by one they will find themselves in this new world. They were there just momentarily however, because the island soon reappeared in its original location, and when it did, there was no tsunami, the sea was calm and everything was still - the great wave had passed them by.

*   *   *

The Alumnians learnt from their experience, and from their glimpse into an alternative reality. They had seen a new and better place, and what's more, they knew how to get there. So in the weeks and months and years that followed, the people of the island mastered the technique of raising their vibration, and they started to live in a constant state of love and peace. As they did so, they began to flit in and out from one existence to another, between the old world and the new. Over time, the piece of land that was Alumnia spent more and more time in this other dimension, until eventually, the new earth became its new home - and that is where it is today.

*   *   *

So the island of Alumnia does still exist, it just can't be seen that's all, although there are occasions when, due to abnormal weather conditions, the island very briefly reappears back in our world. It will only be for a moment, but if someone happens to be in the right place at the right time they may see it, which has in fact happened on more than one occasion.

One such time was way back in the eighteenth century, when a pirate by the name of One-Eyed Fred had become separated from his ship during a spell of extremely unsettled weather. Fred had found himself adrift in a small rowing boat, when he spotted a beautiful island in the distance. He made his way over, and as he got closer he could make out the large fruits hanging down from the trees. His mouth began to salivate in anticipation of biting into the succulent bounty, but then, just as he was about to reach the shore, the island disappeared right before his eye.

The stray pirate was eventually picked up by his ship and reunited with the crew, but when he told them about the island they laughed and said that it was just an hallucination brought on by the lack of food and water; and even Fred himself believed them.

Another event occurred much more recently, in 1969 in fact, when a cruise liner passed by the island en-route to its destination. There was an electrical storm and Alumnia became visible. It was witnessed by several passengers, including members of the crew who were perplexed. Having made the same journey many times previous, they had never seen the island before. They alerted the captain who became concerned that they may have gone off course, but a check of the ship's navigational equipment confirmed that they were exactly where they were supposed to be. The captain was not aware of any island in the location either, and no landmass was indicated on his map. He intended to report it when he returned home, but decided against doing so when, on the return journey, there was no island to be seen in the same location, so he thought best not to mention it. In later years, the incident was occasionally brought up during after-dinner discussions, but always discreetly and only in private circles.

* * *

So please, do remember the island of Alumnia, and if you hear reports of a piece of land somewhere that has mysteriously vanished without trace, then you know where it has gone. And if ever you find yourself on a ship, out in the middle of an ocean somewhere, then keep a lookout - for you never know what you might see.

Cloudland

Tom was telling his friends about a film that he'd recently watched on TV, an adventure story about two explorers who'd set off together to find gold in a stream. Jack, Laura and Alex listened intently as he described what happened, and it gave them an idea. They figured out that if there was gold in that stream, then it was highly likely that all streams had something in them worth finding - so why not have an adventure of their own.

The four children decided that they would go exploring for themselves, to discover treasure, or gold, or anything that would be an amazing thing to find. They'd heard about a stream that was supposedly at the far side of the woods, none of them had ever been there, but some of their friends had and they'd told them all about it. To get there you needed to follow a long trail all the way through the woods, and that's where it was. So, the exploration party gathered up some tools, comprising a small spade and bucket, a piece of old rope, a magnifying glass, a compass, a pair of broken binoculars, and an old metal sieve that Alex had found in her dad's shed - and off they went.

* * *

The adventurers joined the trail at the end of the high street, where the little post office stood. They followed it through the farmers' fields, down the hill, then across a flower meadow to where the trail met the woods.

Stepping into the woods was like entering a different world, the children found themselves amongst hundreds of trees of all different shapes and sizes. There were small trees and tall trees, fat trees and thin trees, some were slender and upright, others were thick and gnarly and looked like they were hundreds of years old. The barks of the trees were different too, most were a certain shade of brown but some were grey and dusty, others still, appeared silver and shiny.

Some of the trees were especially tall, these were very impressive, and they cut out the sound from the outside world. The children were immediately aware of how silent it had become, and noticeably cooler and darker too, because the canopy blocked out much of the sunlight. But as they made their way through, there were areas of dappled light where the trees thinned. Beautiful wildflowers grew in these patches, some that they had never seen the likes of before, and they came upon mushrooms too, and berries and fruits.

As they trundled along, the discernible silence was occasionally broken by birdcalls, probably alerting other animals of their presence. The intrepid explorers were enjoying their adventure, even before they had reached their intended destination, making their way through unexplored territory was exciting.

* * *

The small group eventually reached the other side of the wood, where they stepped out from the shade into bright open sunlight. The sun was glorious, and as they stood together on the green grass they saw it for the first time. It was right there, just as they had been told - a delightful stream. They were pleased to have found what they were looking for, and hurried over to take a closer look.

The stream was perfect. Its water was so clear that you could see the stones and pebbles on the bottom, and it was shallow enough in places that you could stand in it with your wellington boots on and the water would not come in over the top. If you rolled up your sleeve, you could even put your arm in and touch the bottom and your shirt would only get slightly wet. This made it the ideal place to pan for gold, and anyhow, even if they didn't find any treasure it was worth coming, just to have seen such an intriguing place.

The treasure hunters soon got to work with their tools. They searched and searched and found some interesting things: unusual plants that grew under the water, schools of tiny fish, lots of different shaped stones, and Jack happened upon a small crab sitting on a rock. But alas, it seemed that no gold or treasure was going to be found that day, so the team decided that they would return home for lunch - all that exploring had made them hungry.

Just as they were about to leave however, Tom spotted something glistening at the bottom of the stream. He reached down, grabbed it, and lifted it from the water. When he held it up in his hand, he saw that it was a stone, but not just any old stone, it was the most striking stone he had ever seen. It was pure white, with tiny pieces embedded into it that sparkled in the light, it looked amazing. Excitedly, he called to his friends to come over and see what he had found, and when they did they were very impressed. Laura said that it was a crystal, and Jack said that the sparkly bits were probably diamonds. Tom wasn't sure about that, but he did know that he had found something very special.

As the four of them walked back home along the trail, they discussed their find, what it might be and what special powers it might have. Tom decided that it was called a cloud stone, because the colour was so white that it was just like a cloud, so that was definitely what it was called. Back through the woods they went, through the flower meadow, up the hill, and then past the farmers' fields to rejoin the high street where the little post office stood.

* * *

Back at home, Tom could think of nothing else but the cloud stone, and he never let it out of his sight. When bedtime came, he placed it under his pillow for safekeeping. Snuggled up in bed, Tom thought about the exciting day that he'd had with his friends, and the best thing about it was his amazing find. He slid his hand under the pillow to hold the stone, it felt good to have it with him, somehow it made him feel safe and secure, and there was definitely something magical about it.

As he lay in bed, with his hand on the stone and a warm smile on his face, he felt contented. But he was also very tired from all the walking that he'd done, his eyelids soon became heavy and he had to close them. As his body melted into the warm soft mattress his breathing became slow and steady, he was now very relaxed, and soon he fell into a deep sleep.

* * *

Tom awoke from his sleep, and he could tell that his body felt peculiarly light, as if it were floating. Then, to his total surprise, he began to rise upwards and found himself hovering in the air. Now if this wasn't remarkable enough, then things were about to get even more so, because he continued to float upwards even higher - all the way to the ceiling.

He had to laugh to himself when he looked down and saw his whole bedroom below. He could see his bed, and the bedside cabinet with its small lamp, and he saw his books on the bookshelf from above. He noticed his clothes that he had left strewn over the floor when he'd changed into his pyjamas, and spotted his pencil and dream-journal book beside the bed.

For a short while, Tom hovered just beneath the ceiling of his bedroom, looking down at the view below. But then, suddenly, he popped straight through the ceiling and out the other side, he was now outside in the open air, floating above the roof of his house. He didn't stop there however, he rose up to where he could look down upon the houses in his street. He could make out all the different pathways, and the road, and the street lamps, it was amazing. What an extraordinary thing to be happening, he told himself.

He was eager to discover more, he didn't know how long the experience was going to last so he wanted to make the most of it. He realised that he could go even higher, just by thinking it, so up and up he went, and he quickly learnt that by using his thoughts he could instruct his body to go in whatever direction he chose. He could go left or right, and round and round, in fact, he could float about to his heart's content and go wherever he wanted to.

"Woohoo," he shouted, and then heard his voice echo out around him in the night air.

The experience was exhilarating, Tom felt as light as a feather and as free as a bird as he drifted over the rooftops, looking down at the spectacular views below. As he went ever higher, everything below him become smaller and smaller, until it appeared as though he were looking down at a model village. The little houses and cottages, how amusing they looked from up so high, he thought to himself. Some of the houses had lights shining out from within, which made them look cosy and inviting, and he could see all the gardens too for the first time, some had lanterns hanging from trees. A few of the homes had smoke coming out from their chimneys, he noticed.

He could see everything from up here, he could make out the roads, the park, the shops and his school, and he spotted the post office at the end of the street where he, Jack, and Laura and Alex had joined the trail earlier that day. As he drifted over the homes of his friends, he thought how funny it was that they were below him in their beds, totally unaware that he was just above them looking down. I can't wait to tell them when I see them all tomorrow, he thought to himself.

* * *

Tom continued to rise, and found himself high up in the sky amongst the clouds, he felt exhilarated as he drifted slowly around them, as though he were a cloud himself. Then, all of a sudden, he was engulfed by a thick white mist, he could see no further than a few inches from his face, everything was pure white - he realised that he must have entered into a cloud.

He had sometimes wondered what it would feel like to pass through a cloud, and now he knew, it felt cool and refreshing and made his skin tingle. He began to laugh to himself, and as he did the white mist began to get lighter, and soon he could see all around him once again; he'd passed through the cloud and come out the other side.

* * *

As Tom floated along, with the expansive sky around him, he noticed that he was drifting naturally towards a very large cloud, one that was much bigger than all the others. When he got close, he saw that it was huge. I never knew that clouds could be so big, he thought to himself, then realised that it was probably because he had only ever seen them from a long way off, from down on the ground. This particular cloud seemed much thicker than the others too, more dense, and he noticed that it had an opening at the front from which light was emanating out, which he straight away thought as being odd. This needs investigating, he told himself, so he allowed himself to drift slowly over towards the entrance - and when he reached it he floated inside.

Tom found himself travelling through a white tunnel which was lit up by a glowing light from within the cloud, it was quite wonderful. The inside of the tunnel sparkled gently as he moved through, and it reminded him of the stone that he'd found in the stream that day. He drifted along inside for a while, enjoying the incredible experience, until eventually emerging out at the other end. Or so he thought, because when he came out the tunnel he discovered that he wasn't outside at all, he was in the middle of the cloud - and that's when his eyes beheld something quite fantastic.

He saw a land, a cloud land in the sky. Beyond him were white fluffy houses, and there were white fluffy roads, and he could make out a castle high up on a hill in the distance. The whole scene was bathed in a gentle light, he was astonished by what he had discovered, who would have thought that such a place existed, he told himself.

His feet came to rest on the soft surface and he realised that if he were gentle, he could walk on the cloud, which felt spongy underfoot, like stepping on a giant marshmallow. So he began to walk, following the white pathway that led up ahead towards the houses and the castle.

* * *

Tom came to a large gate. He was so excited and couldn't wait to enter, but when he pushed on the gate nothing happened. So he tried pulling, but it still didn't budge, it seemed that the gate wasn't going to open for him, that he could go no further and wasn't going to be allowed into the cloud land.

The thought of returning home without having had a proper look at this strange world in the sky was disappointing, but then, just as he was contemplating heading back, he heard a noise. It was the gentle coughing noise that someone makes when they want to get your attention - someone else was there.

Tom turned his head to the direction of where the sound came from, and saw the most extraordinary person he had ever seen. The strange fellow was sitting all by himself at a little round table, he was small in stature, with a round body, and his face was round too, with red cheeks and large sticky-out ears. He wore a blue jacket and yellow baggy trousers, and his jacket was open at the buttons, revealing a plump pot-belly and what looked like a silver medallion hanging down from his neck. On the man's feet were black boots, which curled up at the toes into spirals. Stranger still, was that protruding from his mouth was a long wooden pipe, from which randomly emerged white puffs of smoke. Each puff of smoke rose up into the air, hovered for a few seconds above his head, then disappeared with a pop.

Slowly and cautiously, Tom approached. The funny little man stood up from his chair, removed the pipe from his mouth and puckered his lips, then began to speak in a rather exuberant voice.

"Hello, hello, hello, how nice of you to come. My name is Mott, and I am the gatekeeper, see, see." He lifted the medallion up from his chest, to show off a large letter G inscribed on it. Tom noticed that the man's ears wiggled when he spoke.

"Oh I see," he replied, "it's a pleasure to meet you." Being as formal and polite as he could.

"And what, what, what, may I do for you today?" asked the gatekeeper.

Tom thought for a second, then said in a rather quiet and timid way, "Erm, well, I would like to go through the gate please."

"Of course you would, of course, why else would you be here?"

Mott then held out his hand, as if expecting something to be put into it. Tom did nothing, he didn't know what to do. There was an awkward silence as the strange character, with one hand holding the pipe and the other extended with palm facing upwards, waited expectantly.

"Well," said Tom, "can I come in or not?"

There was another pause, and then, as if slightly losing patience, Mott spoke again.

"The stone, the stone."

"But what stone would that be?" enquired Tom.

"Well the cloud stone of course, you can't get in without the cloud stone, it's what I do, I am the gatekeeper, see." Once again holding up the medallion in full view.

Tom then remembered the stone that he had found with his friends that morning, and realised that the man must be referring to that.

"Oh I see," he said, "yes of course, the cloud stone. The problem is, I don't actually have it with me."

"Of course you do," Mott said, "of course you do."

"No, I'm afraid I left it behind."

"Well have you tried looking for it?"

"There isn't really much point," he answered, "because I know that I don't have it. I left it at home, underneath my pillow for safekeeping."

"Nonsense," said Mott, as he leaned closer.

The gatekeeper's eyes looked to the left, and then to the right, and from the left to the right again quickly. He then stretched up and whispered in Tom's ear.

"Your pockets, check your pockets."

"Well I'm sure that it's not in my pocket," Tom replied, feeling in his pyjama pockets just to prove that he didn't have it. "You see, as I said, I left it at home under . . . . . ." Tom suddenly stopped speaking, and took from his pocket the cloud stone.

"I don't understand, I didn't actually . . . , I was positive that I left it under my . . . "

"Of course you took it with you," Mott interjected, "how else would you have gotten here?"

"But I distinctly remember it being under my pillow and I can't remember taking it."

"My dear fellow, you took the cloud stone with your mind, that's how it works."

And with that said, the odd-looking figure took the stone, removed a small pair of pliers from a pocket of his baggy trousers, then snipped a tiny piece off from one of the corners before handing it back. He then proceeded to drop the snippet of stone into his pipe. 'Poof' went the pipe, and a puff of powder-blue smoke rose up from out of it. The gate then slowly began to open, and the gatekeeper sat back in his chair with a broad smile on his face and inhaled deeply from his pipe. As puffs of smoke floated above his head, he held out his arm and said, "Welcome to Cloudland."

* * *

Tom could not believe his eyes, as he stepped forward a whole new world opened up before him, a world that looked as if it were made of mounds and mounds of white candy floss, as far as the eye could see. He proceeded to walk along the soft, spongy, cobbled road that lay ahead, fascinated by the surreal place in the sky that he found himself in; he'd had adventures before but nothing quite like this. The road gently undulated up and over small hills as it went, at either side were small fluffy houses with windows and doors and chimney pots, and there were fluffy bushes and trees dotted around in the gardens outside.

The strangest part of Tom's adventure was yet to come however, it was when he encountered the floating creatures. These bizarre-looking beings floated around in the air and were like puffs of cotton wool with faces. They had big round eyes and came in all colours and sizes. The biggest ones were the size of a beach ball and were white in colour, they must be the parents Tom presumed. The smaller ones that followed along behind were various colours, and they must be the children, he realised.

It was rather comical to observe, the floating creatures bobbing along in a line with the largest ones leading the way and the others following behind in descending order of size; some of those at the very end of the line were merely the size of ping-pong balls. The colours of the smaller children were bolder, he noticed, purples, greens, reds and oranges, whilst the bigger ones tended to be pastel shades of yellows and pinks; they certainly looked a colourful sight as they bobbed along together in mid-air. He wished he had a camera with him, so that he could take a picture to show his friends when he got back home.

There was another thing that Tom noticed, which was quite extraordinary. When a floating creature moved swiftly, it made a faint whooshing noise, like the sound of someone gently blowing air from their mouth, and the quicker it moved the louder the whoosh. Occasionally, one of them would float right up close to him, hover in front of his face as if to take a closer look, then smile and vibrate excitedly before moving off. I suppose I must look as strange to them as they do to me, he thought to himself.

He liked the little cloud beings a lot, they were delightful, and one family in particular were very friendly to him. As they showed him around their fluffy world in the sky, Tom bobbed up and down alongside them as best he could. They took him to some fantastic places and showed him some incredible sights, such as a beautiful mountain range, some snow birds, a lovely waterfall that sparkled and shimmered, and a crystal garden where he saw hundreds of stones that were just like the one that he had found in the stream.

* * *

The gentle sound of wind chimes suddenly filled the air, and his floating companions told Tom that it was time for them to go. He thanked them for their hospitality, and watched as the line of colourful fluffy beings drifted away. When he looked around, he noticed that all the other floating creatures were doing the same, and they all appeared drowsy. It seems they are gliding off to their homes to sleep, Tom thought to himself.

He realised that he too had become very sleepy, and wondered if it was something to do with the sounds that were emanating from the cloud. His eyes were getting heavier and heavier, and he couldn't help but close them; he was succumbing to the hypnotic tones of the music. He let his body sink softly and snuggly into the cloud, it was blissful, the softest bed he had ever laid on, like sleeping on a huge ball of cotton wool. As he listened to the soothing sounds, he fell into a deep and peaceful sleep.

* * *

When he awoke, Tom found himself in his bed at home. What an amazing adventure, he immediately thought, and he couldn't wait to tell his parents. He jumped up, dressed himself quickly, then dashed downstairs to join them at the breakfast table. He told them all about his experience in Cloudland: the strange little man at the gate called Mott, what he'd seen as he'd first entered in through the gate, and the floating creatures and the amazing things they had shown him. His parents smiled.

"Well you certainly do have a fantastic imagination," Tom's father said.

"I wish I had dreams like that," said his mother.

He looked sadly down at the table. Was it all just a dream, he thought to himself - but it seemed so real.

* * *

After breakfast, Tom made his way upstairs to his room. He lay on the bed in deep thought, thinking about what had happened to him up in the sky - could it have really been all in his mind? He thought about telling his friends when he sees them later, but then thought better of it, after all, it was only a dream.

He suddenly remembered that he still had the cloud stone, and put his hand under his pillow to retrieve it. He held it in his hand momentarily, then brought it closer to his face to get a better look - it sparkled in front of his eyes.

"It certainly is beautiful," he said softly to himself.

As he lay, staring at the magical stone that glistened in his hand, he realised that there was something different about it. A tiny piece was missing from one of the corners, a little snippet that looked as though it had been nipped off by a pair of pliers. His eyes immediately lit up, and a big smile appeared on his face. He will tell his friends after all, in fact, he couldn't wait, they could all have a go with the cloud stone. We can take it in turns with sleeping with it under our pillows, he told himself excitedly, until the whole stone has been snipped away by the gatekeeper.

THUNDERER PRESS
thunderer-press@outlook.com

CHECKLIST

- ☐ The Doll's House
- ☐ High-Strangeness Day
- ☐ Snowbound
- ☐ The Legend of Albert Hubble
- ☐ The Lighthouse
- ☐ Nine White Clouds Above an English Village
- ☐ Amazon Expedition: 1866
- ☐ Anna
- ☐ The Dream-Bed
- ☐ The Wise Old Man and his Beard
- ☐ Grey Wolf and the Firefly
- ☐ Tale of Walt Pepper
- ☐ The Big Old Tree
- ☐ Umpiddipompus
- ☐ Reunion in the Night
- ☐ Quark Strangeness
- ☐ The Ox and the Oxpecker
- ☐ Train Journey in the Fog
- ☐ Haya - Composer of the Stars
- ☐ A Time Before Humans
- ☐ Extraordinary Occurrence in Takayama
- ☐ The Stream from the Otherworld
- ☐ The Gift
- ☐ A Space Story
- ☐ The Shmungen
- ☐ Event on Strumpshaw Common
- ☐ The Great Dig in the Earth
- ☐ Carnival of the Cosmos
- ☐ Brachyura Odyssey
- ☐ The Glass Submarine
- ☐ Alumnia - The Invisible Island
- ☐ Cloudland

Printed in Poland
by Amazon Fulfillment
Poland Sp. z o.o., Wrocław

29057472R00179